# THE SEA ABOVE THEM

22 / 12^{TH} / 93 /

TO,
22 / 1^{ST} / 94 /

# The Sea Above Them

JOHN WINGATE

NEW ENGLISH LIBRARY
TIMES MIRROR

First published in Great Britain by Arthur Barker Ltd in 1975
© by John Wingate, 1975

*

FIRST NEL PAPERBACK EDITION FEBRUARY 1978

*

*NEL Books are published by*
*New English Library Limited from Barnard's Inn, Holborn, London EC1N 2JR*
*Made and printed in Great Britain by Hunt Barnard Printing Ltd., Aylesbury, Bucks.*

45003730 4

*To the Submariners of the Free World*

Through their lonely vigil, they keep the peace:
because of them, each one of us, whatever our political
creed, can sleep o'nights without fear.

## AUTHOR'S FOREWORD

This book is dedicated to our submariners, but we are in debt also to those whom they leave behind, waiting in the lonely ports for their men's return. Without the loyalty and the fortitude of our women, 'the boats' could not remain so long at sea in times of peace.

I am indebted beyond measure to those in The Submarine Service who made possible this book. Too numerous to mention them all individually, I thank them for their courtesy, their help and, above all, their friendship.

I am particularly grateful to Commander Richard Husk, Royal Navy, and to his officers and men of HMS *Valiant*, wherever they may now be dispersed; to Lieutenant-Commander B. O. Forbes, Royal Navy, Flotilla Escape and Diving Officer, HMS *Dolphin*, and his magnificent team; to Captain Peter Cobb, Royal Navy, who was The Captain (S/M), Second Submarine Squadron; and to Captain Hugh Oliphant, DSC, Royal Navy, HMS *Dolphin*, who made me welcome at Fort Blockhouse.

Finally, I wish to thank three Flag Officers, Submarines: Vice-Admiral Sir John Roxburgh, KCB, CBE, DSO, DSC★, who started it all; Vice-Admiral Sir Anthony Troup, KCB, DSC★, who made possible the research; and Vice-Admiral Iwan Raikes, CBE, DSC, who so kindly helped me finish the job.

All characters in this book are entirely fictitious but, if anyone should recognise him or herself, the fact is coincidental and I offer my apologies.

# Part I

# CHAPTER 1

## *Emergency Stations*

In the submarine service, the primary cause of an eventual disaster can be initiated hours before the emergency becomes apparent. Minor errors can multiply to generate a major emergency: so it was in Her Majesty's Nuclear Submarine, *Mars*.

In this SSN (the Hunter-Killers are thus designated to differentiate them from the Polaris nuclear submarines) events accelerated so swiftly that, even with Commander George Carn, Royal Navy, in command, the final catastrophe became inevitable. The initial cause was human failure: the event passed unnoticed, five hours before the accident; the mistake was a routine affair, an everyday error of judgement . . .

Lieutenant Peter Sinclair, RN, Navigating Officer of *Mars*, had taken his last visual fix for the day, 3 July. Visibility had reduced considerably and he was able to identify only the two peaks at the south-western extremities of Novaya Zemlya. Their outlines, dark and bleak in the pale light of the midnight sun, were barely sufficient for a good fix, but using radar for bearing and distance was out of the question: the object of this *Zed* patrol (the nomenclature used in the sailing orders) and for *Mars* to remain undetected; she could amass little intelligence, if the Russians knew she was there . . .

Peter Sinclair leaned over the chart table in the starboard for'd corner of *Mars*'s control room. After eight months in this boat, and under George Carn's benevolent eye, he had learned how exacting a navigating officer's job could become if he were to be reliable. The mahogany edge of the chart table bore witness to the time he spent pouring over his charts: the edge was polished to the bare wood and the chart drawers were already due for re-varnishing.

Selecting a pencil, Sinclair began completing and checking the day's log, that vital record common to all Her Majesty's ships. In the logs, which were finally stored in the archives of the

Admiralty, lay the secrets of thousands of ships and of countless men's lives. He filled in the column for 2000: barometer was falling; wind, light airs only, leaving an oily calm up top; visibility, poor and decreasing. It was as well that he had snatched his bearings when he did, for a visual fix would now be impossible. He turned to the officer of the watch who was about to stop the boat for a few moments to check the trim. After six hours' steaming this precaution was prudent submarine practice: with such power and travelling fast, *Mars* could be thousands of gallons out of trim, heavy or light, and no one would know . . .

'Better tell the captain, Jake,' Peter said quietly. 'Vis. is clamping down.'

Jake Soper, a tall, gangling figure standing in front of the diving consol, turned and nodded curtly. He did not appreciate being reminded of his duty: a prickly character and always had been, Peter thought. Soper tended to over-compensate for his lack of self-confidence, and this made him conceited and arrogant. He left the consol, strode across to the bulkhead screen and leaned round the corner:

'Captain, sir,' he reported loudly. 'Visibility is shutting down – about a mile at the moment.'

A hoarse voice growled from within the dimly-lit box that served as the commanding officer's cabin.

'Why didn't you let me know earlier?'

'Pilot was fixing the ship, sir.'

The captain emerged, eyes sleep-encrusted, but he was immediately alert as he swung his massive frame into the control room. He grasped the periscope handles and heaved himself into the seat. A swift, all-round look in low-power, the thin pencil-line of light piercing the black irises of his pupils, and he snapped the handles shut.

'No use staying here,' he said. 'Three hundred feet.'

'Aye, aye, sir. Three hundred feet.'

Peter Sinclair turned to his chart of the Barents Sea. The chart was secret, criss-crossed with Decca bearing lines, but annotated fully with the assessed temperature gradients for the area, horizontally and vertically. A good layer between the submarine and an enemy hunter was like a suit of chain-mail to a medieval knight. Peter felt the bow-down angle come on her – *Mars* was going deep.

*The first error had been made. Soper had failed to complete his drill: he had not stopped the boat to catch the six-hourly trim . . .*

'Three hundred feet, sir,' Soper reported.

'Very good. Watch-diving.' The captain turned to his navigating officer. 'Show me our position, Pilot.'

Peter stood aside to allow the captain's bulk to lean over the chart table. Those dark eyes missed nothing, and Peter felt relieved that his fix was already on the chart. The neat pencilled circle with its bearing lines, less than half a mile from the ship's track, was as accurate a position as could be expected.

'Here at eight o'clock, sir,' he reported quietly. 'South-west corner of Zemlya is fourteen miles distant.'

Carn grunted. Peter noted the set jaw, felt the intelligent mind at work. From his profile, George Carn resembled a boxer: large ears, slotted neatly beneath the mass of untidy black hair; broad forehead, with the V-groove of worry etched between heavy black eye-brows; broken nose that had never straightened after a rugger accident; generous mouth with broad lips – a kindly face and one that, when not stressed, would often break into an infectious grin, taking the world with him. In George Carn's presence it was difficult to remain miserable for long . . .

'Position *Zed*'s not far off now, Pilot,' he said. 'What speed do I need to arrive there at dawn?'

Peter picked up the brass dividers and snipped off the distances. *Mars* would have to steer a dog-leg course to reach position *Zed*, which was on the far side of the headland: the Russians had chosen an ideal base for their vast project. Remote; protected from the sea from all quarters except the east; and, above all, secure from an intelligence angle. What spy could infiltrate this loneliness? Which is where *Mars* came in, wasn't it?

Peter smiled inwardly – it was fun sharing a secret with Carn: besides himself and the captain, only Sinden and Number One, Terence Culmer, knew where they were and why they were tooling about off this benighted lump of barren Russia.

'To arrive at twilight, sir, even though it will be broad daylight,' Peter said, 'you should reduce to six knots at 0200.'

The captain nodded. 'That's good,' he murmured. 'We'll slide in silently, first thing tomorrow. I'd prefer to enter their territorial waters during the day: there's more chance of their shipping being about which might confuse the issue. I'd rather have time in hand, Pilot, and take a good look around, before reaching *Zed*. I'll have enough water presumably?'

'Plenty, sir: over 500 feet up to the beach. The cliffs of the islands are sheer, right up to the entrance of the base.'

'I'll get my head down then,' Carn said. 'Call me if you need me, Pilot, but I'd like a shake when we reach the shelf.' He nodded and shuffled off in his carpet slippers towards his cabin, which was five yards down the passage and within earshot of the control room.

Peter always felt the weight of added responsibility when once George Carn had left the heart of the boat. He was that sort of man: everyone felt better when he was around – competent, kindly and a good submariner. When he was absent from the control room, things could go wrong more easily and very quickly . . .

*The second cause of the impending disaster had slotted into place . . . inadvertently, by remaining at relatively high speed,* Mars *would be steaming at the critical moment through a deep patch of a lower density level . . .*

The time was now 2024. It would soon be Friday, 3 July – young Peter Junior's birthday: Peter Sinclair smiled again to himself as, working at the chart table on tomorrow's DR, he imagined his family settling down for the night in the married officers' quarters at Faslane.

Peter Junior would be six tomorrow . . . frightening how time was rushing by. It was only yesterday that Jeannie was nursing him in that crummy house they'd rented in Fleetwood when he'd been in trawlers. But that was a different world, when Mate Sinclair was struggling for his first stern-trawler command. That savage confrontation with the Russian fleet off Iceland would be a period in the planet's existence which historians would never forget . . . the world had held its breath, as it did over Cuba. But it was the calmness and efficiency of the Royal Navy and the Royal Air Force that had won the day.[1]

The incident had settled Sinclair's mind for him, for at twenty-five he had still not found his feet . . . He had applied for his special entry into the navy and had never looked back. His trawler experience had been invaluable and so had the long N course he had taken before joining submarines. But time was slipping by and he had now reached twenty-eight . . . he was becoming ancient, and he furtively bent his knees to catch a reflection of himself in the thick plate-glass that boxed in one of the SINS' (Ships' Inertial Navigation System) components . . .

[1] *Below the Horizon,* by the same author, Arthur Barker 1974.

11

The face that peered back had certainly lost its youthfulness . . . it was difficult to ignore the faults when looking at one's own image.

His wasn't an unpleasant dial, was it? Lean, more angular than most of his brother officers' faces, perhaps harder: those lines about the corners of his mouth registered the years he'd been at sea since he was seventeen – and mucking in with the lads in trawlers hadn't always been a picnic. He knew that Jeannie liked his brown eyes; she'd said that the freckles he'd picked up last year off Borneo had added to the touch of humour never far absent from his gaze, but she was prejudiced. One or two grey hairs had even begun to fleck his mouse-coloured hair, as Jeannie called it . . . beloved Jeannie – what a marvellous wife she'd been to him. Wonderful in bed, she still cared desperately for her house and her brood. Peter Junior was well on now, but little Nicola had been difficult: though she was only four, she needed a father at home, even more than her elder brother.

He glanced at his watch: 2230. He'd check that all was well with the officer of the watch and then he'd turn in . . .

The time was 2258. Able Seaman Ron Cheeseman was trying to keep awake in the sonar room. He tried to count the seconds and make them coincide with the second-hand of the electric clock as the red pointer crossed the hour: 2300. He was the UC (Underwater Control) rating on watch and he was longing for his bunk in an hour's time. He'd wring Lofty Willis's neck if he over-slept again . . . he was a holy terror for relieving his watch on time.

The sonar room was a peaceful haven, particularly at watch diving. The mass of orange and fluorescent dials, with their soothing luminosity, gave the compartment a space odyssey atmosphere. His duty was to report any sonar contacts, but this desolate ocean was hardly Piccadilly, was it? He grunted as he slumped forward, his mind far away, his imagination with a certain Miss Mary Johnson of 16 Camden Way, London. He enjoyed these all-too-rare moments of privacy, when a man could snatch a grain of comfort with his dreams: two months without mail or leave was too bloody long . . . he found himself mouthing the name he loved so dearly . . . *Mary, Mary, wait for me until I get out of this* . . . and his head slumped forward momentarily on his chest. Twenty seconds later, he jerked upright, shaking his head . . . he mustn't nod off again, for God's sake, or he'd be in the rattle.

*In those vital seconds, at 2307 to be precise, UC 2 Cheeseman should have noticed a scarcely audible change of pitch on his sonar – and, a few seconds later, the familiar 'tick . . . tick . . .' of a surface warship in contact. The transmission had ceased as abruptly . . . and, when Cheeseman had recovered his awareness, the sonar was operating as it had before . . . for days and days and bloody days on end.*

*But the third link in the chain of errors had been cast . . .*

Lieutenant David Tregant was the officer of the watch for the Middle. He was never at his best in the early hours and woe betide anyone that crossed him. Small and efficient, he never enjoyed taking over from Jake Soper: that bastard never failed to remind him that David Tregant was the Fifth Hand and very much a 'makee-learner'; but apart from the antipathy between them (who in the boat liked Soper anyway?) Jake often failed to hand over his watch adequately: he was too slick – *wham – wham – wham –* and he was off to his pit, quicker than the TI off on a run ashore. He usually missed something, and the rest of the watchkeepers were becoming sick of covering up for him with the Old Man.

'Watch the bubble, Burnley,' he murmured quietly in the Leading Seaman's ear. With the boat now peacefully at watch-diving, the fore and after hydroplanes were linked for one planesman's combined control. Burnley sat in the black leather arm-chair, controlling the six-thousand ton boat by means of the joy-stick. Just as a jet-pilot controlled his airliner, so did the modern submariner operate his boat: finger-tip control by one man, both of depth-keeping and, by turning the stick in the other plane, of steering. The trimming was in the hands of the officer of the watch: by working through the outside ERA on the pump-order consol and by watching the flow-meter, he could compensate with internal trimming changes.

Tregant enjoyed sharing a watch with Leading Motor Mechanic Hennessy, Blue Watch's Outside ERA. He was older than the others, and blessed with a wry sense of humour. Tregant had known him slip up only once, when he had failed to check that one of the 'on' and 'off' red lights on the pump order consol was not reading correctly. The bollocking he'd received from the Old Man had cured Hennessy of any further complacency.

13

'She seems a bit heavy for'd, sir,' Burnley said from his control seat. 'I'm using a bit of rise most of the time.'

Tregant nodded: he'd already noticed the tendency. Couldn't be far out though, for Soper would have caught a stopped trim during the First Watch . . . Tregant felt reluctant to alter things: he was still green in the art of trimming a boat of this size – funny how, after hours of going deep, there was a tendency to resist taking action. He could now understand this in-built human failing, which affected lonely, round-the-world yachtsmen. He turned towards Hennessy:

'Shift five hundred gallons from H and put it into X.' He hoped the trimming adjustment would not wake the Old Man. He added quietly: 'Let me know when four hundred gallons have passed.'

Hennessy repeated the order. The red light blinked and the flow-meter on the trimming panel began to move.

'Four hundred gallons passed from H to X,' the Outside ERA reported.

'Very good.'

It was still difficult not to appear self-conscious. The newness of the two gold stripes on his shoulders still proclaimed his lack of experience, and nonchalance was not his *forte*. He'd been press-ganged for submarines (they were restoring to this wartime practice, now that the problem of manning the submarine fleet had become so acute). On the whole, most of his shipmates showed kindness, though Dick Freemantle, a chum of his from training class, was being made miserable by his sense of inadequacy. Pressed men were, unconsciously, a different breed of submariner, and it took a good man to combat successfully a sense of inferiority.

'She's still heavy for'd, sir,' the planesman reported, glancing over his shoulder at Tregant. He was obviously dropping a hint, trying to help. Should he send for Terence Culmer, the First Lieutenant, who had the overall responsibility for the trim of the submarine? Tregant glanced at the clock: 0048. Three quarters of an hour of his watch gone . . . at this moment, the captain walked into the control room.

'What's going on, Officer of the Watch?' he asked, an understanding smile curling at the corners of his mouth. 'We're heavy, aren't we?'

Commander George Carn stood behind the young lieutenant, watching him at the controls as he grappled with the trim. Tregant would make a good submariner one day, when he'd

14

gained confidence. But the boat was heavy, Carn felt sure . . . strange when the stopped trim should have been carried out several hours ago. Soper had been the OOW of the First, hadn't he?

Carn glanced around the control room, his dark eyes flickering over the instruments. A built-in warning system was flashing inside his mind; he had a feeling in his bones, an instinct that came to experienced and born submariners . . . something was wrong.

'Give the First Lieutenant my compliments,' he said to the bosun's mate, 'and ask him to report to the control room.'

It was at this instant that the Outside ERA raised his voice. A red warning light was blinking at the fire-monitoring panel. A telephone shrilled and, when Tregant grabbed it, he heard a voice gasping from the other end.

'Fire in Number Two reactor protection circuit, sir,' Tregant reported, turning towards his captain. 'The watchkeeper's injured, sir.'

Carn felt the adrenalin surging in his blood-stream: he knew then that a full emergency was on his hands.

CHAPTER 2

## *Scram*

'Emergency Stations . . .' The captain's command rapped like a pistol shot through the control room. Tregant lunged for the general alarm push and the electronic hooters whined throughout the boat, their weird cacophony a summons to immediate action for every man-Jack in the boat.

'Emergency Stations,' Tregant broadcast, 'Emergency Stations . . .' The summons was demanding, imperious . . . Men tumbled from their bunks, resignation etched on most faces: they'd known it so often before, but this time was for real – they could smell the smoke through the ventilation trunking.

Carn glanced again at the alarm consol – there it was, the agitated red warning light, blinking in its tiny square: REACTOR PROTECTION CIRCUIT – 2. To prevent the reactor running wild, these protection circuits provided a fail-safe system. If there was a major fault in two of the protection circuits, the safety measures sprang into operation and the rods were withdrawn automatically . . . he recognised the stink of scorching insulation as a black, sticky smoke issued from the tell-tale.

'Fire in the reactor circuits room . . . ' Tregant broadcast again, his duty as Control Room Officer of the Watch being to inform the ship's company of the whereabouts and type of emergency. 'Stop ventilating . . . ' He ducked beneath the periscope and hurried for'd to his diving station, as Soper relieved him at the control panel.

'I've got her,' Soper said.

At this moment, Peter Sinclair scrambled into the control room to man his position at the navigational and plotting complex. This was no exercise: he could feel the real emergency. His first duty was to obtain an accurate position for the W/T officer. He saw the fire party hustling down the passage, men already asbestos-suited as they jammed on their breathing sets. In charge was Petty Officer Schuman and he was hustling the others along.

'Get a move on, Kinley,' his voice rasped. 'Ain't got all friggin' day: someone's hurt down there.' The unfortunate seaman tripped as he ran out the hose; he slammed his head against a valve and, bleeding, carried on unreeling.

'35 bulkhead door shut and manned, sir,' came the report from for'd and, seconds later:

'Number 101 bulkhead door shut and manned.'

The patter of tumbling, soft-soled feet immediately ceased; the control room was in relative quietness, disturbed only by the gentle whine of electric motors.

'Trim line pressurised, sir,' Hennessy, who was also the Diving Stations Outside ERA, called out. That was quick, Peter thought: the fire parties can deal with the fire now. The boat then lurched violently, as she took on a steep, bow-down angle.

Planesmen were in the act of exchanging places when the major power failure sprang upon them. With both the planes jammed at hard-a-dive, the boat was now out of control. The reactor had 'scrammed' and, at the same moment, the generators had gone 'off the board': a mass of six thousand tons was gathering momentum and hurtling for the bottom.

Radio Operator Morgan's voice on the stornophone continued calmly to pass the reports to the officer of the watch:

'After part closed up, sir; spare hands mustered in Junior Ratings' Mess . . . ' Then, seconds later, 'Fore part closed up and

16

spare hands mustered in Senior Ratings' Mess . . .'

As Sinclair turned to pass the ship's position to the radio office, it was difficult to keep his feet. The bow-down angle was increasing rapidly, and gear had begun to break adrift . . . there were few emergencies worse than a full power failure, a boat of this complexity being operated entirely by electricity.

'Two hundred feet . . .'

This was the captain's voice, rapping out his orders, as if this was a drill day off Portland.

'Full astern . . . Rate air to both planes and hard-a-rise . . .'

The seconds were flying past, and now it was impossible to stand. The emergency lighting had snicked on, and by its pale glow Peter could see the fear in men's eyes. By the hard lines on Carn's face, all knew that this was a major emergency: they were fighting for their lives in hostile water. The needle on the depth-gauge was flying round the dial . . . four hundred and ten feet and going down fast . . .

'Shut main vents – air emergency . . .'

Thank God, Peter thought with relief. Carn was taking the last resort of all submarine COs – but would the main vents shut swiftly enough whilst in the process of transferring to air emergency operation?

The air screamed above them and Peter felt the thunk! thunk! of the main vents as they sprang shut.

*There was no time*, for only Peter and the captain knew that they were in only 500 feet . . . and was the bottom here sand – or rock?

'*Blow one, two and three main ballast . . .*'

He saw Carter, a senior POMEE, wrestling with the main air blows – then the precious stuff screamed through the hydraulic HP line. There was an instant hush in the control room as men froze rigid, waiting for the acute bow-down angle to right itself . . . there was a sudden trembling throughout the hull, then Peter felt the deck beneath his feet begin to lift. The slithering of men's feet ceased as the bow began to right itself . . . The depth gauge was now showing 460 feet and Peter braced himself for the annihilating shock . . . the emergency had so far lasted exactly ninety-three seconds.

From the first few moments after the uncontrolled dive, George Carn had been steeling himself for the impact when *Mars* was to hit the bottom. When the reactor scrammed and he had lost total power, he knew then that there was no time to recover control.

The boat was seriously out of trim, thousands of gallons heavy for'd . . . he needed more than 200 feet, when steaming at twelve knots with planes jammed and no power. But he carried out the instinctive drill, for he knew there was nothing else he could do . . .

'Stop,' he snapped. 'Revolutions to thirty. Machinery state telegraph to "stand-by" motor . . .'

The Chief's voice crackled through from aft, but Carn knew it was no use, pointless in these few seconds to attempt a fast recovery . . . the reactor had scrammed itself intentionally – the protective circuits had seen to that. *There was no time*, even now the HP air was screaming through the lines to the main ballast tanks, to blow the hundreds of tons of water – but to arrest the momentum of six thousand tons plunging downwards took some doing.

'Disengage the clutch and propel on battery drive . . .'

Tregant was doing well – he'd remembered the drill, but he had turned his white face towards his captain for reassurance. Carn nodded in approval, as he grabbed the pipes above his head to take the weight when the crash came . . . 470 feet, 475 . . . and slowly, degree by degree, she began to lose that crazy bow-down angle. Carn waited, that vital split second – God, but she must *now* stop her downward surge: then the main ballast began suddenly to take charge . . .

As swiftly her bows began to soar, the deck lunging up at him beneath his feet . . . the bubble on the inclinometer slurped forwards and, at the instant that Carn thought she was clear, there was a strange grating noise from aft. Swiftly the bows lurched downwards: then, with uncanny ease, she settled on the bottom. *Mars* shivered, then gently took on a moderate list to starboard.

'She's touched right aft,' Carn said. 'Stop blowing main ballast.'

The scraping and hissing ceased abruptly. In the silence, all eyes in the control room were on the depth gauge: 508 feet. Then, reality suddenly cruelly clear, each man turned his gaze on the one character upon whom their lives depended. Carn stood there, a rock amidst their crumbling world. He shoved his hands in his pockets and turned towards the navigating officer:

'Well, we know where we are now, don't we, Pilot?' he said, a sour grin on his face. 'All compartments make their reports.'

# CHAPTER 3

## *Killer Hunted*

Nuclear submarines, and particularly Hunter-Killer Fleet Submarines, do not appreciate bottoming. This fact was immediately apparent.

'Sonar fails to function, sir.'

'Generators off the board, sir. Cannot circulate.'

'Stopping fast recovery, sir,' the chief engineer reported. 'I daren't risk it until we get off the bottom, sir.'

The reports streamed into the control room, both from the machinery spaces and the living compartments.

One of the occupants of the control room was not a permanent member of the ship's company. An observer and a passenger for this trip, Commander Alastair Sinden, had been appointed 'additional' for this patrol only, to under-study George Carn. The next Hunter-Killer of the class, *Hector*, was to be commanded by Commander Sinden, and he had been sent to *Mars* to gain as much experience and background as he could before his own SSN joined the operational squadron covering the area. He had deliberately made himself scarce while the emergency developed, but now George Carn had turned towards him. His words were mocking, but Sinden knew that the captain of *Mars* was stretching out a hand for moral support.

'Well, Alastair, you didn't expect the real thing, did you?' Carn asked, grinning. 'This will give us time to think, anyway.'

Sinden smiled back. 'Couldn't have bottomed more gently, even in an old A-boat,' he said. 'Pity you don't carry a drop-keel, George.'

Carn grimaced. 'Shan't need it. I think she's just about ready to break clear, by the feel of her. She's pivoting amidships, don't you reckon?'

Sinden nodded. It was difficult to feel depressed when George was in command. A phone shrilled and the operator handed the instrument to the captain:

'First Lieutenant, sir.'

'Yes, Number One?' George answered. Sinden noted the eyes clouding with anxiety.

'How badly burned is he?' Carn was listening intently. 'Good. Tell the LMA to make him as comfortable as possible. Very good. I'll be coming to periscope depth shortly.' He handed back the phone and spoke aloud. 'Leading OEM Turnbull was on watch,' he said quietly, 'He's burned in the face, but he's not too bad.' He turned again towards his friend standing by the navigational plot; he waited while the reports continued and then the two older men's eyes met. He picked up the stornophone:

'D'you hear there?' He spoke quietly into the microphone, 'this is the captain speaking . . . ' He paused as he collected his thoughts:

'There's no need to tell you all, that we've a major emergency on our hands. We've had a small fire in the reactor protection circuits, but it's been an extremely important one: we've had to scram . . . the loss of power and our bad trim have caused us to bottom, but luckily we've hit soft mud or sand. No compartment has reported flooding, so the pressure hull must be okay.' He paused again, gathering his thoughts.

'You must have guessed by now that we're on the Russians' doorstep off Zemlya: obviously I don't want to give away our position. That's why I'm staying where we are for a bit – to give us time to sort ourselves out.

'One thing is certain: we'll have to return to base, because bottoming has damaged our sonar and underwater gear. We've *got* to conserve all our electrical power to maintain the reactor's circulating water: and you all know how many amps that takes . . .

'Use as little electricity as possible and give the chief engineer and his boys a chance. They won't be able to restart the reactor, because the fire has burnt out the circuits. As soon as we're ready, I'll come to periscope depth to start snorting. We'll have only the two diesels; the reactor will need to be kept cool, so we'll have only enough amps for four knots.'

The confident voice paused for just a moment, for an instant uncertain of itself. 'Remember, everyone,' Carn went on, 'we're virtually at war here, in enemy waters. If we're to get back, we need every amp we can get. Keep quiet, don't move about – and remember your drills. All we need is patience, because the old girl is about to surface on her own, without any urging from me . . . ' He stopped again, then spoke conversationally on the VO to his second-in-command: 'Is all well for'd?'

The stornophone crackled and the calm voice of Lieutenant-

Commander Culmer came on the line:

'All well for'd, sir,' he said. 'Turnbull's under sedation and is recovering from the shock. He's got his head down, sir . . . '

There was subdued laughter over the amplifier . . . Turnbull was famed for his powers of eternal sleep. Then the chief engineer took over, his Scottish voice a reassurance that nothing was impossible for him and his over-worked team: .

'All well back aft, but can you give me a few minutes?' he asked. 'I'd like to check the snort gear so that there can be no hang-ups.'

'Very good, Chief, but buck up – we need every amp and the battery can't last long. I'll have an all-round listen if I can, while we're waiting.'

'Aye, aye, sir.'

Sinden saw Carn nod towards Elliot, the electoral officer. 'All-round sweep, if you can, please . . . '

'The hydrophone works, sir,' the Lieutenant said, 'but I'd like to nip down to the sonar room to check up.'

The captain hesitated. He did not want to open up the watertight doors, but it was vital to know whether it was safe to come up from deep. There could well be shipping up top, and none too friendly at that. He had a horror of surfacing from deep, without knowing whether it was safe to do so. He'd nearly lost his periscope in *Antelope*, his first conventional command . . . the danger of flooding was over now. He picked up the mike again.

'Open up bulkhead doors.' As the doors swung open, Lieutenant Elliot hustled out towards the sonar room.

Alastair Sinden was a sensitive character, receptive to the moods of others. He caught the sense of relief in the compartments as once again the boat opened up to become a whole unit. Only those aft of 63 bulkhead, pierced by the two-ton door which separated the nuclear plant from the rest of the boat, were now isolated from the remainder of the company. In SSNs, 63 bulkhead was the real trouble: 63 bulkhead was the end of the world, dividing the ship's company in two. It was a pity, Sinden thought, that life wasn't like it used to be in submarines. Before these incredible monsters appeared, everyone knew everyone else's job . . . There were only two occasions now when a seaman mixed with a stoker back aft: if the batteries were charging and gassing, when the seamen could not smoke for'd; and when there was trouble with the cooling system for'd, so that the seamen were forced to go aft to keep relatively cool.

George, Sinden noted, was doing his best to remain patient.

He paced his control room, saying nothing, but mentally counting the seconds as the small battery exhausted its life-giving energy. Once all power was lost, everything would stop, including the life-support systems, the oxygen-making machinery and the $CO_2$ absorbent. Sinden knew that the low visibility was what worried George most, the full moon being irrelevant in these latitudes. The radar masts would be of use only when the boat was at periscope depth ... Speed was vital now – so what was delaying Elliot?

'All-round listen completed, sir,' the sonar room broadcast announced, as if in answer to Sinden's thoughts. 'I'm doubtful, sir, on a bearing of 340°. Request permission for another check?'

'Carry on.'

Bill Elliot was a Cambridge graduate: to escape the rat race, he'd joined the Royal Navy and he found the life fascinating. He was an excellent electrical officer and enjoyed the complexity of his job. Though he wasn't the sonar officer, he spent much of his life in the sonar room. Modern sonar had made incredible strides since those early asdic offices of the wartime submarines wherein one man crouched over a set in the port after corner of the control room. In *Mars*'s vast sonar room, the 'eyes' of this incredible submarine, Elliot watched intently as the operator slowly continued his search.

'Petty Officer Harris,' he said, nodding to the Torpedo Anti-Submarine Instructor, 'take another all-round sweep.'

'Aye, aye, sir.' The most experienced sonar operator in the boat slipped the earphones back on his head. Watched by the eight other men in this secret room, Harris methodically swept around the compass in five-degree steps. Listening with all his concentration, he had covered all sectors and was reaching the north-western quadrant when Elliot saw the man suddenly stiffen. Elliot leaned over his shoulder: 325°, then on again to 330° and 335°, then cutting back to 325°, checking and cross-checking ... Harris worked silently, then completed the sweep to 360°. Swiftly he returned to 330°. He took off his headset and handed it to Elliot.

'Listen, sir,' he said, and there was a query in the man's blue eyes as he turned his head upwards towards his departmental officer.

It took one and a half minutes for Elliot to re-acclimatise himself to the old method of listening, that of using the sonar receiver as a hydrophone. There was nothing on 320° ... nothing but the familiar water noises of the sea; then, at 325°, the note changed to a gentle whispering which, on 330°, developed into a definite pulse, a staccato beat ... tick – tick – tick ...

He renewed the sweep – there it was: tick – tick – tick ... He picked up the broadcast microphone:

'Captain, sir,' he reported. 'Sonar room here. There's a warship in contact with us on a bearing of 330°.'

# CHAPTER 4

## *Dawn Encounter*

Peter Sinclair leaned back, his hands taking his weight on the edge of the chart table. He'd indicated to the captain the ship's estimated position: an encircled dot in pencil, 218° – southern edge of the sheer cliff at the south-eastern end of Mezhdusharsky Island – 13.7 nautical miles. Peter had typed out the position and given a copy to the radio room, just in case . . . and now he could do nothing but wait, as so many of the others.

Peter knew that the captain was worried about the visibility ... it had been barely over a mile when they went deep last night – and now, with enemy surface forces up top, the risk of collision was very real. If these Russian frigates (if they *were* A/S frigates) were in contact, what were their intentions? Capture probably; or if that failed, then destruction of the intruder who had trespassed into the waters they considered their own. They would ask no questions . . . only an oily patch for a day or two, and no one would be the wiser – not even 'grave' representations by the politicians in the sacrosanct marble halls of the world's forum would ripple the diplomatic sea.

'Ask the executive officer to come to the control room.'

Sinclair was surprised. This move was the first indication that the Old Man was worried. He made his own decisions and needed no help from his second-in-command. Seconds later, the gingery-haired, tired face of Lieutenant Commander Terence Culmer peered round the dividing bulkhead of the sonar room. He was freckled, but the boyishness that had once smiled from that strained face had long since vanished. His grey-green eyes were serious as he reported to his captain.

'Like to come along too, Alastair?' Carn asked, his gaze meeting momentarily that of his friend and passenger.

The three senior officers in the boat moved to the privacy, five yards away, of the ward-room. When existence was in the balance, Carn was man enough to seek the advice and the support of others. It was during those few minutes of deliberation, that the sonar room made another report:

'Enemy appears to have lost contact.' Harris was reporting, and Peter could sense the relief in the PO's voice. 'Slow HE, sir, disappearing 345°.'

So the frigate's hydrophone effect was decreasing, was it? That, at least, was a bonus, unless she was merely stopping to listen – a well-worn, war-time ruse to lure submarines to the surface. Peter glanced at the clock above his chart table: 0108 – seventeen precious minutes of those vital amps had been consumed. The circulating pumps had to be kept running or the reactor would run wild . . . Peter watched the captain returning to the control room, at his heels the XO and Sinden. Carn's face was set as he picked up the stornophone to speak to his company:

'Captain speaking . . . I've just taken counsel with the executive officer and Commander Sinden who, as you all know, is with us on this patrol to gain knowledge of this part of the world before he brings *Hector* up here. I've asked their opinions of the courses of action open to us, because the decisions I am about to take will affect the lives of all of you. You'll be relieved to know that was are all in agreement.'

Carn paused a moment, coughed, then went on:

'Our choice, as I'm sure you'll realise, is quite simple. As I said just now, because the reactor must be kept cool, we have to use amps on running the reactor cooling system – that's our first priority, or the kettle will boil. If I stay here on the bottom, we have another fifty minutes of battery power and then we lose everything . . .'

Peter was watching the silent men who, for a moment in time, seemed like marble statues as they stood, motionless, awaiting their fate.

' . . . if we are to survive, we must snort to get the diesel going. That means periscope depth, and as soon as the chief engineer can give us the generators, we'll be in business . . .'

He paused once again. The lines in his heavy cheeks grooved deeply; his eyes were hard and determined, as he held those of Sinden.

'I'm not sure what's going on up top,' the captain continued.

'There may be trouble because someone (so the sonar room thinks from their bow-and-arrow gear) could be waiting for us. There's the choice . . . ' He stopped, waiting for his words to sink in. 'We either stay here to wait for the kettle to blow up. Or we come to periscope depth and try to get the boat home – two thousand miles.'

Once again he hesitated. He seemed, Peter felt, uncertain whether to amplify his anxiety.

'I've decided to come up and try snorting – even at four knots we could get home – but it would take a day or two.'

The momentary mounting of their hopes was soon dashed by his next announcement.

'You all know that, whatever happens, we can't let *Mars* fall into enemy hands. So I've asked the First Lieutenant to be at immediate notice for opening main vents, if the enemy looks like boarding. If I decide on this last resort, I'll order *Abandon Ship*: you'll have to look slippy to get out . . . '

Before the impact of the final decision could penetrate, he snapped out his statement.

'All hydraulic systems are now back on line. We're in almost perfect main ballast trim. I'll try to hold her on the planes as we come up . . . ' He put down the mike and turned to his XO:

'Take over the trim, please, Number One. Try to hold her on the planes when I go slow ahead. Shut all bulkhead doors and remain at emergency stations.'

Peter felt his heart racing against his ribs: the next few minutes would decide their fate.

The captain picked up the mike again and talked to his company. 'Resume emergency stations,' he ordered. 'The general alarm will not be sounded . . . *Emergency stations, emergency stations, emergency stations . . .* '

Peter felt the thump of the bulkhead doors slamming shut: the compartments were once again sealed off, each an isolated capsule. The loudspeaker crackled again:

'101 bulkhead shut, door manned . . . 35 bulkhead shut, door manned . . . '

The captain nodded at his executive officer. 'Take her up, Number One,' he said quietly. 'Slow ahead, 15 degrees bow up.' He turned to Hennessy at the panel.

'Crack one main ballast,' he ordered. 'A quick puff to lift her bows.'

The HP air screamed momentarily. 'Stop blowing,' snapped Carn. 'Stand by to snort.'

Peter held his breath – she was stuck – nothing shifted. Then gently, almost imperceptibly, her bows lifted. He felt the deck come up to meet him: the needle on the depth gauge flickered, began to move.

*Mars* was coming up from deep. She was blind, she was out of trim and no one knew what was up top. But these were secondary fears: she was on the way up.

'Periscope depth.'

The captain's command brought Alastair Sinden's concentration back to reality: for too long his thoughts had been in Scotland, in the Ayrshire village nestling in the birch-woods north of Faslane. Jacqueline Carn and her children would be tucked away there at the moment, totally oblivious of the drama being played out, the head of the family its principal actor: it was a far cry to Dunbrae House from Novaya Zemlya . . .

George was a remarkable guy . . . there he stood, four-square in the control room, a workman if ever there was one: squarely on his splayed legs, his huge frame poised to balance against this steep bow-up angle, his rolled-up sleeves showing the thick-set forearms, dark with their covering of hair. Hands on hips, his intelligent eyes were everywhere, assimilating the data from the innumerable gauges, monitors and dials . . . if anyone could extract a sixty-million-pound, 6,000-ton submarine out of this mess, he could. Carn was certainly one of *Dolphin*'s most competent COs: he had not been boss of the 'Perisher' Attack Teacher for nothing – all the recent generations of submarine captains had been dragged through their COQC (Commanding Officers' Qualifying Course) by him.

'Hard-a-dive on both planes . . . ' It was the XO, his voice low-key but incisive. All eyes were on him now, for in his hands he held their lives.

'May I speed up, sir?'

He had turned his head momentarily to meet those of his captain. Carn shook his head – and Sinden understood the reasons for the refusal: there could be little battery power left and that was needed for cooling the kettle . . . to group up and, by the extra speed, hope to hold her down now, was unrealistic with this monster under a main ballast trim. If she was going to break surface. nothing would stop her now, except perhaps opening main vents and risking plummeting again to the bottom.

'400 feet, sir.'

Culmer was methodically carrying out the drill. Trained in

26

conventionals for fifteen years, there was little he did not know about trimming. 'I can't get this angle off her, sir. D'you want me to compensate?'

If he shifted water from X to H, he might get this 40° bow-up angle off her; but, once again, with a main ballast trim, she could decide to put her nose down again . . . there would be no second chance of recovery from a deep plunge now.

'Yes – but watch it . . .'

Alastair Sinden would have done the same. He was watching Carn like a lynx, fascinated by the man's reactions: the worse the trauma, the quieter the guy became. There was complete silence now in the control room: the light of the reduced lighting reflected palely on the white faces; the tense commands, the swift repeats, were now all that could be heard, except for the whine of the motors and the forced draught of the ventilation.

'Let me know when seven hundred gallons have passed . . .' And Sinden's eyes, like all those in the control room, watched for the tell-tale indicator lamp to blink.

She was coming up fast now . . . 150 feet, 140, 130 . . . fast, apparently out of control – and there seemed no sign of the bow-up angle coming off – she was shooting upwards, and it was difficult to keep one's feet. Sinden swore softly as a tool-box broke adrift, careered across the deck and smacked him across the ankle.

'One hundred feet, sir,' Culmer reported. 'Coming up fast, sir. I can't hold her.'

'Very good.'

Sinden knew then that things were bloody serious – until now he hadn't realised how desperate the emergency had been. George Carn was uncertain whether *Mars* would remain in a positive trim and he would not permit her to resume a negative . . . he would ensure that his troops could bale out, rather than risk a fatal catastrophe . . .

'Up periscope.'

The rap of command jerked Sinden back to actuality. If there was anything up top now . . . George Carn was taking her up from over 500 feet and she'd shoot out of the water like a floundering whale . . . if some unfortunate ship was overhead, *Mars* would slam straight through her bottom.

'Eighty feet, sir.'

Carn was grasping the periscope handles firmly, waiting for the glass to break surface – a quick all-round look and, all being well, the welcome command of 'Start snorting . . .'

'Open number one main vent.'

27

So the captain was trying to hold her down, risking another dip . . .

'Shut number one main vent . . .'

A quick open-and-shut, to reduce momentarily the leap upwards . . . Alastair felt the check, the pressure beneath his feet suddenly coming off: the bubble was moving swiftly . . . 25° now – damn sight better and easier to stand.

'Seventy feet, sir . . .'

This was the moment of truth. Sinden held his breath, waiting for the sickening judder, the screech of metal and the roar of the inrushing deluge . . . he watched Carn, tensed at the eye-pieces of the periscope as he waited for the shaft of light to flicker through to his eye-ball. When the glass broke surface, the water would stream off it, to reflect a clean image to the eyes and the brain some seventy feet below.

'*Don't flood, Number One . . .*'

There was urgency in Carn's words as the pencil of light pierced his eyes. He had sighted something. There was now nothing he could do to prevent a break surface. He was swinging round the whole arc, swiftly scanning the horizon by using the Mark I Eyeball Method . . .

'There are five destroyers here,' he said. 'They've been waiting for us . . .' Then, savagely, he rapped his final commands, the orders he had dreaded to give:

'Surface,' he ordered. 'Stand by to open main vents.'

He dipped into the conning tower, as Soper flicked the clips off the lower lid. As he climbed the ladder, his voice boomed in the tower, echoing in the clammy vault:

'Stand by to abandon ship,' he called. 'All hands remain at diving stations. Pilot – man the periscope.'

The boat lurched wildly. Then, suddenly levelling-off, she jerked men from their feet. She wallowed drunkenly, helpless on the surface, like a harpooned whale in its death throes . . .

'Blow one, blow two main ballast.' Culmer's orders resonated clearly from the tower, above the thunder of the seas walloping against her pressure hull.

The pressure vented suddenly as the upper lid opened. Water splashed downwards and Peter felt the wetness as he grabbed the periscope handles. He caught his breath as he swung across the horizon: five lean, grey shapes were rolling gently in the swell, less than a mile away. In the early Arctic dawn, their silhouettes stood starkly against the horizon, where the black outline of Zemlya's cliffs hung like a backdrop to some Shakespearean tragedy.

One destroyer, larger than the rest, seemed to be the control ship. Another, steaming in from the north-westward, was less than five hundred yards distant, a bone in her teeth as she swept in to ram. There were seamen on her fo'c'sle and they were leaning over the guard rails, arms outstretched and pointing . . . less than four hundred yards and plunging straight towards them. Peter could see her knife-edge bows plunging in the swell, her dark-red anti-fouling rearing momentarily . . . sheets of spray flung across her fo'c'sle and bridge; her CO stood motionless, mesmerised on his bridge as he conned his ship towards the hated enemy. Three hundred yards and decreasing rapidly . . .

'Dive, dive, dive . . . ' The cry echoed from far away in the cavernous tower. Peter knew that the order came too late: *Mars* took seven minutes to get down. He braced himself, waiting for the shock. He forgot even to lower the extended periscope.

# Part II

# CHAPTER 5

# *The Falling Leaf*

For that millionth part of a second which the human brain takes to make a decision, Commander Carn was undecided as to his next action. He was standing with his back pressed against the fore edge of the fin, his legs astride the slippery, dripping deck. His eyes were rivetted on the destroyer tearing in on *Mars*'s port quarter: the brute was almost on top of them.

The periscope head reared above the submarine's bridge personnel which consisted only of Carn, Soper (the Surface Officer of the Watch) and young Dean, the Radio Operator (General), who had the best eyesight in the boat. All three pairs of eyes were glued on the grey monster charging down upon them: her bows sliced a white bow-wave from the green water to spill spume and spray across her fo'c'sle as she lunged in the swell.

'Dive-dive-dive . . .'

Perhaps it was the submariner's natural instinct for conceal-ment that clicked Carn's mind to this decision; perhaps it was because the only alternative was to do nothing . . . the Russian was hell-bent on ramming to destruction, so why wait for it? At least, by going through the motions of diving again, the boat would be in the first degree of water-tight integrity.

Dean was already sliding down the tower; Soper was half way through the upper lid when Carn jumped for the hole. His glimpse of the surface world was one he would never forget: their executioner was upon them, her bows rearing from the water as her fore-foot struck the rounded casing of the submarine's after part.

It was the screeching of the torn metal, rather than the shock of impact, that appalled Carn's sensibility – and then the sickening crunch when the destroyer's bow bit deep through *Mars*'s pres-sure hull. The destroyer's bows rocketed into the air from the impact; then she slumped, her fo'c'sle shoved backwards like corrugated paper; Russian seamen were leaping clear into the boiling sea, as Carn glimpsed the precise point of impact: some thirty feet abaft 63 bulkhead. A huge gash, like some obscene amputation, showed momentarily – and then as suddenly disappeared as the destroyer's side, leaping upwards, rolled over the mortally wounded submarine. Carn felt the shock of the impact as he fell through the upper lid.

'First clip on . . .'

He shouted the report when the hatch slammed shut above his head, his words pygmy and unintelligible in this cacophony. The boat was being laid over on her side, until Carn could no longer gauge the angle of heel – must be over sixty degrees – and *could* she be turtled, a boat of this immensity and displacement? Suddenly she catapulted back as she wrenched free from the lethal embrace of the destroyer. Carn heard a cry of pain beneath him (sounded like Dean being flung against the lower ladder) and then he knew that *Mars* was on her way down.

It was the bow-down angle that shook the captain most. *Mars* was standing on her head, with a bow-down angle of at least sixty degrees – and Carn, head downwards, had to hang from the lower ladder in order to reach his control room. Sinclair was there, face white as he turned towards him with outstretched hands. Tregant, the Diving Officer of the Watch, was clutching the planeman's seat and was trying to yank himself upwards, back on to his knees.

The depth gauge showed 93 feet.

Lieutenant Peter Sinclair had watched the collision through the periscope. He was snatching a visual bearing of Novaya Zemlya – (he succeeded in taking three good ones in those vital seconds) when he too became mesmerised by the destroyer mounting *Mars*'s gleaming turtle-back. He'd also seen the point of impact, the terrible wound opening up abaft the fin, some thirty feet abaft 63 bulkhead.

'Where's she hit us, Pilot?' Carn gasped as he collapsed into the control room.

'Abaft 63 bulkhead, sir,' Peter said. 'I saw the collision.'

Carn nodded, his mouth working as he yelled something in response, unintelligible in the prevailing bedlam.

The cataclysm began when *Mars* reached 180 feet: a deafening, underwater roar accompanied the screech of tortured metal. Each hideous wrench plucked at their nerves; each shock hurled men against the boat's sides, and into their countless projections. A high-pitched scream, barely sonic, swamped the overwhelming screech of massacred steel. A hideous thump! a crash! . . . and the boat reeled, as if struck by a blow from a giant's fist.

3                                    33

Then, just as swiftly, the cacophony ceased . . .

This sudden silence was more unnerving than the appalling noise that had gone before. The control room adopted an even worse bow-down angle: Sinclair had given up trying to estimate the angle now, but the remains of the submarine must have been at an angle of over seventy degrees.

'The after part has broken adrift,' Carn said. '63 bulkhead was the fulcrum – the after part's gone.' He was numbed by the shock, unable to speak clearly. Peter glimpsed the agony in the man's face but, even now, Sinclair could not assimilate the magnitude of the disaster.

'Hold on,' the captain was shouting. 'We're heading straight for the bottom. All of you,' he commanded, 'flatten yourselves on the deck, feet first. We're about to hit the sea-bed.'

Sinclair could feel her now, plunging downwards in a spiralling motion, like a falling leaf, 300, 370, 380, 400, 440 – faster, faster, gathering momentum now, bows down straight for the arctic floor.

'*God save us*.' Peter averted his eyes from the gauges.

Alastair Sinden was crouched close to him and his eyes were closed. There was a twist of a smile at the corners of his grim, tightly-shut mouth.

Alastair Sinden braced himself for the devastating shock that was about to disintegrate the remnants of HM SSN *Mars*. It was possible that the after part had broken free; it was considerably longer than the section in which the for'd half of the ship's company were now incarcerated; the reactor compartment was in the forward section and must weigh at least three thousand tons: a mass of this magnitude would carry some momentum when it hit the bottom. He stretched himself on the control room deck and tried to compose his mind for the end . . .

Sinden wasn't surprised that he found himself praying. He believed in his Maker, not for all the intelligent reasons, but because he had discovered the nearness of God when his marriage with Claudia had collapsed. During those days after he had left their home in Weymouth (he'd been running *Truncheon* out of Portland) he had reached the depths of misery to which only a man of sensitivity could descend. He realised later that, to have survived the crisis, particularly when he was concentrating on his first conventional submarine command, was due to the discipline which had been hammered into him at Dartmouth. If nothing else, at the college you learned to tolerate conditions which you

34

hated; and he, with his innate longing to paint and his penchant for music, had learned early in life that a man could not escape his misery: the only solution was to lump the misfortune and to get on with the job.

In the moment of despair, he had crept into All Saints, the little church at the top of the hill, and prostrated himself before the altar; he had stretched out his hand and placed it in the hand of God. He had never been alone since then and had weathered seven lonely years since the divorce. Mercifully, they had chosen to forego a family until they could afford a decent house . . . he bore her no grudge and, thank God, she'd married again.

'Stand by₋₋.'

George Carn's warning stabbed through Sinden's thoughts. From his position on the deck, he could watch the reflection of the depth gauge against the perspex backscreen of the plot. The image of the dial was arse-about-face, but 500 feet was coming up fast . . . he clenched his fingers around the periscope wires to allow his body to go limp. God, how he hated this waiting game, he'd never . . .

The shock was not as violent as they had expected. There was a sickening scrunching of metal from for'd; a shock as they were all thrown forward; and then she decelerated . . . she slid sideways to take up a more civilised angle as she finally smashed her way to a halt across the sea-bottom.

'Her outer casing must have saved her for'd,' Carn said in the strange silence that followed. 'The rock here must be silted over.'

He turned towards Sinclair, as he expressed the thought that racked all their minds. Had the fore-ends survived, with their thirty-seven occupants?

'Rap on the bulkhead, Pilot,' he ordered. 'See if they're all right.'

The clock above the chart table had stopped: the hands were stuck at exactly 0119.

# CHAPTER 6

## *Facing Reality*

The knocking from the other side of the for'd control room bulkhead was not long in its response. The Old Man was right: the fore casing must have acted as a shock-absorber to take the full force of the impact. Those rounded bows, like the nose of some grotesque whale, must have rolled backwards like butter. But, Sinclair wondered, what had happened to the torpedoes? The fish were armed for an operational patrol: two warheads were conventional and four were wire-guided acoustic Mark IIIs. And what of the tube-space crew?

'Make your reports . . . ' the captain ordered briskly, while men clambered to their feet. 'Dean, are you fit enough to try your morse on the bulkhead?'

The captain advanced the few paces towards the radio operator, who had damaged himself in the tower. Carn stretched out a hand to steady the nineteen-year-old, who seemed still groggy from the blow on his head. 'You okay?'

'Fine, sir.' The pink-faced youth smiled nervously, abhorring the attention being forced on him. 'I'll have a go, sir.'

So, the picture began to piece itself together like a jig-saw. The morse tapping laboriously spelt out the situation in the fore-ends and tube space. Things were not as grim as all in the control room had at first thought; once the morse tapping was perfected, it was only the slowness of communications that became critical. But through 63 bulkhead there was no response, the captain himself having beaten upon the two-ton hydraulic door which separated the reactor compartment from the fore-part. They tried down below also, deep in the pump spaces next to the periscope well. The sinister reverberations from the reactor were the only sounds in the lower compartment.

As the hollow ringing of the wheel-spanner against the steel bulkhead died away in the stillness of the control room, men remained silent, each with his unexpressed, but smiilar, thoughts: the after part, with some sixty-five of their messmates, had broken away . . . this after section, like the fore part, must be lying inert on the bottom, at a depth of some 500 feet . . .

Sinclair respected George Carn – and this was not because Carn had married Jacqueline, Peter's sister. Peter had always liked George, but he had never appreciated more the steadiness of the man than at this moment, when disaster overwhelmed them. As Carn turned to await the final report from for'd, Peter caught his eye, and, for a second, a sense of mutual understanding passed between the two men. Carn knew that he enjoyed the confidence of his men, but there were moments when even those at the top needed reassurance.

The maddening clatter of the tapping had ceased. Dean turned his pale face to make his report:

'Tube space is flooded, but the fore-end bulkhead has held. No water coming in, sir.'

'Tell the XO I'm opening the bulkhead door.'

Peter felt better for the order that Carn had just given. The tube-space crew must have perished, but those who had survived in the fore-ends could endure the agony together and gain strength from each other. The clips clattered as they fell free and then the steel door swung open: in its entrance stood Terence Culmer, a streak of drying blood staining his freckled forehead. He slid across the sill of the doorway and climbed into the control room.

'The tube space crew got out, sir, before we shut the door. One casualty: Marine Engineering Mechanic Gallo, sir. I suspect a fractured skull.'

A sigh rippled round the control room. Though Gallo was seriously hurt, it was a miracle that no one had perished. They handed the unconscious man into the control room and laid him on the desk alongside the plotting table. He was suffering from internal bleeding from his head for blood was seeping from his nostrils.

'Number One,' the captain said, 'let's foregather once again in the ward-room.' He nodded also at his friend, Alastair Sinden, and then raised his voice so that his words would carry through the control room:

'We're intact,' he announced, his voice rasping from the over-worked chords. He cleared his throat and wiped the sweat from his forehead with the back of his hand:

'The after part has broken adrift and can't be far away. What is left of us is sound; we're not making water; and, apart from cuts and bruises, no one is hurt. The unpalatable bit is that, with the reactor automatically fully SCRAMMED, we've no power. You know what that means: we've got only what is left of our emergency lighting. That means no life-support system either, so we have to move fast, with so many of us to share the residual air in our two compartments. Our great bit of luck is that we're at only 500 feet: you all know that it is physically possible to make a rush escape from this depth: it's been done from six hundred.' He turned towards the Coxswain, CPO Ronald Hebbenden:

'Cox'n, call a rapid muster. Get yourselves organised to stand by for a rush escape from the fore-ends.' He faced Peter.

'Lieutenant Sinclair, take charge.'

Peter felt a jerk of relief. Since giving the captain their last known position, 13.2 miles from Zemlya, the collision point, there had been little that he could do. The coxswain could carry out the muster, while he and David Tregant counted the immersion suits.

The pale light from the single emergency lamp shone dimly upon the glistening faces sitting round the ward-room table: Carn, Sinden and Culmer. Their beards were shadows now on their faces and sweat dripped from their foreheads.

'It's warming up, sir,' Culmer said. 'The kettle?'

'Yes – reckon so; it should be fully scrammed on its own – God knows why it's boiling away like this . . .' Carn was speaking quietly, his mind racing for the decisions he knew he must make swiftly.

'As I see it,' he said, tapping his finger on the table, 'we're in 500 feet of water and, if Sinclair is accurate, we're just outside Russia's territorial waters: 1.2 miles outside their 12-mile limit.'

'That means that she shouldn't interfere with any rescue attempt?' Sinden was talking to himself. 'Once FOS/M (Flag Officer Submarines) mounts the sub-smash, the RAF could soon get a team here, provided the Russians will play ball. They might even lend us a salvage ship . . .'

'Yeah, that's okay, Alastair,' Carn snapped shortly, 'but we haven't got the air, mate . . . I haven't had the count yet, but there must be over sixty of us. There's precious little air left – the only hope is a rush escape and you know it.'

Culmer was surprised at George Carn's sudden terseness – he was rarely terse with anyone, particularly with his friend and contemporary, Alastair – the fatigue, tension and shock were enough to make a saint short-tempered.

'It's fifty minutes already, since the collision,' Sinden added. 'You're quite right, George: we've got to get out – and at the rush.'

There was a silence between the three men: no one wanted to express their common fear – 500 feet was a theoretical possibility for a rush escape, but should anyone panic, what then?

There was a shuffle of footsteps, and then the navigating officer and the coxswain appeared round the corner of the screen:

'I've had three counts, sir, both in the fore-ends and the control room,' Sinclair reported. 'There are now seventy serviceable immersion suits. The rest have been damaged by fire . . .'

Culmer said: 'We put it out, sir, without difficulty, but it was very intense while it lasted. The shock of bottoming sparked off an electrical fault.'

The four officers turned their heads towards Hebbenden.

'Seventy-three of us, sir,' he said as he swept the sweat from his forehead. 'That includes you, sir, and MEM Gallo.'

Carn met his senior rating's eyes squarely: Hebbenden was a fine man, loyal and utterly dependable. At forty-two he was the boat's 'father' and, for most of the junior ratings, father-confessor in addition. With his short, greying hairs and humorous brown eyes, he was instinctively trusted and liked. The tight lines – half-moon indentations at the corners of his mouth, told the story of his life of hardship and thrift: his devoted family (the two boys were grown up now) had learned to live all their lives by doing without. Now Hebbenden spoke up, his eyes meeting his captain's.

'I'd like to stay with MEM Gallo, sir,' he said quietly. 'The LMA is missing: he must have been abaft 63 bulkhead, and I'm the only chap qualified to care for Alfie, sir.' They all knew who Hebbenden meant. Alfie Gallo was the boat's comedian.

'Sit down, Coxswain,' Carn said, indicating the wardroom settee. 'Pilot, you might as well join us too. Keep quiet, please, about the number of suits.'

Peter Sinclair squeezed past Culmer and slumped down on the vinyl seat. He disliked the heat more than the cold, and his legs were feeling weak.

'Speak up, any of you, if my logic is wrong, but this is what I propose to do.' Carn, concentrating his thoughts, his head between his hands and his elbows on the table, spoke softly, as he deliberately chose his words.

'With no power, we have no air for a long wait. There are too many of us. To give Gallo a chance, we have to wait for him to regain consciousness – right?' He paused and Sinclair heard the soft affirmative from the other three.

'That forces several of us to remain behind and wait until Sub-Smash is initiated. The fewer the better, because the control room is a big compartment and we could last a long time, what with the external oxygen bottles. Right . . . ?' The three men nodded silently before he continued.

'So the quicker the rush escape is made, the better. A large crowd of you, floating up there in your orange suits, will provide a good chance of being found, providing you all stick together . . .'

'The Russians will have us on their sonar,' Sinden said. 'They'll be waiting for you . . .'

Culmer smiled. Even a hostile Russian was better than the emptiness of the Barents Sea and its icy greyness.

'There are seventy suits, so we're three short,' Carn said. 'Alastair and I are bloody good swimmers, so we'll get out in a free ascent – we don't need any damned suits.'

'With respect, sir,' the coxswain said firmly, repeating his previous suggestion, 'I'm an ex tank instructor. I'll stay to help the rearguard party, if I may, sir. You'll need me, and I can look after Alfie here.'

It was obvious to Sinclair that the captain accepted defeat. Hebbenden's obstinacy had triumphed. Carn nodded, then said:

'We can decide who's going to stay behind while the fore-ends are sorting themselves out.' He turned to his executive officer. 'I'm ordering you, Number One, to take charge of the rush escape. Flood up the fore ends: you know you can all get out if the drill is carried out properly.' Wanting no heroics, the captain was curt to the point of rudeness. 'Carry on, please, Lieutenant Commander Culmer,' he said, rising to his feet. 'You're my second-in-command and I want you to tell 'em up top how to get hold of us. They might even get that American mini rescue submarine here in time. It was designed to lock on to our escape towers.'

Culmer rose slowly from the settee. 'If those are your orders, sir, there's nothing I can do,' he said quietly. 'Good luck, sir.' He stood awkwardly, then moved quickly into the control room. 'I'll muster the hands now, sir.'

Peter Sinclair followed the small convoy. His heart raced: he'd always know that every man, once in his life, was put to the ultimate test – and this was *his* moment of crisis. He could not explain his reaction but he could not desert the captain and the others who were standing by Gallo. For the rest of his,

Peter's, life, he would never be able to look a man in the face again. He'd bloody well stay – he'd analyse the reasons later.

'Sixty-three minutes have gone,' Commander Carn said, addressing the sweating men gathered around him. They moved silently like a swirling tide as they donned their awkward orange immersion suits.

'Look like penguins,' Peter thought to himself. He wondered how many would reach the surface alive. There they stood, those splendid men, a homogeneous mixture of humanity, highly trained in the art of submarine escape. Thank God that they had been so well trained. The risks in the escape tank were worth taking, in spite of occasional fatalities – none of us, Peter realised, would have a chance if those devoted men in the tank hadn't trained us so patiently – it was disciplined drill that counted, when a man's instinct was only to panic.

'Sixty-three minutes,' the captain was repeating, 'and that's too bloody long. When I tell the executive officer to carry on, the rearguard party will shut the door on you: you must carry out your drill quietly, without fuss, just as you did at *Dolphin* . . .' His eyes travelled around the men, some of whom he knew so well; some of whom he'd been forced to punish; some to whom he'd been a friend in difficult times . . .

'If you carry out the drill calmly and correctly, you'll all get out without any bother.' He half turned to Hebbenden who was standing behind him:

'A rearguard party of about half a dozen will remain with MEM Gallo. We reckon we'll have a better chance than you lot, because you'll be waiting for us with cuppas at the ready.' He paused again, searching for his words.

'Commander Sinden, whom you all know, will be staying with me. So will the coxswain and, I believe, Lieutenant Sinclair.'

Peter felt the moment come and pass. He nodded: the die was cast. He felt better already.

'I'm a navy swimmer, too, sir . . .'

It was Soper's voice, cool and arrogant as ever. He edged behind the periscope and elbowed his way to stand by Sinclair.

'You'll need someone to read morse, sir.' Pinky Dean's high-pitched voice interrupted the awkward silence. The nineteen-year-old radio operator was pinker of face than normal, as he picked his way through the throng.

Carn gave a half smile. He shook hands with the three of his remaining officers, Bill Elliot, the Electrical Officer; Best, his

41

Fourth Hand and Franklin, the Torpedo Officer. The Chief and the two others had been in the after part.

'Good luck,' Carn said brusquely. 'Don't waste time.'

Culmer was waiting by the bulkhead door. He waited until Franklin had passed through, then turned to meet his captain:

'We'll be waiting for you, sir,' he said quietly. 'If the Russians play ball, we'll soon have you out . . .'

Peter watched the two men as they faced each other momentarily – and then Culmer was gone. As the door swung shut, he heard the XO's final order to the escape party:

'Stand by to carry out a rush escape,' he ordered. 'Plug in breathing units and check BIBS hull valve is open . . .'

The locking wheel spun and the door was shut.

'They'll be flooding up now,' Sinden said quietly.

He gently took Carn's elbow and guided him back to the silence of the ward-room. As they reached the screen, the boat shivered; a rasping sound, metal grating on rock, rumbled through the structure of what remained of *Mars*. She trembled as the bows suddenly dipped again:

'She's pivoted about the conning tower,' Carn said quietly. 'I thought she was doing that, after we'd settled. Did you feel her swaying, Alastair? I reckon we're perched on an underwater mountain-top.'

The boat groaned. There was a whistling sound from the other side of the bulkhead.

'Pressure will be equalising,' Sinden said. 'First man will be on his way up soon.'

As the rearguard party slumped off to the ward-room settee, there was a distant thump, a metallic ringing from the far side of the fore-end's bulkhead door.

'They've opened the upper lid,' Carn said, glancing at the clock which showed 0230. 'First man's away – good luck to 'em.'

Peter Sinclair closed his eyes. The pressure at 500 feet must be at least 330 pounds per square inch – would he stand the excruciating pain when his final test came?

# CHAPTER 7

## 'Sub Smash . . .'

Michael Boyd, Commander, Royal Navy, was Duty Operations Officer for the night. In his office below ground, at the heart of Britain's Defence Headquarters, it was difficult to believe that *Mars* had not made her routine signal. His orders were clear: the clock showed 0257 and in three minutes she would be officially designated overdue. He pushed back his chair, smoothed his black hair; donning his cap with the new gilt of his 'scrambled eggs', he passed down the passage to the exit door leading in to C-in-C's private quarters at Admiralty House. Admiral Sir Malcolmn Driver, C-in-C, Fleet, would not enjoy being shaken at this hour . . . but then, the orders were crystal clear should a nuclear boat become overdue . . . but this was going to be tricky, with *Mars* on a secret patrol . . .

'Admiral, sir . . . ?' He picked up the direct telephone sited by the entrance door of Admiralty House. He hoped that Mrs Admiral would not be disturbed: she was a holy terror. The instrument clicked at the other end . . .

'What is it?' The soft voice was alert, clear-cut.

'Duty Officer here, sir. *Mars* is overdue. Permission to institute Sub-Smash One . . . ' Once the procedure was set in motion, nothing could stop the wheels rolling . . .

'Her last position was about sixty miles south-west of *Zed*, wasn't it? That's Michael Boyd, isn't it?'

'Yes, sir, Boyd here. You're correct with her position.'

'Get me Flag Officer, Submarines, at Dolphin House,' the voice snapped. 'I'm coming down.'

Vice-Admiral Sir Frederick Clewes was an outspoken man, even for a submariner, for such had been his career until he became, to his surprise, Flag Officer, Submarines. The head of the Submarine Branch was not always a man of The Trade, Clewes's predecessor having been a gunnery officer (even that specialisation had vanished – there were no guns now). FOS/M detested being woken in the early hours, but he was surprised to hear C-in-C's unmistakable voice at the other end of the direct scrambler. Had there been an accident to one of the boats?

'What's up, sir?' Sir Frederick asked.

'*Mars* is overdue by twenty-three minutes. What are we going to do about it?'

FOS/M did not reply at once. Standing bare-foot in his red pyjamas, he rubbed the stubble on his chin. His own orders were clear enough, leaving no room for doubt – but if *Mars* had sustained an accident, should secrecy be jeopardised? No rescue attempt could be mounted without giving away the game to the public – and once the press sank its teeth into the news, the mass-media would be baying after the drama like hound-dogs. *Could* a rescue bid be attempted without the co-operation of the Russians? He doubted it.

'It's unlike George Carn to be adrift.'

Vice-Admiral Clewes chose his words carefully. He sensed that the emergency which was materialising could develop into the crisis of his eventful life. 'He must have had an accident, either to the boat or to his communications.' He paused a moment, before continuing his conversation with the sea-going navy's chief. 'You'll realise, sir, that every second will count now, if *Mars* is in trouble; it's a long way to point *Zed*.'

'The choice is clear, isn't it, Fred?' C-in-C summed up. 'We either show our hand to the Russians and disclose that we are aware of their $H_3O$ project; or we ignore *Mars*'s plight: you may not be able to achieve much, anyway, from this distance.'

'That's the choice, sir.' Clewes's voice was deliberate, ice-cold. 'I'm a submariner. I can't abandon George and his men, without lifting a finger. To hell with the national interest: *Sub-Smash One* is my decision.'

C-in-C did not reply immediately. The phone crackled again:

'Carry on with *Sub-Smash One*: make all your preparations, but, until I've had the PM's concurrence, everything is to remain secret.'

'Aye, aye, sir,' FOS/M acknowledged. 'Understood, but there's no hope of a rescue attempt unless the Russians help. If *Mars* is outside their territorial waters, they might co-operate. If *Mars* has lost her life-support system, we've probably thirty-six hours in which to extricate the survivors. Until we learn something, there's little we can do except to alert the salvage teams and the Royal Air Force. Sir, *we've got to get through to the Russians*: use the Hot Line, for God's sake. The Russians may need help from us one day: point that out to them.'

'Right,' the Admiral, Fleet, snapped. 'And don't forget, for the next hour, this operation is Top Secret, Fred . . . bye.'

The line snicked, went dead.

*Action*: Sir Frederick Clewes was happier on his own ground, if he could pursue his own profession. Would telephoning Bill Adams, his opposite number in America, constitute a breach of secrecy? Damnit, they were on the same side, weren't they? Bill could fly their rescue mini sub across, in one hop, to Zemlya, if the Russians would allow him to land. He'd alert him, anyway. He picked up the *sub-smash* telephone:

'That the Duty Officer, Faslane? Good. Execute *Sub-Smash One* and ask Captain s/m to speak to me – at the rush . . . ' He sensed the shock at the other end. Duty Officers at Faslane and in Blockhouse were not shaken by FOS/M for a *Sub-Smash* every night of the week. While the Vice-Admiral waited for Jack Quincey, Captain s/m Four, to emerge from his pit, he flashed the operator on the red telephone:

'Get me Admiral Adams in Washington,' he snapped, 'and be quick about it.'

By 0430, every man-jack in *Dolphin* and Faslane knew of the *Mars* emergency. By 0445, the Prime Minister, realising that the *Sub-Smash* was about to become world news, lifted his veto. The only course now, politically, was to appeal to the Russians for their help; if they refused to provide physical salvage assistance, they might provide aircraft landing facilities; or, at the worst, they might be asked not to be bloody awkward.

The Prime Minister, yawning from his bed, was about to pick up the telephone to speak to the President of the United States. He hesitated a moment: should he get through himself, direct to the Russians? While he hesitated, the red telephone shrilled on his desk.

'The President here. Good morning, Prime Minister, I'm sure sorry to hoist you from your pad at this hour, but something hot's turned up. The Russians have been on the line: they are accusing me of sending one of our submarines to their northern coast. They've picked up a red marker-buoy.' (The President pronounced it 'booey'.)

The Prime Minister tried to interrupt but the President was, as usual, in full spate. 'There's a name, *Mars*, on it. It's not one of ours.'

The Prime Minister seized his opportunity:

'Thank you. I'm afraid she's ours, Mr President. One of our

nuclear submarines is missing in that area. I'll get on to the Russians – tricky, isn't it, what with operation *Zed*?'

'Yeah . . . but you can count on me. I'll ring the navy now. They'll give you all the help they possibly can . . . So long.'

The grey-haired, distinguished but unshaven Prime Minister lowered the instrument on to its rest. He picked up the red phone again.

'Put me on direct to the Russians please. I want Mr Yarnoff.'

The Prime Minister was unlikely to enjoy the next few minutes. Yarnoff had succeeded Brezhnev and company, but, as boss of Russia, he was just as intransigent and tough. The Russians were unpredictable: when men's lives were at stake and, if there was desperate urgency, they might well co-operate to prove to the world that they *did* possess a heart – *could* react in a civilised manner. The least that Secretary Yarnoff could do was to release information on *Mars*'s position . . . the receiver snicked; the Prime Minister's wrist-watch showed 0452 . . . the minutes were ticking away now and every wasted second was a condemnation.

Captain Jack Quincey, DSC, Royal Navy, Captain of the Fourth Submarine Squadron at Faslane, was one of the few surviving captain S/MS who had served in Hitler's war. He had won his decoration in the Pacific as First Lieutenant of *Tantaliser*, one of the last T-boats.

He had put in train all that he could for *Mars*'s Sub-Smash, so had decided to call on Jacqueline Carn himself: no one else should break the news to her – she'd suffered a basinful of sadness already. Jack Quincey pulled the muffler more tightly around his neck.

'Get a move on, Jenny,' he said curtly to the WREN driver, still bleary-eyed from her sudden awakening. 'I haven't got much time.'

The captain's official car surged forward to weave its way up the narrow lane to Dunbrae House, the Carns' temporary home overlooking Loch Long. COs often exchanged their family houses when taking over their boats, and the Carn family had been no exception. With all their problems, the Carns could have found in the neighbourhood no better retreat than Dunbrae. Quincey rubbed his stubbled chin – this was no way to call on a submariner's grass widow. He'd known the Carns since his own early days as First Lieutenant of *Amphora*. George had married early: he had been an RNR Midshipman and had volunteered for submarines way back – he'd soon gone ahead, first as Fifth Hand, then as Third Hand of *Walrus*. Then he had married Jackie; he had been a junior lieutenant, with three years in.

As for so many, the early years had been penurious, but happy: four sons, all in a row – regularly, after every sixth patrol – and Jackie, a natural warm woman, had revelled in the joys of motherhood. Four sons – and Quincey knew how much Carn had longed for a daughter. Then their personal tragedy had hit them. They were under stress now, with having to cope, but something more had happened to Jacqueline.

He sighed – what a bloody job this was, this personal side of his lot . . . he dreaded how she'd take the news of *Mars*'s accident . . . *she* would realise, in her heart of hearts, that the chances of recovery were remote. The car slowed; the WREN's fingers twitched the indicator and the green lamp flickered on the dash-board. The car swung through the white gate which, typically George Carn, was always left open, the gravel scrunched beneath the tyres as the car snaked up the drive. Jack Quincey was peering through the side window: a house curtain was being drawn aside and, as he clambered out, he heard a child's cry.

Jacqueline Carn turned over once again, restless in her wide, empty bed. She was aware of Stephen's crying, but this awakening was normal now – the little mite barely knew what he was doing. His lack of understanding had made his upbringing so difficult – another difference between George and herself: he could not accept that they must treat Stephen differently from the others.

Slowly she regained consciousness, to the delicious love-duets of the wood-pigeons and the doves cooing their dawn serenades. She could hear the whispering of the leaves from the birches near the mossy rocks leading down to the loch's edge. She enjoyed this moment, every morning: a mid-summer dawn in western Scotland belonged to fairy-land; she could smell the dampness of the leaves and the sweetness of the bracken . . .

When George was away on these patrols, she had learned to tolerate the long separations; she refused to brood over the problems, preferring to count the blessings which God had granted her. Having to cope with Stephen had, in a strange way, brought its compensations: particularly with the new friendship she had made. She no longer felt so lonely, but she dared not tell even her mother – who could never understand, with her narrow views on propriety and what she considered to be 'the right thing'. Mum knew little of the warmth of love.

George had, she knew, always felt in his heart that *Mars* was his first unlucky ship. Since that near-grounding on her launching day, and after the refit accident, he had remained silent when she had asked him if he was happy with the boat. His silence had worried her, because he had never ceased to discuss his previous commands with her: she'd had to listen to interminable shop, but she had always been patient, knowing that the release of talking to her was a help: a captain's life was a solitary one.

There was little object in staying a-bed. Stephen was crying for her now (she could recognise the plaintive anxiety in his voice when he needed the reassurance of her presence). She'd get on with the chores so that she could be ready for the day's callers – but even the visitors had decreased since Stephen had complicated their life. She knew their sincere friends now, those who helped and those who truly meant to share their problem.

She rolled from the bed and tip-toed over to the mirror: what a sight! She raised her hand to brush her hair, but in the act she hesitated, to regard the woman peering back at her . . .

'I love your hair like that,' he had whispered the last time. 'Don't tidy it for me, my love . . . ' and she half closed her eyes, relishing in her imagination the delicious tenderness of his loving.

Her dark hair was coarse, like flax, and now streaked with grey – she kept it short and swept it back, like a tom-boy's. The quiff which she set across her forehead added a simplicity that breathed the wildness of the Scottish highlands.

She considered carefully her body, the outline of which showed clearly through the cotton nightie she always wore when she was alone and the nights were close. For her thirty-two years, she was remarkably slim after five babies: her stomach sagged more than it should, but her breasts had stood up well to the demands of motherhood – George had insisted that she should nurse her own children. Oh God, how she had longed to present him with their first daughter – she could never forget the moment when time stood still, on that morning he had rushed into the nursing home, straight from patrol . . .

Surprised, she heard the scrunch of the gravel, as car wheels rolled up the long drive between the wild rhododendrons. She moved swiftly to the curtains: a car was swinging slowly around the approach corner; it was black and it was official. Good Lord, it was Jack Quincey . . . what a mess she looked, but what on earth brought him here at this hour?

Suddenly she knew: the instinct of every submariner's wife was alerted, setting her nerves on edge . . . something had happened to *Mars*. She flung her quilted house-coat about her and moved swiftly into Stephen's room. His troubled eyes cleared with reassurance as she turned him over. She pattered down the bare staircase; she crossed the hall as she heard the car halting on the gravel. The door-bolts rattled as she drew them free; she swung open the oaken door to welcome the Captain of the Fourth Submarine Squadron.

She knew then that there was nothing to say: Jack was standing there, unshaven and with a scarf about his neck. His face, always so full of fun, was stern and uncommunicative.

'May I come in, Jackie, just for a minute?' he asked. 'I wanted to see you myself.'

The cry escaped her lips as she nodded and beckoned him inside. She stiffened when he put his arm about her shoulders. She allowed him to lead her into the kitchen: instinctively she filled the kettle before sitting down.

'What is it, Jack?' she asked softly, eyebrows raised in query. 'Something's happened to *Mars*?'

After he had let himself out, the car had crawled down the drive until at last there was no noise, nothing to remind her that, during those few minutes, her life had changed. Save for the sight of the wind through those distant pines, there was nothing, not even Stephen's cry to disturb the silence of these early hours of this most terrible dawn of 3 July.

When she reached the bedroom, she stood by the window and tried to analyse her thoughts: she longed, like most women, to alleviate the pain through the merciful relief of tears. As always, she succeeded in controlling herself: she had learned the art during these past few years: no one must detect the agony behind the façade of what was once Mrs George Carn (*'wonderful wife, you know, to George; he's devoted to her and the children. He's one of the successful* COs, *isn't he, my dear . . . ?'*) – and so went the coffee-time gossip, day after day . . .

Bitterly, she slipped silently back into bed, drawing the double blanket over her. She lay on her back, outstretched, waiting for the tears but come they would not . . . and, in misery, she mused on her relationship with George since his Devonport accident.

Had she *really* tried hard enough? What had happened to her, why did he repel her now? Was it the fear of another pregnancy with the repetition of its terrible result . . . ? Or was she using these natural revulsions as an escape to the lover she had so wonderfully, suddenly found? She flung herself on her side to bury her head in her arms. She felt the scalding tears streaming down her cheeks. As the sobs racked her thin body, she knew the meaning of despair. There was no one to whom she could confide her agony, share the frightful dilemma . . . God, surely, couldn't be so unkind? He was a God of happiness, wasn't he? Not a murderer of the finest of his children – why, oh God, why, why, why?

# Part III

# CHAPTER 8

# *The Rearguard*

Six men sat around the table in the ward-room of what was left of HM SSN *Mars*, the intact control room compartment: the seventh man, still unconscious, lay along the passage-way skirting the officers' mess. Apart from the normal external water noises, his heavy breathing was the only sound to disturb the silence in the steel tomb lying on the bottom of this arctic sea. The men at the table were listening, ears strained for any unusual sound from outside. The largest of them glanced at his wrist watch: 0342 on 3 July.

'They must have all got out,' Commander George Carn said. 'We would have heard something otherwise . . . '

'We've come a long way since the war in our escape procedure,' Alastair Sinden said. 'The experience of those who were kept down helped enormously our knowledge of the dangers of air under pressure: *United*, one of the U's was one of them, wasn't she, George?'

Carn nodded. He'd served as a fourth hand with Andrew Brough who'd known one of the war-time boys. He'd had a tale to tell – thirty-six hours, wasn't it, that she'd been kept down – and survived?

'Yes – that was her – I met her one-time CO once. He became FOSM wayback. He once told us how they'd coped.'

George Carn remembered then the day he'd listened to them yarning at the bar in *Dolphin*: and, come to think of it, their own predicament was little different. For all the advance of technology in these nuclear submarines, when once the power had failed, they were back to basics – seven men breathing air in a locked compartment whose cubic capacity would be little different from that of one of the diminutive U-boats. *Mars*'s control room compartment was probably a trifle smaller than the total internal volume of *United* . . .

Thirty-six hours . . . from the instant of impact at 0115, some three and a half hours ago, a similar ordeal would take them until

1300 on the day after next, Saturday, 4 July. Carn remembered the FOS/M saying that if he'd had the choice over again of whether to bale out and risk being shot in the water, or re-living their thirty-six-hour dive, he'd have picked the former . . .

The oxygen plant was kaput and so was the carbon dioxide absorbent apparatus; today no protosorb, the carbon dioxide absorbent, or tin trays were carried in these modern marvels. So during the next thirty-three hours, life would be very much the same as earlier submarines had known it. George Carn guardedly considered the six others who were endeavouring to sleep around the table; he had told them to stop talking and to move as little as possible, in order to conserve oxygen, and they were doing their best.

First, there was Gallo, Marine Engineering Mechanic (or 'Stoker' as an MEM was traditionally called), unconscious and stretched out as comfortably as possible along the deck. 'El Greco', they christened him in the fore-ends: he was the boat's comedian and arch-skiver, was up to all the tricks to dodge any matter official or ceremonial. He had been known once to appear at Divisions in the depot-ship at Faslane, but that had been for the Queen's birthday. A mutual truce had been declared between Gallo and the coxswain, who was simulating sleep in the corner of the settee. The 'Swain' and El Greco enjoyed the undeclared war between themselves, sharing the camaraderie of men who respected each other.

Gallo was in a bad way. Since the collision, when he'd been crushed by the torpedo that broke adrift in the fore-ends, he had lost consciousness from his terrible injuries. His skull must be fractured and he was bleeding internally: they could not stop the blood smearing beneath him on the deck.

Carn realised that only Alastair and 'Heb', as the coxswain was known, would have an inkling of what the next thirty-three hours would bring: and even they were barely old enough to have had contact with a hot war. For the other three, Soper, the unreliable Lieutenant; young Dean, the nineteen-year-old Radio Operator; and the Pilot, Peter Sinclair, only the mass-media or American films could offer any clues to the ordeal that lay ahead . . . This was just as well – and Carn sighed deeply. What a bloody awful mess he'd got them into. He'd have to compose his thoughts, consider carefully the various factors. If he kept his head there might conceivably be some sort of chance for one or two of them.

After scramming the reactor, there was the collision; then the torpedo breaking adrift and the fire in the fore-ends. When he'd asked Culmer to discuss things in the ward-room, the First Lieutenant was the only other who could have realised the gravity of the final disaster that had befallen them: the fire had destroyed a large proportion of the immersion suits in the fore-ends.

Sufficient immersion suits were carried in each compartment for the total ship's company, but the fore-ends' fire had destroyed nearly half the outfit. After the sixty-five men who had made the rush escape had been catered for, there were only five suits more – and one of these was damaged and dubious.

When Dean and Hebbenden had insisted, too, on remaining behind, they had known that there were five immersion suits (and one shaky) for seven men, though one of them was unconscious. It was too late, but Carn wished that he had not asked Sinclair to remain.

The whole damned thing was a tragic paradox. Two of them certainly would not have remained behind had it not been for Gallo: Dean was El Greco's 'oppo'; and it was Gallo's injuries which had swayed Heb's mind.

Gallo was dying, Carn knew that; he could see death in the pallor of the man's face. The quick breathing and the blue lips – he couldn't possibly last another day, let alone thirty-two and a half hours – and how could they possibly dress him in a suit and eject him from the tower? Carn wouldn't let the cat out of the bag yet: he had personally locked up the suits in the radio office so that Soper and Dean should not know the worst.

And Alastair, what of Alastair Sinden, his passenger and prospective fellow SSN CO? He'd been unusually subdued this trip. What had got into him? There was a suspicion of a gulf widening between them; was he apprehensive, perhaps, of being in the way and an embarrassment? If so, this was a different Sinden to that of the old days when they'd shared a cabin up at Rothesay – that had been a wild party, then, a Perisher of Perishers . . . but these nuclears needed a different breed of captain: the piratical flair had to be discarded if a sixty-million-pound monster was to earn her keep and survive. Alastair would make a good SSN CO – and, if anyone really *knew* Sinden, it was George Carn: it was typical of Alastair that he had quietly stood behind Carn in his hour of need, even if the choice meant certain death.

So here they were, Sinden, Sinclair, Soper, Hebbenden, Dean, the stricken Gallo – and himself. It was probably easier for him to face the inevitable, than for the others. He knew he'd have to be the last to escape – and from 500 feet without a suit, there wasn't a cat's chance in hell. He preferred to sit it out alone and face his Maker – the gentle kiss of death could be a lot less unpleasant than being crushed by the pressures outside. Five suits, seven men – and as he was to be one of the unlucky ones, who was to be the other? Or the other *two*, because the fifth suit was very suspect – he wouldn't like to escape in it . . .

Sinclair? He was probably the most inflexible of the other five – obstinate as a Turkish mule when he thought he was right. The guy was a good one, even though he'd come in by the back door, rather like he, Carn, had done. Ex-trawlers was an unusual entry, but so was Carn's as an ex-midshipman RNR. What was pleasantly normal was that Jackie adored her brother – and that sometimes led to difficulties when Carn had to rebuke his navigating officer – but, fortunately, the necessity arose seldom.

Sinclair would have made a good CO: it was like him to stay behind without protest, but it was a damned shame, with his Jeannie so proud of her submariner husband. The Sinclairs were a delightful family, and Jeannie, with her independent training as a trawler mate's wife, was quietly competent in bringing up the two children. Jeannie was expecting their third, and it was sad to think that it might be born fatherless if they didn't get out of here alive. She would have to bring them up alone – but she would marry again, for she was an attractive girl, warm and out-going, the ideal woman for someone like Peter, who needed reassurance.

In the half light, Carn regarded the navigating officer and brooded upon the young man's open face, with its amused, brown eyes: an honest face, with few secrets to conceal. The big, pro-truding ears and the wide, broken nose, gave him an Honest-Joe look . . . You could trust Sinclair, but he was not always as self-conscious as he seemed: when he gave an order, the troops jumped – and that was what was needed. He badly wanted to be recom-mended as a Jimmy for the fast disappearing conventionals, so long as he could stay the pace . . .

One of the lieutenants, Sinclair or Soper, would have to escape without an immersion suit: whom to choose was a monstrous decision for Carn to make: for one of them, it would be a sentence of death. He could not select Sinclair just because of the family connections: Soper had as much right to live, though he had always been the odd man out.

Carn had never been able to trust Soper . . . perhaps it was the over-confidence of the one-year-in lieutenant that made Carn wary of him? Three years younger than Sinclair, he enjoyed the advantage of the training and polish which Dartmouth was supposed to afford. Good-looking in a smooth, self-satisfied way, with his fair hair always immaculately brushed back on either side of its neat parting, his face had the buttoned-up look of a well-cut waistcoat. With his looks, it was not surprising that the girls flocked around him at parties; it was perhaps his arrogant unconcern for the company around him that attracted the flashy sort of woman. Carn had always been dubious about Jake Soper's love-life – he seemed disinterested in the female sex, and at twenty-five appeared to have no bird in the nest. This had been noted by his evil-minded messmates, but the assumption they made probably bred the chip on the shoulder which Soper undoubtedly possessed.

There were times when the chap was very unpleasant to Sinclair; because Soper carried a year's seniority over Peter, there was no need for him to show his dislike for a man who was ex-trawlers. If ever they got out of this, Carn would have to be firmer with Soper about his attitude: his abrasiveness was already affecting *Mars*'s ward-room. When he had volunteered to remain with the rearguard, Carn had been pleasantly surprised . . .

The final member to be considered was that strange little bloke, Radio Operator (General) Perry Dean. The youngster's face was half turned towards him, and Carn could see why the troops nicknamed him Pinky. The roundness of his face did not promise the so-called toughness required of men summoned into submarines. They'd given the boy (nineteen now, wasn't he?) a rough time in the fore-ends, but that was before Gallo had knocked seven bells out of one of Pinky's tormentors. From then onwards an indissoluble friendship had developed between the stoker and the radio operator – an unusual comradeship, because the lads in the engine-room department tended, because of the different watchkeeping system 'back-aft', to stick together for their runs ashore. Pinky's loyalty had landed him in this mess . . .

Carn glanced at the ward-room clock which mercifully worked mechanically as well as electrically – some designer must have been a far-sighted, one-timer submariner: 0412 . . . dear God, how the time had dragged – three and a half hours passed and thirty-two and a bit in which to survive . . .

Then he heard a 'tick', 'tick', 'tick . . . tk', 'tk', 'tk . . . ' a faint ticking pervading their surroundings and coming from all directions. He was already double-checking his reactions when Chief Petty Officer Hebbenden sat up slowly from the settee.

'Sonar transmissions,' he said softly. 'D'you hear them, sir?'

'Same moment as you, Coxswain. Wake the others.'

By the dim lighting (they were using only one emergency lantern now) Carn watched each recumbent figure jerk to life. Sinden and Sinclair listened in silence.

'What's up?' Soper asked.

'Listen,' Carn said. 'Try to pin-point the bearing . . . '

Then, in the stillness, disturbed only by the rapid breathing of the prostrate man on the deck, the flutter of a ship's propellers whispered above them.

'That's a destroyer in contact, I'm certain,' Sinden said. 'Could be Portland all over again, George.'

Carn smiled. Bit of a contrast: crippled on an arctic sea-bed instead of ping-running peacefully in the blue waters of Weymouth Bay . . .

'She's speeding up, sir.' That was Hebbenden again, experienced and reliable. 'She'll be running overhead in a moment.'

'Not much point in shutting off from depth-charging,' Sinden said, his forced humour grating on Carn's nerves.

'There's nothing else to shut,' Sinclair said.

'Except your mouth,' Soper said, barely audibly. 'Dry up, Peter, for God's sake. We're running out of air – or didn't you know?'

Carn heard the bitterness in the man's voice. Soper was right, as usual, but he had no right to talk like this.

'Keep still, all of you,' Carn snapped. 'If anyone is going to yap, it will be only me . . . Listen, all of you, to what I've got to say.'

The hydrophone effect crossed overhead and slipped down the port side – the whisper receded, stopped, then started again; but now the noise grew louder as the destroyer attempted, once more, to turn directly overhead.

'Can't hear any charges on their way down,' Sinden said. 'Perhaps they've some other ploy up their sleeves.'

No bangs, no explosions . . . yet.

'While you lot have been sleeping your heads off,' Carn said, 'I've been coming to some conclusions. I'm open to correction, but, as I see it, the Russians have picked us up . . . don't ask me how, but I reckon they were waiting for us when we were run down.

'Since then, keeping in contact will have been easy for them. By now, they must have seen the XO's party: this destroyer is probably picking up our survivors. Our marker-buoy must have been released before the rush escape and this will be pin-pointing our position. If Number One is up there, there won't be much time wasted.'

'So long as the Russians are friendly,' Sinden said. 'They're a funny lot: over a thing like this, they might even try to help . . .'

'You're right, Alastair,' the captain said. 'Our best hope is to assume that they're basically human beings like ourselves. FOS/M will have been on to them, because Sub-Smash must be operating by now. Our job is to stay alive long enough, so listen to what I've got to say . . .'

Carn glanced round the table. Sinden smiled; Hebbenden nodded; Sinclair and Soper stared him in the face; Pinky Dean bit his nails; and Gallo's rapid breathing was a depressing accompaniment to which they had grown accustomed.

'We're down to basics – the only air we have is what's left in our wrecked compartment. 63 bulkhead has held and so has the fore-end section. We're not making water, so we should have enough air to last at least . . . ' and here he paused, uncertain whether to be over-optimistic. He decided on facing the facts. ' . . . thirty-six hours from when we lost power, judging by past submarine disasters. We've already used up nearly four hours of our ration, so there are thirty-two hours left. If we are sensible we can last out that long and Faslane won't waste time in getting cracking. It doesn't take long to fly gear around the world now, and the Yanks might lend us their prototype rescue sub . . .'

'At least,' Sinden said, 'the constructors provided us with a built-in pad, before they clamped down again on the estimates . . .'

'And before they stopped the tank training at *Dolphin*. . .' Soper added.

There was silence then. Too many politicians had their fingers in the pie: it was the old, old story, but then parliamentarians did not risk their necks in the service of the sovereign. Carn watched the bitterness reflected in Soper's face. If another half million had been spent on this boat, she might have been more comfortable – and, certainly, there would have been a better chance of escaping, had the estimates allowed for the rescue pads to be built into the new-construction SSNs.

'Don't talk, don't move about. We eat only when we have to,' Carn continued. 'One of us will remain on watch, while the rest of us sleep. I'll finish the first trick until eight, and then you can relieve me, Pilot. You will also be in charge of the air when we need oxygen later on.'

Sinclair nodded in acknowledgement, but there was an uncomfortable silence while they waited for the captain's vital decisions. Carn forced himself to continue:

'Some of you won't know this, gentlemen, but when we hit the bottom, the fire in the fore-ends destroyed nearly half the immersion suits. The xo reported the fact to me, but I saw no point in letting you know. I thought the first escape party should be properly equipped.' Hebbenden was nodding his approval, but there was no comment from the others.

'We can use the fin as our escape tower. I reckon we can squeeze three in there: two to escape, and the third man to shut the upper lid after the others have gone.' He glanced at Hebbenden. 'You were a *Dolphin* tank instructor, weren't you Coxswain ... ? Any objections?'

The Swain remained silent for a moment. 'Seems all right to me, sir. We could drain down several times, I imagine, without pressurising the remaining air too much.'

'That's the risk: $CO_2$ and oxygen under pressure, but I can't see any alternative at the moment.'

'We'll need only two drain-downs,' Sinden said, 'before the last pair have a go.'

'Right,' Carn said. 'That's three escape attempts.'

'Should be easy.' This was Pinky Dean, his voice pitched higher, even, than usual. 'It's been done from 600 feet, hasn't it, sir?'

'Of course it has,' Carn said kindly. 'It's only a matter of keeping our heads ... One other thing: each one of you, to pass the time, try to remember the details of the nearest escape you've experienced during your time in submarines. You have evidently all survived the emergencies so perhaps some bright idea might be remembered which could help us.' He glanced at them – five men, with no trace of bitterness now:

'We've five suits between the seven of us – and one's shaky,' he said. 'Some of you might have some ideas on how to resolve that little problem ...'

He smiled then and felt the warmth of their trust as they returned his gaze.

'Get some sleep now,' he ordered. 'I'm starting my watch.'

As they lay down and turned on their sides, a ship ran in again, her HE fluttering across their starboard bow as she drew away. When she thundered overhead, *Mars* shuddered, then trembled throughout the length of her twisted remains. She seemed poised on her beam-ends – balanced on a knife-edge and weaving in the current on the sill of some abyss ... Carn closed his eyes.

# CHAPTER 9

# SSN Command

There was no need for Commander George Carn to recall the worst submarine emergency in which he'd been involved – he was in the midst of it now, up to the neck in it. Though he knew that there was nothing they could do but pray for a miraculous rescue attempt before the next thirty-two hours ran out, at least he could try to keep their minds occupied, until conditions became intolerable. He opened his eyes and eased himself more comfortably into the corner by the passageway.

The last two years had not been easy. It had all started, he supposed, when he'd been sent for by the MOD, twenty-two months and two weeks ago, before he launched *Mars* down the Barrow slipway. As long ago as that, Britain had obviously been on to this gigantic Russian enterprise: one of our conventional boats, on passage off North Cape, had picked up a drowned man, a seaman by all appearances. At the post-mortem, they had discovered that he had been tortured; he had died of self-administered poison. They had also found a message concealed in his anatomy. The Russians were resolutely committed to their $H_3O$ project at Novaya Zemlya: the attempt to convert the heat produced by nuclear fission directly into electrical energy, without its having to pass through the steam and turbine processes. From then onwards, the Russia secret was to be known by the American and British as project *Zed*.

*Mars* had been the first boat designated for *Zed* patrol. The builders had wasted no time, in spite of the Communist-inspired strikes, but one of the sacrifices had been the omission of the proper locking-on gear for the rescue mini subs. At least the pad was fitted, forward of the fin.

*Mars* had earned her name as an unlucky ship from the earliest days, when she had run aground on the mud at her launching; she had overset a tug, with the loss of skipper and mate. Six weeks later she had run foul of a dredger's wire in Gibraltar, when the 'egg-beater', the manoeuvring propeller for harbour use, had failed when entering the base. Both incidents had not been forgotten by superstitious sailormen.

She was the first of her class, larger than the *Valiant* but designed for the role of an SSN, a Hunter-Killer, working as a fleet unit in the distant oceans. Her advanced sonar was the best in the world, though, after the Portland spy case (ex-PO Hough, wasn't he?) the Russians had probably now caught up.

*Mars* could range far ahead of the nuclear surface fleet. Her incredible underwater communication system allowed her to report any contact which she might pick up many miles ahead. Provided she carried out her homework twice a day to make sure of the temperature gradients, she could find any target, surface or underwater, whatever the layer conditions. The problem remained the same as it always had been, and it was hoped that the Russians had not yet mastered it. Britain had hitherto been behind in this field, the Germans having produced ocean charts of the North Cape density layers, even before the end of Hitler's war.

Stationed ahead of the fleet, an SSN acted as a deep sonar platform. Apart from investigating contacts, she could be despatched to attack targets picked up by aircraft or surface ships. She could operate either in company with another SSN, at depth without disclosing their positions; or on her own or with the fleet, her job being essentially to act as an anti-submarine killer.

The lurking SSN could communicate with a surface ship who was either in the fleet screen or disposed to one side. This vessel was known as the 'link ship', and the SSN could talk to her on underwater telephone, even at speed and without betraying her position. By using this system in conjunction with the incredible efficiency of our modern sonar, one Hunter-Killer stationed ahead of the fleet could cover a very large area of ocean. If the SSN 'went active' on her sonar, not only would she be picking up any enemy at great distances, but she would scare the hell out of a lurking submarine: whatever evasive tactics the enemy boat might attempt, our SSNs could hunt it to destruction.

Our submarines were not for nothing reported to be the most silent in the world. If *Mars* could operate below a layer, she would pick up the enemy before being detected herself. By then she would have passed all the relevant information to the link ship; the opposition would never know what had struck them.

If *Mars* stayed passive, she would keep listening on her sonar, and at the same time maintain contact with her link ship. By using her variable depth sonar, she could also choose beneath which layer to sit. Then, when she went active, she would scare the pants off any enemy in the area.

George Carn often wondered whether we were not too damned cock-sure of our theories. Supposing the Russians refused to play our game and had totally altered the rules? And what of their anti-submarine measures? Their attacking destroyers with their homing torpedoes; their killer helicopters; their own hunter-killer submarines; their nuclear depth-charges; and their nuclear-headed torpedoes . . . but it was surprising how trials had proved, just as in war-time, that even a nuclear warhead had to explode very close to a submarine before it was lethal. Even rocket projectiles, like sophisticated 'hedgehogs', were relatively close-range weapons: the Russian attack information would have to be very slick. Even with these fearsome nuclear A/S weapons, the enemy would have to be very up-to-date, because the SSNs could travel like the clappers: the 'time-late' factor would have to be minimised if the Russians were to be successful. In one minute, *Mars* could be a considerable distance from the scene of detection.

George Carn glanced at the men who had preferred to remain behind: it was difficult to believe that the problems of manning our nuclear submarine fleet were becoming almost insurmountable. The 'Boomers' (Polaris) were easily manned: they ran a fixed routine – three months operational, a month's leave and training before putting to sea again. The man's family could rely upon the date of the breadwinner's homecoming, because the Boomers' programmes were planned months in advance. In spite of this advantage, the divorce rate in the Boomers was sadly much too high; but in SSNs the rate was considerably worse: their routine was too erratic, and this forced wives and husbands to lead unnatural lives. Whilst the rest of the country enjoyed the peace bestowed by the Polaris and SSN submarines, their crews were leading war-time existences. Unacceptable strains were being inflicted, and this stress affected the sea-going crews. It was difficult to know how to alleviate this vicious circle.

Carn sighed. The worst strains appeared, as usual, amongst the overworked watches of the engine-room department. The reactor was an insatiable tyrant, needing constant surveillance. This entailed twenty-four-hour watches, day in, day out, for years on end, the reactor needing re-fuelling only every three years. To operate the machinery in harbour, the engine-room crew ('back-aft') were in a five-watch system, whereas, the rest of the ship's company (for'd) were in four watches; at sea, there were four watches back-aft, and three for'd: inevitably, there was a distinct partition between the two worlds. It was at 63 bulkhead, a physical as well as a psychological barrier, that the division occurred.

George Carn was never happy with the arrangement, but he tried hard enough to break down these divisions in his company. There were so many new faces on each patrol (some for training, others on leave), that it was normal for him to accept twenty per cent of his complement as new and untrained. On this trip in particular, these untrained men had been an embarrassment, because they had had to be wet-nursed by the others, like sheep to the slaughter . . .

It was impossible for him to know all his men – and, as he was a traditional submarine captain, this failing went deeply against the grain. Because the passageway led beneath the control room, no longer did the younger and inexperienced ratings have to pass through the brain cell of the submarine. In a conventional boat, it was customary for the hands to slip into the control room to check up on what was happening; in this way, the captain met and talked with everyone – an impossibility in these boats.

In Carn's opinion, this was an unforeseen but serious fault in the boat's design – no one had considered the human aspect when the SSN was on the drawing board – and now, the complete engine-room crew were entombed not far away in their steel coffin, 500 feet down. He wondered how many had died in the onrush of water or whether any had managed to escape the deluge. With the chief there, they would stand a chance, because the Chief Engineer, Charles Macgregor, with his ginger beard and his six foot three, was a tower of strength. If he had perished, the loss would be a sad blow for the submarine service.

How the chief stood the pace, Carn never ceased to wonder: he would never let up. Every second of the day, he had to be on the ball, with that maze of high-pressure machinery. The din of the three steam generators; the heat between 110° and 120° all day, in spite of the vital refrigeration plant to cool down the machinery space; and the constant strain: these factors alone would break men of lesser fibre – which was what made the chief engineers of these nuclear boats the men they were.

There were few moments, Carn ruminated, when a thinking submariner could take stock of what he was doing with his life – but with death less than thirty-two hours away, this was certainly a moment when he should try to make his peace with his Maker . . .

He wasn't in this business for the money and certainly not for the easy life. Admittedly, he had always loved submarines: not to escape the more 'pusser' attitude of general service existence, but because there seemed to be a better type of man here. In a 'boat', as a submarine was known, everyone, officer and rating, sank or swam together; this fact bred a sense of loyalty to one's fellow shipmates, a quality notably absent in life ashore where, in modern Britain, ruthless selfishness seemed to be the order of the day. When trade unions wielded the power of life or death over simple folk by dictating whether hospitals continued to function, it was time to call a halt. Whether we slothful British would ever realise that, one morning soon, trade union commissars would be deciding what was best for the people, was a nightmare which kept him awake o'nights.

There was an attraction about submarine life which he likened to the appeal that a motor-bike held for an adolescent youth: the smell and the grease and the challenge of making things work were very akin to the attraction of submarine life. The unforgettable smell of torpoil and corticene; the whine of the fans and the hum of electric motors; the comfort and privacy of one's bunk when collapsing into it, dead from fatigue; and, above all, the comradeship: these were the things one remembered. Carn smiled to himself: but he should have known better, after the incident which had changed his life – Stephen's birth.

Secretly, he had been a proud man when he'd been appointed CO of the Attack Teacher, which meant running the perisher for two and a half years: to be responsible for training Britain's future submarine COs was no mean responsibility. When, next, he had been selected to command *Mars*, the first of this new class, he had had to guard against a swollen head, but the Devonport incident had swiftly corrected that malady.

*Mars* had been undergoing her first inspection refit, after her designated six months' running. She was lying in the nuclear dry-dock in Devonport, less than five hundred yards from the depot ship. He would never forget that Sunday, one of those beautiful Devonshire early-March mornings when the families came down to the depot ship for a horse's neck. The day was hot and sunny; he had left Jackie and the boys with his friends in the ward-room and, unable to resist the temptation, had sauntered down to the boat to see that all was well and to make his number with the officer of the day, Tommy Forrester, his new Fourth Hand.

He distinctly remembered being irritated by not being received on board, even the quartermaster being absent. As he crossed the brow on to the casing, he caught sight of Forrester emerging from the screen in the dry-dock's side, the special shelter which concealed from the public gaze the guts of the reactor, whilst it was being inspected after being lifted out of the boat. The undertaking was gargantuan because the specially designed section above the reactor compartment had to be lifted out of the pressure hull.

Forrester was speaking rapidly to the quartermaster. As the seaman saluted and began to double up the dry-dock's steps, Forrester turned towards the bow, and he instantly spotted his captain.

'There's something wrong with the kettle, sir,' he shouted across the intervening gap. 'I was just coming to report it . . .'

There was a blinding flash, a roaring noise that overwhelmed his senses, and Commander George Carn remembered no more.

He regained consciousness in a ward of the naval hospital. It was days before he could speak, and then they sent him to Haslar for special treatment.

'You'll be all right, Carn,' the PMO had said kindly, but his eyes had not smiled. 'As you know, we must take every precaution in a case of this sort.' Carn had received VIP treatment. They eventually told him of Forrester's death in the bottom of the dry-dock. The quartermaster had been two yards inside the passageway leading upwards through the masonry of the dock: the thickness of the stone had saved him . . . and George Carn had escaped apparently unhurt.

He had convalesced impatiently at home, whilst they held an inquiry and replaced the defective reactor. Jackie and he had enjoyed a second honeymoon and they had taken no precautions. For so long, he had yearned to bring a daughter into the world and Jackie had yielded to his persistent love-making. Four sons were undoubtedly a quiverful, but she, too, wanted a little girl, and this had seemed their opportunity.

In August, he had taken *Mars* out of dockyard hands, ready, at last, for engine-room and sea trials. She had passed these successfully, and so, by the end of September, after a hectic ten days' work-up, he'd been able to report to Captain S/M that *Mars* was, in all respects, ready for operational duties. By this time, Jackie was most definitely *enceinte*, though the pregnancy was not proceeding as easily as her previous experiences of motherhood.

One month's work-up patrol off Greenland and Spitzbergen

5                                            65

was followed by a week's leave from Faslane for each watch. Jackie had reinstalled the boys in Dunbrae House, but, when he arrived home, he had been shocked at her appearance. Her face was grey and puffy, and her legs were painful from the varicose veins which had always been a nuisance. He spent the seven days in a frenzy of straightening up the house and caring for the boys, who were still enjoying their last ten days of holiday. Their youngest, Mark, was looking forward to his first term at the village school: Carn could not continue to pay those high fees for a dubious private day-school. For the past four years, the others had been despatched to boarding school, to give them some educational continuity. A sailor's home was not an easy one for the children.

For the first time, Jackie had broken down when they parted for his three-month's patrol. She would be expecting the birth ten days before *Mars*'s return date and she desperately wanted him at her side for this last child of theirs – 'I so long to give you your daughter,' she whispered, biting her lips as he gently pushed her away to pick up his travelling grip. 'I want you to be the first to see her.'

She had been so sure that this time she had succeeded in conceiving a girl – but what did it matter, he realised, what sex the child should be, so long as Jackie kept in good health.

The patrol had been difficult: there was much to put right in the boat, and the ship's company needed time in which to shake down. He had been forced to deal with several stupid offences: he detested punishing men at sea – the process was so wasteful, when all their concentration should have been bent towards working the boat. He realised now that his worry over Jackie's confinement had probably made him niggly and that this irritation may have permeated throughout the boat.

He had done his best to foster joviality in the boat for a Christmas at sea, but life at 200 feet beneath the ice-fields was hardly conducive to a festive spirit: there were many men in *Mars* whose thoughts were blacker than they should have been on 25 December. As the second week in February approached, the week of the expected birth, he could not suppress the worry that was gnawing inside himself. On the homeward passage, off the Lofotens, Jackie's expected confinement day had come and passed.

He knew that Captain s/m Jack Quincey, would have been the first to send a personal signal during the routines, but nothing had arrived until, within a day's steaming from Rockall, the

RS (Radio Supervisor) had personally handed him the signal: 'Jacqueline entered hospital today for expected confinement. She is well.' A thoughtful gesture of Jack Quincey's and one which Carn would never forget.

He'd manoeuvred *Mars* alongside at dawn on Friday, 17 February. She would not have cracked an eggshell, so gently did she slide alongside the jetty. Captain S/M saluted from the jetty, as the boson's call shrilled the traditional honours. The white ensign streamed in the cold breeze blowing from across the loch. When Number One had secured the springs, Carn scrambled down the fin and over the brow towards the black saloon which Jack Quincey had placed at his disposal. Quincey said quietly:

'Jackie's in labour, George. I'm coming with you – I've got to go to the hospital, anyway.'

'I'd rather go alone – if you don't mind, sir.' He had been discourteous, he knew that.

''course, George. Carol said she was having a pretty rotten time.'

Mrs Quincey had always been good to Jackie and often took care of the boys. 'Thanks, sir,' and he had clambered into the car. Captain S/M's personal driver, the red-headed WREN, drove to the hospital in Dunoon.

'Don't wait,' he told her, as the car slid up to the entrance door that was begging for a coat of paint. 'I'll be some time.'

The WREN smiled with that wistfulness which women reserve for the mysteries of birth, which only they understood. 'I hope it's a girl,' and she had laughed shyly. He realised then that the entire base was wishing a girl for Jackie and himself – self-interest, probably, because life was more comfortable for all and sundry, if Carn was not under stress.

He walked down the corridor until he found the side-ward which proclaimed MATERNITY. He gently pushed against the double spring-doors and peeped inside. There was a smell of antiseptic, and from the far end of the small ward he heard the cry of a child. A harassed nurse, in a violet uniform, rustled past him. She was carrying a white bowl and, obviously irritated by his intrusion at this moment, she asked shortly:

'Yes? Can I help you?'

He realised that he was still in uniform, the three stripes on his sleeve out of place in this world of fundamentals.

'Commander Carn,' he said. 'I've come to see my wife. She's expecting our daughter ...'

He had smiled shyly, hoping that the ruffled nurse would understand.

The girl caught her breath and glanced up at him. Her black eyes flickered across his for an instant, before she looked away.

'How is my wife?' he asked gently. 'Is all well?'

'Your son was born an hour ago,' the nurse said abruptly. 'Will you sit down, please, Commander? I'll tell Sister you're here.'

Carn's head jerked upwards. He had been day-dreaming and had nearly dropped off. But now he was summoned back to this nightmare by the unmistakable sound of a ship manoeuvring overhead. Something clanged against the hull, and, seconds afterwards, the methodical tap-tapping of morse echoed through the stricken submarine.

# CHAPTER 10

## *The Seafaring Tradition*

Kapitan Stavislaus Isokov was proud of his new ship. One of the latest *Kurovs*, his frigate, *Krakvilsk*, was certainly among the most efficient working out of Novaya Zemlya's naval base, the newly constructed, advanced port for the strike arm of the modernised Baltic fleet. He had been stand-by emergency frigate when *Kulmanov* had picked up that suspicious contact yesterday. After *Kulmanov* had limped into port, at dawn, with her bows stove in and with her back broken abaft the funnel, all hell had been let loose in the base, and prudent men kept clear of the Admiral. Kapitan Isokov glanced at the hands of the clock glowing in the half darkness of his enclosed bridge: 0532, almost exactly four hours since *Kulmanov*'s emergency signal.

Unless his college-mate, Ili, unfortunate commanding officer of *Kulmanov*, had imbibed too much vodka the night before (a distinctly possible explanation), it was difficult to believe his report that he had rammed an unreported submarine: mercifully, all of the Russian submarine fleet, and there were many of them, had been accounted for. *Kulmanov* had sunk alongside the jetty, but the Admiral had despatched the entire Tenth Frigate

Squadron and put Isokov in charge. There had been no need to institute a search: *Krakvilsk* had picked up the target contact on her first sweep over point zero, the collision position.

Kapitan Isokov stifled a yawn: those young officers had to be set an example, and he was determined to maintain his reputation as one of the up-and-coming generation of senior officers. He did not believe in mixing politics with his profession, so he particularly resented Commissar Borinov whom he was forced to tolerate on his bridge. Because of the dangerous mood generated by the new intellectuals in Mother Russia, the political arm had been strengthened in each ship: every ship larger than a frigate was now blessed with a commissar.

After communicating with the base for instructions, he and his squadron had settled down to a long wait. The target seemed to be lying in about 170 metres of water on the edge of a rocky shelf. What was difficult to explain was the size of the echo: she must either be a large submarine or have shattered into several pieces after the collision. Isokov was a man of action, irked by having to wait for C-in-C's reply.

The affair could well develop into a political row, for he knew what the political boys were like from his experience in Marine Headquarters in Moscow: they never missed a trick. He was thankful it was not winter, with its miserably cold nights – the day, at least, would soon warm up now that the sun was out at last. He checked that the look-outs were alert, then turned towards the chart table. As he did so, there was a shout from the fur-capped seaman in the starboard wings.

'Buoy in the water, Kapitan,' the man shouted. 'One hundred metres and abeam.' His arm was outstretched and the unshaven face reflected his excitement as he turned towards his Kapitan: 'It's got a flashing light, Comrade Kapitan.'

Isokov spun round. He levelled his binoculars on the orange spot in the water: a buoy, with an aerial on the peak of its cone, was bobbing in the swell. As the Kapitan peered along the bearing ring of the compass, an orange flotation suit emerged close to the marker-buoy. For a long moment the lifeless dummy floated on its back: then an arm waved desperately, summoning aid.

'Hard a starboard,' he shouted. 'Slow ahead port, half astern starboard.' As the propellers bit into the water, a second orange bob appeared; then another and another. 'Away lifeboat's crew,' he shouted. 'Lower scrambling nets and tell the doctor to come and see me.'

Kapitan Isokov had been in submarines. If the survivors had escaped from this depth, he knew the physical condition they might be in. He wondered whether they were Americans – but what mattered it? They were sailors, were they not?

'Get off a signal to base,' he called to his senior signalman. 'From Kapitan, Tenth Frigate Squadron,' he dictated, carefully selecting his words. 'Am picking up survivors from unidentified submarine in point zero. Am monitoring marker-buoy sighted in same position. Time of origin . . . ' he glanced at his watch: '0548.'

He hoped the authorities would co-operate swiftly: over four hours had elapsed since the time of collision.

# CHAPTER 11

## *All Possible Despatch*

Flag Officer Submarines glared impatiently at the signal which his Chief of Staff had brought in from the teletape that clicked and clacked from the machine in the office outside.

'Good news, sir,' the bald-headed Captain Colin Spense said, without raising his voice. 'The Russians have sighted *Mars*'s marker-buoy and have picked up seventeen survivors. They're playing ball, sir – '

'Bloody miracle,' Vice-Admiral Sir Frederick Clewes said. 'Now we can get cracking. Colin, get me America and quickly.'

The gaunt Admiral, in his mid-fifties, with greying hair immaculately groomed, paced his office overlooking the black submarines lying alongside the *Dolphin* jetties in Haslar creek. He prowled the room like a caged tiger. The agony of waiting for information was worse for him than anyone. He could take no decisions until he knew whether the Russians would co-operate. The American President and the Prime Minister on their hot lines had achieved the miracle . . .

The red phone trilled from the corner of FOS/M's desk. The long sleeve, with its one broad and two thin stripes, stretched across for the phone, and the Vice-Admiral was in touch with his opposite number four thousand miles distant.

'Your American call, sir,' the WREN operator announced.

'Thank you . . . That you, Admiral?'

A voice, hard and rusty, croaked in answer, as clear as if he had been in the same room.

'Okay, Fred. They're playing ball, I hear . . . ' the US Admiral grated. 'I'll despatch the mini sub right away. Her Commander, Lieutenant Commander Dugan, will be accompanying her in the same aircraft.' The American paused momentarily. 'The plane's mission is to lift *Lily-One* (that's our name for the mini sub, Fred) to the Russian's base at Novaya Zemlya. Can you arrange for liaison on landing, in case the Russians hold up things with red tape?'

'Yes, all taken care of, Bill,' the British admiral replied. 'What's the ETA, *Zed*?'

'About 1345, I guess. The aircraft is flying as high as it can to clear the head winds.'

'Thanks, Bill. We owe you a lot.'

'It's a pleasure. Pleased to help you limeys, anytime.'

'I'm moving up to Faslane, Bill,' Clewes said, grinning to himself, 'so you'll be able to reach me there. I'm sending Captain Jack Quincey off to *Zed* to take charge locally, so if there's anything else you need, just let me know. Jack will take care of all salvage operations, under the Russians. He'll try to set up a joint team there, if your boys would like to join us . . . '

'That's good . . . sure . . . fine. Good luck, Fred. Will be thinking of you . . . '

The phone clicked. Vice-Admiral Clewes slowly put down his handset. He pressed the buzzer, and seconds later his Chief of Staff stood in the doorway.

'Colin, I want you to stay here and look after things. See if Lee-on-Solent can fly me up to Faslane, will you? Ask the RAF to deliver Jack Quincey to *Zed* as soon as possible, and let me know their ETA.'

'Who'll be taking over from Jack, sir, while he's in Zemlya?'

'Commander S/M of course; he'll look after the squadron. I'm personally taking charge of the Sub-Smash, and it will be easier up there, if I'm on the spot.'

The Flag Officer, Submarines, was once more alone in his office. The fate of George Carn and his men would depend upon the ability of the rescue team and the trapped men to communicate and to read each other's intentions. Until communications were established between himself and the rescue team, the rescue bid would not get off the ground. If he, FOSM, could be

71

at the heart of things at Faslane, he would be much closer to the technicians who maintained the nuclear boats: their skills could make the difference between tragedy and success.

Captain Jack Quincey, Royal Navy, was one of the youngest captains S/M. He was more bone and muscle than his rotund figure suggested. As captain of the nuclear S/M base at Faslane, he had little time for recreation, but when he could, he would try to fit in a three-quarter-hour game of squash, often to the chagrin of his younger staff. He was short, he was tough and he enjoyed the reputation of being an excellent seaman; and that in spite of his many years in submarines, which, because of the technical knowledge required to run a boat, tended to divorce a submariner from the more prosaic demands of seamanship.

It was precisely thirty-seven minutes past six when FOS/M had rung him up from Blockhouse, as *Dolphin* was better known; the RAF's chopper was picking him up at 0800 to lift him to Prestwick, where one of their Nimrods would fly him to Zemlya. He had dashed home to pick up his grip; Carol, bless her heart, was nipping around like a fussy hen as she collected his warm clothing: his (once white, but now a worn, battered thing) woollen submarine sweater, a pair of half-wellingtons, his old working suit and his toilet gear. Carol, an attractive woman still, after years of service life, was sharing a cup of coffee with him when Jenny, the WREN driver, brought the car to the door.

'Good luck, dear,' Carol said softly, holding his hand and offering her lips for him to kiss. 'I'll take care of Jackie.'

As the car door clunked behind him, he heard the phone ringing in the hall. Carol rushed inside and, when he reached the front door, she was standing there and holding the instrument for him.

'It's the base,' she said. 'Tom wants to speak to you.'

Commander S/M, Tom Bolitho, spoke briskly:

'Wanted to catch you, sir, before you left. Blockhouse has just come through.'

'Yes?'

'The Russians are really pulling out all the stops, sir. They're sailing *Kronstad*, their submarine salvage ship, for the collision position, which they've designated as position "X". Her ETA is 1600.'

'That's good, Tom. I'll drive direct to the pad, so don't bother to see me off.'

'Aye, aye, sir.'

The phone went dead. He pressed Carol's arm and jumped back into the car. As Jenny let in the clutch, he heard the grandfather clock chiming in the hall.

It was a quarter to eight: over seven hours had already slipped by; less than twenty-nine were left.

## The Navigating Officer

When Peter Sinclair took over from the captain at eight, morale needed a boost. All six men had heard the surface ship endeavouring to communicate, but young Dean, the one man well trained to read morse, could not establish communications, in spite of their banging on the pressure hull where they had, with a wheel-spanner, ripped away a section of panelling.

Peter had found their spanner when he had groped his way into the darkness to do his rounds. At the top of the ladder leading down to the periscope wells in the lower compartment, Soper had waited, holding the emergency lantern. They had had to take it from the ward-room in order to conserve the precious light, because they could muster only seven lanterns. As each lantern had a total endurance of ten hours, and they were already reduced to lantern number six, that meant they must limit themselves to twenty minutes each hour, if they were to have any light thirty hours later.

'We'll need the light even more later on,' the captain had said, 'so I suggest we put up with the darkness as much as we can.'

As Peter had been floundering about on the slippery decks of the lower compartment, the light at the top of the ladder had dimmed, faltered and then extinguished.

'For God's sake, hurry up, Peter,' Soper called down to him. 'I'll get another lantern.'

Peter stood motionless. He'd wait here until he could see again. He could hear only his own breathing, and it was eerie to feel that, within a few yards on the other side of this plating, the remainder of *Mars* was also lying. The silence was total down here, and the plating was unusually hot beneath his feet. He was baffled until, groping about in the dim light, he touched the bulkhead. He sprang backwards from the pain of the burn across his fingertips.

'The kettle's hotting up.'

He shouted towards the ladder, and heard his words echoing in the emptiness of the steel tomb. A pale light shone again from the top of the hatchway and, as he stumbled towards it, he spotted the wheel-spanner hanging from a valve-wheel spindle. He collected it after his final search for any emergency oxygen bottles – there were none.

With the built-in, high-pressure breathing system in these modern submarines, the old-fashioned oxygen bottles were considered superfluous. Each compartment was supplied with two breathing lines fitted with sufficient connecting tubes for the crew, plus a few spare. Clean, dry air, stored at a pressure of 3,500/4,000 pounds per square inch in bottles outside the pressure hull, was available through these air lines; after passing through reducing valves, the air provided a perfect breathing mixture of 100/130 pounds above the pressure of the compartment during flooding-up time. Peter had not checked the system yet, but it was good to know that it was there when they needed it.

'Shake it up, Peter,' Soper called from the head of the ladder. 'We've only got four more lanterns.'

Peter felt irritated, but resisted the temptation to retort. He clambered through the hatch and followed the pale light back to the ward-room. Before Soper snicked out the lantern, Peter glimpsed Gallo lying along the passageway. His face was grey, and his lips blue-tinged. Beneath the saturated blankets, there was still a wetness on the corticene. Peter knelt down to listen to the man's heart. He could barely feel the beat of the pulse, and the breathing was shallow and rapid.

Peter sighed as he sank back on the empty patch of the settee – the corner which was to become his home during the coming ordeal. It was strange, he mused, that in a crisis of survival the human animal craved to be close to its kind for mutual protection. He heard Soper turning on his side. There was no more that Peter could do: he closed his eyes to allow himself the luxury of dreaming of Jeannie and the children . . .

0845 at number 44 – she would have been up for some time now. She'd be scurrying Peter Junior out through the front door of their semi-detached house in the new officers' married quarters. He could see her now, key turning in the red door, in a flat spin as she tried to collect herself. She'd have to take the push-chair with her because Nicola could not walk very far yet and it was some way to the bus stop. Beloved Jeannie – what a good wife she'd been to him since their earliest days together when the going had been really tough. Those trawler days, three weeks off Iceland in all weathers, winter and summer, and perhaps three days in harbour before sailing again – three hectic days when they had clung together through the nights, trying to hold on to time. But slip, it would, through their fingers until the agony of parting came around again.

At least this life in the navy was easier for Jeannie. She lived amongst friends who were in the same boat, so to speak . . . but now, what would be the atmosphere on the estate? The other wives would be trying not to intrude, but it was difficult when a boat was missing . . . they'd all know now that *Mars* had been overdue for more than seven hours. Captain s/M, Captain Quincey, was a stickler for keeping everyone informed.

Peter wondered how often Jeannie thought of the possibility of his not returning one day. She'd miss chattering like an old hen with the other wives on the quayside, as they waited for the familiar, black, slug-like fin to come sliding round the point and into the loch – and how would she fare as a widow, once the shock had passed?

They rarely discussed the eventuality but, one night, as she lay with her head in the crook of his arm, he had told her that he hoped she would marry again quickly, if an accident befell. She was a warm-blooded, passionate creature, so she must not, through loyalty to his memory, allow her life to become a blighted, sick thing, when she had so much to give a man. In the darkness, he smiled to himself, relishing the memories. He shook himself – the pleasure of his thoughts was making him drowsy and he still had half his trick to go . . .

He'd been happy in *Mars*, since the day he joined. He had liked George Carn at first sight, long before these ssn days, when, as an up-and-coming 'two and-a-half', George had married Peter's sister, Jacqueline Sinclair. Peter had managed to be best man at their wedding, but until the *Mars* appointment he'd seen little of Jackie. Paradoxically, now that Jackie was living in Faslane, he and Jeannie tended to keep away from Dunbrae House, for obvious reasons. The situation could have been difficult for Peter and for George Carn, but both were very conscious of the dangers of possible accusations of nepotism: Soper had been swift enough to insinuate these thoughts but then Jake Soper was a bastard anyway: it was fortunate that submarines very rapidly taught tolerance, because every man had his own idiosyncracies.

The rift between Soper and himself was beginning seriously to worry Peter. Admittedly, their two backgrounds were very different, and even in egalitarian, socialistic modern Britain, the class barrier had not yet been demolished – or, at least, snobbery died hard. There was a world of difference between Peter's back-door entry to the Royal Navy and Soper's traditional entry via the Royal Naval College, Dartmouth.

In Peter's eyes, Soper was like an efficient machine, ably designed, moulded and maintained by the state, which needed officers to man its defence forces. Yet, there was something missing in the Dartmouth training which was difficult to pin-point: did not that great sailor, Andrew Cunningham, express somewhere in his memoirs that he preferred the élan of the public school (eighteen-year-old) entry to the more prosaic but excellent training of the Royal Naval College? However unpleasant Soper's intentional attitude was towards Peter, he (Sinclair) had to put up with it because, though a year older than Soper, Peter was two years his junior in the seniority list.

Peter would not forget the day he joined *Mars*. He had been wandering back from the fore-ends and had lost his way en route to his manoeuvring station. Chief Petty Officer Hebbenden had waited for him to pass in the narrow passageway by the pump space: he had asked, his face as wise as an old owl's, 'Good God, sir, lost your way?'

Peter had enjoyed his long navigation course at Southwick; its back-up, for long N officers transferring into submarines, had also been excellent, practical and comprehensive. So the SINS (Ship's Inertia Navigational System) had provided Peter with few headaches once he had used it for a spell. SINS took most of the heat out of today's submarine navigation; he smiled to himself when he recalled the day he had deliberately set a trap for the staff at home, when *Mars* had been on an underwater passage back from Norfolk, Virginia. They had rung him up:

'We reckon you're five minutes late altering course,' the watchkeeper had said from his headquarters some ten hundred miles away. But Peter had laid on a course of 080°, making a great circle. In fact, he came round to 070°, but they were using a magnetic reader, so that it looked like 080°. *Mars* had been very chuffed about this, out there in mid-Atlantic after days at sea.

Peter reckoned now that he was on top of his job, but it was a full-time one to keep his plotting team fully efficient. With every contact to be monitored, sonar, radar and visual, his young ratings had to be of high calibre – the Service had been having a hell of a time trying to cope with its manning problems, ever since the Polaris programme had gobbled up all the technicians and, necessarily, the senior rates.

It was the operation of the sonar room, with its attendant machinery space, that accurately typified the calibre of man now required to work the Hunter-Killers. The SSN's role being to search out, pin-point and destroy an enemy submarine, the sonar and the guidance systems for the modern torpedoes were the last vital components required for the SSN to deliver its weapon. The sonar department was numerically the largest, for'd of 63 bulkhead.

The sonar room's machinery space was a compartment immediately below the sonar room, and with a petty officer watchkeeper permanently on watch. This machinery space was full to the brim with electronic boxes: the watchkeeper's task was fault-finding, to ensure that all went well, twenty-four hours of the day. Even in this complexity, no one knew when an accident might occur.

Petty Officer Harris had been on watch when the boat took on a dangerous bow-down trim. He had been standing inside the doorway and holding on to a sonar set with one hand, while he tried to keep his balance with the other. Gravity was forcing his body against the bulkhead, so he could not move. Without warning, the sonar set shot outwards, over a hundredweight of it, stopping within two inches of his face. Another six inches and his skull would have been pulped.

It was during that emergency also that an incredibly similar accident proved almost fatal: it was the suddenness in the angle of trim that caught people unawares.

The laboratory, a small compartment for'd of 63 bulkhead, was used regularly by the Leading Medical Assistant, Thompson. There, shut away in his protected cell, he possessed all the facilities for the chemical and general physical control of the atmosphere which provided life support; his role was that of the ship's doctor, and, in emergencies, he was empowered to carry out simple major operations. Having attended a nuclear medicine course at Alverstoke, he was proficient in radiation safety practice, once he had passed his City and Guilds examinations. At sea, Thompson concentrated upon the safety of the ship's company from the radiation hazard; in harbour, he saw that the general medical routines were carried out methodically: that no one missed their jabs or their Pulheems.

To help him at sea, each man who was likely to pass through the nuclear compartment wore around his neck a tally, which consisted of a photographic film that measured and differentiated between various forms of radiation; the tally could pin-point whereabouts in the ship the hazard existed. When the boat was dived and running, the radiation dose was less than when she was surfaced or when men walked ashore in the dockyard.

Thompson was carrying out his routine work of counting the radiation samples. To achieve this he had to punch the tallies into the solid lead cylinders which were hollowed out in the middle to receive the samples.

For some reason, the cylinders were not properly secured. When the boat shifted its angle too suddenly, these cylinders, over two-hundredweight each, shot straight past his head. They smashed against the bulkhead having missed his head by the fraction of an inch: if he had been in the way, he would have been decapitated. The shocked man was trembling for over an hour afterwards and needed medical care himself . . .

Peter smiled to himself: what would they have done on board this boat without God's gift of humour? But Gallo lay there, the boat's comedian, and even his unsettling moans were silent now. When the captain had handed the watch over to Peter, he had detailed him to become responsible for the boat's air supply during their ordeal. Carn had left the ward-room with Peter and, out of earshot of the others, explained in detail the problems that inevitably lay ahead of them.

'I don't know how the heat will affect us, now that the reactor is hotting up,' the captain said quietly, 'but I can tell you what life's going to be like otherwise – pretty bloody, if some of the experiences of the war-time boats are anything to go by.'

They were groping their way through the grotesque shadows thrown up by the cold light of the emergency lantern. Carn was searching for the air gauge of the built-in breathing system to see that all was well.

'When things get bad, we can open up the breathing mixture, Pilot. We may not have oxygen bottles like they used to, but we'll be much better off with dry, clean air to breathe. Where's that damned gauge?'

They groped to the panel. Carn held up the lantern beneath a group of valves, situated at a distance from the remainder of the complex panel.

'There it is, sir,' Peter said. 'Just to your right . . .'

'If you open up the supply valve, Pilot, we'll be getting high-pressure air from the dry-air reservoirs,' said the captain. 'Crack this air valve regularly, when we become short of oxygen. I suggest you crack it every hour when once we start using it. Have a go now, so that you can find it in the dark, if need be . . . '

The captain held up the lantern to help Peter to see the identifying label on the hand-wheel. There it was: 'Dry-Air Breathing Mixture'. Peter reached up and, taking the wheel-spanner which he had now attached by a lanyard to his waist, locked on to the spindle. Giving the valve a sharp twist, he waited for the HP air at 3,500 pounds per square inch to scream along the line. He watched the pressure gauge immediately above the valve: he must conserve this life-giving stuff, so he'd better shut the valve as soon as the pointer jumped. He waited for what seemed an interminably long time – *no scream of air, no needle jump . . .*

'Open right up,' Carn snapped. 'There's something wrong.'

Peter yanked at the spindle; the valve spun open . . . no sound . . . Carn rapped the dial.

No movement in the gauge . . .

He turned and stared at Peter.

'The line's smashed,' he said roughly. 'We've no clean air for when the going gets tough.'

He lowered the lantern, twisted its head; the control room plunged into darkness.

'We've got no protosorb; and now no clean air,' he said softly over his shoulder to Peter. 'Have you any ideas, Pilot? We'll be in a hell of a mess by this time tomorrow, if we haven't . . . '

Then Peter remembered the laboratory. He was sure he'd seen the emergency medical oxygen cylinders down there, some six of them, small, and neatly strapped into their racks.

'Get 'em when you can, Pilot. Have them ready at hand. We may be needing them earlier than we thought.'

As they groped past the screen door, a low rumble echoed throughout the pressure hull. The boat was bouncing again. She seemed to be balanced on some knife-edge of rock, and each time she swayed in the current, she took on a steeper angle. The two men had to haul themselves up the passageway. By the time they reached the settee, Carn was struggling along on all fours to prevent himself slipping backwards. Peter followed and finally reached the corner seat which had become his home. For the first time, his breathing was more rapid than usual. The luminous hands of his wrist-watch glowed: 0910 – eight hours since the disaster.

He'd fetch those oxygen cylinders when he'd handed over his watch to Commander Sinden. Now he'd try to catch some rest and to reflect upon his own problems.

No emergency oxygen. No carbon monoxide absorbent. Well, that was the classic situation, wasn't it? Mercifully, there were few survivors left: seven men in a large compartment, so the air should last at least another day. They could survive this, surely? Twenty-eight hours was a long time to mount a rescue bid, but remarkably little had occurred so far. Had the XO and his boys got out all right? Peter realised that his mind was grasshopping, so settled his thoughts upon an accident that he could remember – and, as he now seemed to be the boat's survival expert, he might as well stick to the subject.

It had always seemed to him that as great a miracle of development as the nuclear reactor which drove the boat for two and a half years, was the revolution that was defined as 'life-support'. Before the advent of unlimited energy provided by the nuclear reactor, a submarine could depend for the power it needed only on the capacity of its batteries; to recharge those life-giving cells, the submarine had to surface at night to run its diesel generators, which required air. The snorked breathing-tube, by which a submarine could run its diesels when dived, was only an extension of the working of a conventional submarine. There was little logic in developing a nuclear submarine which could run for months on end, unless the human material could also survive. Hence the vast research into life-support.

The life-support machinery was concentrated in a forward compartment running across the whole submarine. The oxygen-making plant was contained inside sealed covers and powered electrically. It drew in sea-water and extracted the hydrogen, leaving only salt and oxygen. Two potential hazards therefore always existed: a high oxygen content and a hydrogen leak. The former, though making breathing easier and the air purer, raised the fire-risk. A sparking armature (there were hundreds of electric motors in the submarine) could produce an intense fire. The latter danger, the hydrogen leak, again produced an explosive atmosphere.

In addition to being *Mars*'s navigating officer, Peter's supernumerary duty was that of fire officer. He was therefore familiar with the whereabouts of all machinery pertaining to life-support.

Not long ago, he had been inspecting the extinguishers and talking to Petty Officer Anthony Tamblin, the reliable PO in charge of the life-support compartment, who was crouched over one of the electrolide boxes, a unit which extracted oxygen from the sea-water and, at the same time, disposed of the hydrogen.

Peter was standing apart from him, waiting for the man to finish his routine work. The box was opened up, but, unknown to Tamblin, a small earth was cutting in on one of the pumps when the current was switched on.

Peter had waited patiently, a morning's work lying before him. Suddenly a jet of the chemical, lye, squirted upwards and into Tamblin's eyes. Peter heard the involuntary yell of fear, saw the liquid streaming down the man's face. A bucket of water stood near, ready for scrubbing out. Peter grabbed it. He forced Tamblin's head, face downwards, into the water; acting instinctively, the Petty Officer opened his eyes to dilute the lethal solution.

The incident happened so quickly that both men shook from the shock for minutes afterwards. The fault was traced eventually: a new hand had inadvertently made the circuit, the earth had operated and cut in the pump – and so lye was squirted into Tamblin's eyes. He was blind in one eye for over a month.

The accident had been a small one and there was no lesson from it which could help their present predicament. What worried Peter most was the problem of carbon dioxide, which, as every schoolboy knew, man exhaled more than he inhaled. Normally, when there was power in the boat, the other compartment in the electroliser took care of the carbon dioxide problem. Absorption units, operated by high-pressure air, devoured the extra carbon dioxide. Now there was no HP air, so without the well-tried protosorb tray method, the carbon dioxide would build up rapidly. It was only nine o'clock, barely eight hours after the accident, and already Peter felt the air becoming stuffy, like the frowstiness that enveloped an over-crowded room on a hot sunny day.

There was no sun down here, in this stygian darkness; only the stench, the heat from the reactor and the build-up of carbon dioxide poisoning. He closed his eyes again, trying to picture his beloved Jeannie. She remained tantalisingly remote, smiling at him, her hands out-stretched, welcoming him home through their garden gate.

Another sudden trembling shook the boat. The agonising crunch of twisting steel tormented Peter's nerves. His companions' deep breathing stopped: the six men in the darkness were awake. They, too, were tense and could not sleep. It was the long wait for the unknown which was the real agony.

6

## CHAPTER 12

# *The Passenger*

Commander Alastair Sinden had succeeded in snatching two hours of restless sleep. He had been wakened at 0900 by a violent tremor which vibrated throughout the hull, but he had continued to half-sleep, half-dream away this illusory forenoon. His luminous watch showed 1105, but surely they must be further into their morning by now? Ten hours since the calamity – and twenty-six to go if the prophets were right.

Was death from lack of air as terrible as one imagined? The end was probably akin to slow strangulation, but he felt sure that George would make an escape bid before they were overcome by poisoning and suffocation. They were at only 500 feet, whereas men had escaped safely from 600 – but they had been properly equipped. And now . . . ? He, Passenger Sinden, would certainly be one of those left without a suit. He'd insisted on his right to stay behind. There was nowt to live for now – and Jackie had her George . . .

It was strange how, during this half-life between the unconsciousness of sleep and the reality of awakening, a man's mind so sharply recalled the details of the past – and, it seemed, his intelligence and memory had become ultra-sensitive, now that his death was inevitable . . . He'd try making his peace with his Maker. He'd believed in God for some time now, ever since that terrible day four years ago.

Claudia and he had enjoyed a rush wedding. She'd insisted on marriage before he sailed east in his first submarine command, one of the old conventionals, *Termagent*. Her father, who owned a chemical factory near Billingham, had spared no expense and the affair had been one of the society 'do's' of the year. Their honeymoon had lasted only five days, but it was long enough to discover that his bride had been around. In bed, it had been a matter of her making the pace, rather than him. He had been bemused at the time, both shocked and delighted: he'd supposed that her experience of the London scene, a life she'd appeared to enjoy so much, had given her sophistication.

She had waited for months before flying out to join him in Australia. Looking back on it now, he blamed himself for his weakness: he should have insisted that she joined him, instead of allowing her to spend his money in enjoying what was left of the London season. When finally she had arrived in Freemantle, he had sensed at once that she had been unfaithful to him. There had been an elusiveness about her, a distant, cold embracing that was more reminiscent of a female automaton than of the hot-blooded woman he'd hoped he had married.

The *mésalliance* had lasted three years, mercifully without the begetting of children: she had been too jealous of her figure for that malarkey. She had always insisted on his taking precautions, because she was fearful of the pill. He turned over on his back, sick with the memories that were still too vivid.

He had tried desperately to forget her, and so bloody hard to prevent the tragedy of his private life affecting his professional career as a submarine CO. He felt that he had succeeded, but only at the cost of cultivating a hard, external shell. Beneath the façade, he hoped there still remained the man who had always been there, the sensitive individual who enjoyed his music, the paintings, the beauty of the written word . . . but it was difficult. He would never forget that last night at the Savoy Grill. When he recalled the incident, even now, he realised he could have tolerated her for no longer.

Claudia enjoyed French cooking, so she had ordered anchovies. The waiter had served her with the silvery fish, while he, Alastair Sinden, had been fascinated by her long fingers, with the deep, blood-red nails, encircling the fish-knife as if it were a scalpel. She had dissected the anchovies, cooked 'au feu' on charcoal; had deliberately held the morsel in her mouth, savouring the taste. Her puckered lips had pouted, like an over-indulged child.

'They've lost their taste,' she said petulantly, looking up with disfavour at the waiter in the white tunic.

'They are out of season, madame,' the French boy said. '*Je suis désolé, madame.*'

'You shouldn't offer them on the menu, in that case,' she retorted, pushing away her plate. She stole a glance across at her husband. 'Send them back, Alastair,' she said softly, her jet-black eyes smouldering. She knew how he detested scenes in public, and he was certain that she was challenging him. If she could stir his anger, he sensed, she would have gained some sort of victory over him. When she had annihilated him between the sheets, her sense

83

of achievement had always been the same. He had always come too swiftly for her, and she seemed to delight in torturing him for his incompetence.

'Send it back, Alastair . . .'

She referred to him by his christian name when she was being unusually bitchy with him. In the early days, or in public amongst his submarine friends, he had always been Al, to her. He faced her squarely and slowly shook his head.

'No,' he said quietly. 'You ordered anchovies.'

This was the moment when the deputy head-waiter, sensing trouble, had silkily approached the table. His eyebrows like crescent moons, he affected an urbane superiority which declared an unspoken distaste for those who disturbed his dining-room.

'Madame ordered the anchovies?' he demanded politely, as he extended his arm to remove the dish. 'Would madame prefer something else, sir?' he asked. He glanced at the naval officer, amused contempt dancing in his Neapolitan eyes.

Alastair had already made up his mind.

'No,' he said sharply, without raising his voice. 'Take it away.'

The anchovies were whisked from the table; the deputy head-waiter vanished: in the background the French waiter hovered, ready to serve the mayonnaised turbot fillets languishing on the waiting trolley.

Claudia, tossing her mink wrap about her shoulders, gathered her bag from the arm of the chair, which grated as she pushed it backwards. She rose from the table. She stared down at him for a moment, her upper lip curling, flashing her dark eyes with anger. She slung her bag about her shoulder and swirled away from him without a word. She made a great exit.

The fat woman, bulging from her carmine robe at the adjacent table, had smiled sympathetically at him as, ensconced between her two gentlemen friends, she besprinkled her mountain of food with pepper from the long, phallic grinder. Even now, in the darkness of *Mars*'s ward-room, he could recall that ineradicable scene in every sordid detail. The amusement in their eyes; their whispered conversation . . . the droll incident could have occurred last night.

He had paid the bill and, endeavouring to maintain his dignity, retired for coffee. The room, a dimly-lit lounge in the modern idiom, with low, pendant lighting throwing pools of brilliance upon the mahogany veneer table tops, had offered him the privacy he needed in which to think things out. The red carpet glowed expensively, whilst a Negro voice was stridently caterwauling the 'blues'. He could remember the words now . . . *Good morning – honey – might as well be wed. Might as well be wed – honey – ; might as well be wed; might as well be wed – good morning, honey . . .* What rhymed with 'wed'? Dreadful stuff, but somehow in keeping with the mood of the evening's disaster.

A broad-leaved palm tree stood in the centre of the room, its fronds, tickled by the draught, shivering silently . . . All this was four years ago. He'd reached the bottom of the pit, alone, unable to share the sense of shame, the guilt, the anger. Then, when he was at his lowest ebb, he had at last found peace. In despair he had crept into a village church, to pull himself together. And there, utterly abased, he had discovered a strength which had steadily grown, like the roots of a tree. This new-found fortitude had remained with him through the years, until this recent crisis had enveloped him, like a flash of forked lightning – and he was *not* thinking of this submarine disaster which was to end his physical existence.

Why had they been thrown together, Jackie and him? Why, for God's sake, why?

Being captain of the port watch crew of a Polaris submarine, he had been able to settle down to a steady routine throughout the year – three months out, three months ashore, preparing for the next patrol. This was the advantage of being a Boomer captain – a regular routine for these picked, steady men.

When he'd been enjoying his rest period ashore after a three-month stint, *Mars* had usually been away on her long patrols. Since those childhood days when they had both been brought up in Woodbridge, George had always been a good friend: it was only natural for Alastair to see much of the Carn family, particularly since, after his divorce from Claudia, he'd been a free agent. He had been one of the Carns' true friends to whom they could turn in their despair after Stephen's birth. He'd noticed the imperceptible change in the relationship between George and Jackie, but could not explain it.

Then had come that Easter Sunday when *Mars* was away on patrol. The dawn of a brisk March morning was shining through the east window of Glenburra's little kirk. The sun's rays streamed upon the clumps of Easter lilies, and, on the sills of the small windows, the gold of daffodils vied for precedence with the bunches of sweetly-scented primroses. In the peace of the early service, he'd seen her, solitary in the pew at the back, alone with her thoughts and burden. He had quietly joined her in the pew and together they had shared that Easter morning; and during the Creed, when the congregation stood, he had gently encircled her rough tweed coat with his arm. She had not recoiled. Instead she had leaned against him, silently, her eyes closed, facing the cross.

There, before God, they became deeply aware of each other. They had remained silent and gone their separate ways, she to Dunbrae House, he to his cabin back at the base. Not a word had passed between them, but each had known that their lives had been touched by some miracle too precious for expression in mere words.

It had been seventeen years since he had last suffered the physical pain of heart-ache, when he had first fallen deeply in love; this was one of the marvels that separated men from the beasts, wasn't it? There was no medical explanation for the metamorphosis of falling in love: there need be no physical contact, not even the intangible connection of two glances meeting each other – and yet, there, suddenly, they had been blessed by this miracle that most people never encountered in a lifetime.

They had met again, after he had rung her up. 'Come to tea, Alastair,' she had invited, and in those prosaic words were the promise of a new life for both of them. No longer were two people alone, encased in shells from which they could not escape. They had fallen in love and neither knew how to halt this headlong, runaway bliss which had enfolded them so suddenly.

They had first kissed at Dunbrae House, when she bid him goodnight. The shock of the contact had overwhelmed them, and for days afterwards they had deliberately stayed clear, one from the other – their feelings could blaze out of control, like a prairie fire.

When *Mars* returned to base for her spell in harbour, he had visited Dunbrae House only once: George and he had behaved naturally, while Jackie hovered in the background, muttering sweet platitudes. Why was it that, when two people were in love, they were so adept at making excuses? He smiled to himself, trying in the privacy of his bunk to picture her, his sweet, beloved Jackie . . .

She was the daughter of a Lancashire family, her father being connected with the fishing industry at Fleetwood. As children, she and her brother, Peter Sinclair, spent their childhood in the foothills of Westmorland, along the shores of Morecambe Bay. Though Peter was younger than her by a couple of years, they had been inseparable; the coincidence that George was Peter's captain made her very happy. She had never breathed to anyone

86

the obvious anxiety, that both her men were in the same submarine – but now, apart from her children, *all* those she held precious were there, trapped in *Mars* and with little hope of survival. How would she bear it, and how had she taken the news?

Jackie had strength, a toughness derived from her Lancashire upbringing. He could picture her, her dark hair, touched with the red-gold of her Scottish mother's ancestry, falling naturally about her head, like a boy's. This swept-back hair-style accentuated the freckled forehead framing her intelligent eyes. Flecked with the golden glints of a moorland stream, her grey-green eyes still reflected the laughter that life had once dealt out to her.

Child-bearing had not noticeably spoilt her adorable figure. At thirty-two she was remarkably trim; her hips were slim and her breasts had begun to reveal the seductiveness of the middle-aged woman. In her open-necked shirts, usually with the top button undone, she was the picture of a fresh country girl; she was only five feet tall, but, dear God, she was beautiful . . .

The opportunities for being alone together had been the terrible temptation. How easy it was: she at Dunbrae House; he alone and free, down at the base; and George away on patrol. How too damned easy – and, at first, they'd recognised their folly and he had stayed away. Then, as time slipped past, their meetings had become more frequent, until, alone on his evening walks, his steps led inevitably over the hills and along the birch-tunnelled lane.

He had tried so hard to save the situation: 'You must give me up, Jackie, *now*,' he had commanded on that April evening in the garden, with the scent of bracken in the air, 'before it's too late . . .'

She had whispered against his shoulder, gently sobbing until the lapel of his jacket was soaked with tears:

'I can't. You know I can't, not now . . .' and the passion had overwhelmed them both.

And weakly he had allowed their clandestine love for each other to flower. There was no harm, he told himself; he had saved her sanity, given her hope again . . . and so they had continued, resolutely resisting the inevitable union towards which they were both being swept.

His temporary appointment to *Mars*, under George's command, had been a terrible dilemma for him. He was about to see Captain S/M, Captain Quincey, to decline the opportunity, but had been dissuaded by Jackie: 'What reason are you going to give?' she had asked. 'You'll have to admit the truth, and that will mean hurting George.'

'I can't tell the world,' he'd replied, 'that I love my best friend's wife.'

So he had remained silent, preferring to wait and hope for a solution he knew would never come . . . All would be well: they would remain, Jackie and he, the best of life-long friends, nothing more – but that was before the picnic, the day they'd spent together, up on Dunbrae Moor . . .

He jolted upright . . . what was that? His heart was beating against his ribs, as he listened to the tapping, distinct and clear; a message was being knocked out in deliberate, decipherable morse code . . . Perhaps only he could hear it because he was sleeping on the outboard bunk, but he was certain of it now . . .

'George,' he said, trying to contain his excitement. 'They're in contact up top . . .'

## From Deep . . .

Terence Culmer, Lieutenant-Commander and XO of SSN *Mars*, could not believe that the impossible had almost been achieved: sixty-two men and three officers had made a rush escape from that flooded compartment. Though he admitted it only to himself, the achievement did say something for the instruction given by that devoted team in the escape tank at Gosport – and for his own perseverance in training *Mars*'s company. The sixty-five had left the compartment successfully, but how many would he find alive when finally he reached the top? And how many would be crippled for life by the bends?

The effects of the pressure in the flooded compartment were rapidly beginning to tell on him: he had been for a long time, watching the others slide into the tower, but if it had not been for these breathing units, he doubted whether many would have escaped . . .

No one had panicked: that was the secret. Fear was the unknown; everyone had known exactly what to do (they had all done a 'refresher' at *Dolphin* the last time they were in Gosport). The escape might have been from a re-scrub requalifying run at Blockhouse, except that it was from three times as deep.

Culmer was alone now, the last to leave. In this intense blackness, he had to feel his way towards the lower hatch. The nose clip hurt and his ears ached from the continuous clearing: hand over the exhaust outlet and blow out . . . repeat continually . . . his orange immersion suit had been inflated for some time now, but it seemed to be taking the strain. *Well, may God help us . . .* and he shuffled towards the tower . . . He inhaled deeply from the breathing unit, wrenched off the connecting tube; dipped under the water and ducked into the escape chamber. Suddenly he was away, more rapidly than he'd expected.

One rip in this suit and I'm . . . God, I'm clear of the tower. Breathe out, breathe out or your lungs will burst . . . 500 feet at seventeen feet a second – how many seconds was that? I'm shooting upwards, too bloody fast – I'll never survive this ascent – too fast, too damn fast – breathe out, you fool, Culmer . . . BREATHE OUT . . . about half a minute, that was as long as he'd have to control his breathing – and then, from somewhere far above him lightness glimmered, growing brighter, brighter with every agonising second – BREATHE OUT, YOU SILLY BASTARD . . .

He must have shot ten feet into the air, he was shooting upwards so fast. He lay back for an instant, dazzled by the light of the arctic mid-summer dawn. He was alive, God damnit, he was alive – and instinctively he lay back in the water to top up his stole and fully inflate his suit. And what about the others? From somewhere he thought he heard the sound of men's voices. He looked about him and there, less than two hundred yards away, wallowed a grey warship. From her yard-arm there fluttered a blood-red flag with its hammer and sickle; along her deck and manning the guard-rails was a row of cheering men. They were dressed in orange suits and their hoods were down. He heard a 'plop-plop-plopping' near him: a motor-boat was lunging into the long swell and growing larger at every second. He could see the bowman heaving a line towards him. He grabbed the rope and, an instant later, felt strong hands beneath his shoulders as he was hauled over the gunwale of the pitching boat.

Captain Quincey touched down at *Zed* within five minutes of the RAF's ETA. The Nimrod was met 500 miles off Novaya Zemlya by a squadron of MIGs which, wheeling and flashing in the forenoon sun, escorted the British reconnaissance plane to the runway concealed in the valley, on the eastern side of the inhospitable island.

Jack Quincey was one of those people who could converse with both a king and a beggar, and be as much at home with the one as the other. Of round face and with a rollicking, bucolic friendliness, he was the right man for the Russians. Within minutes he had metaphorically rolled up his four-striped sleeves and was moving things in the right direction . . .

The problem of language was solved immediately through the offices of an intelligent, thirty-year-old Russian lieutenant. The pressed uniforms seemed incongruous up here, Quincey thought, as did the tunic collars and the flat shoulder epaulettes, but the Russians were sticklers for etiquette.

'I want to get out to position X,' he said, speaking slowly and deliberately. 'The collision position. I understand that your salvage vessel, *Kronstad*, is on her way there with all her heavy lifting gear?' He raised his bushy, ginger eyebrows in question. The senior man amongst the circle of officers still surrounding him on the tarmac nodded his large head, the metal fillings in his teeth accentuating his grin. He smiled the whole time, an idiosyncracy which disconcerted Quincey, who, at first, could not decide whether the Russian was friendly or obstructive.

'A helicopter is waiting for you,' the interpreter said. He indicated the chopper waiting on the runway, the paraffin exhaust squirting its jet haze high into the air. Its rotor blades drooped, but the white-helmeted pilot was waiting patiently in the cockpit. 'It will fly you out to the frigate. Kapitan Isokov in *Krakvilsk* is expecting you.'

'One thing, sir,' Quincey said, as he began to stride towards the helicopter, 'the Americans should be arriving here at one o'clock with their mini submarine. They have head winds against them, but could you lift the craft out to position X as quickly as possible?' The jovial face had lost its grin. 'We haven't much time . . .' He glanced at the watch concealed in the fuzz of his hairy wrist. 'Just over twenty-four hours left, gentlemen – eleven hours have passed and we haven't even established contact with the submarine yet . . .'

The brawny Russian Staff Kapitan encircled Quincey's shoulders with a bear-like arm. 'Have no fear, Comrade Kapitan,' he said. 'We have our submarines too, you know . . .'

Quincey shook hands and clambered into the helicopter. The whine of the jet became a scream and then suddenly they were off, lurching and pirouetting into the sky; they skimmed the shoulder of the black mountain, then made for the speckled grey sea heaving beneath them, its white horses gleaming in the sun. After ten minutes, he spotted a large salvage ship following in the wake of a smaller, lighter craft. Both were steaming fast, their wakes threshing white. The pilot nodded: *Kronstad*.

Another twelve minutes of crazy swooping and the happy-go-lucky Russian sighted the frigate group, dead ahead. He spoke rapidly through the mike of his R/T and then the chopper was spiralling downwards towards the leading ship of the squadron: a fine-lined frigate with a low freeboard and a squat funnel. On her quarter-deck was the white-circled landing pad where overalled men were standing by and flapping their hand flags to assist the landing.

Quincey barely felt the bump. He jumped out and shook hands with the pilot before turning to the officer waiting to greet him:

'I'm Kapitan Isokov,' the broad-faced Russian said. 'You are welcome on board my ship, sir.' He smiled expansively and swept wide his arms: 'She is the *Krakvilsk*, leader of this squadron.' He spoke understandable English, but with the typical Russian rolling of the Rs.

'It is good of you to be so helpful, sir,' Quincey said. Then, smiling broadly, he added, 'under somewhat unfortunate circumstances.'

The Russian burst into gales of laughter:

'That is good, Comrade,' he bellowed, belting Quincey across the back. 'Very good. One day you too perhaps may be able to help us, yes?' His black eyes were dancing with merriment. 'You too are surrounded with our submarines, yes?' He led the way forward to his bridge. 'Come, please . . .'

Quincey was careful not to allow his eyes to roam over Russian secrets, but he was surprised to find how similar the enclosed bridge was to those of our own ships. The main difference was one of Action Plot presentation, the ops room being part of the bridge, but on a lower level.

'Please . . .' Kapitan Isokov picked up a headset and placed it across his own short-haired head. 'You, sir . . . ?'

Quincey took off his cap and donned the headset. Above the clatter of water noises, he could hear the rhythmic pulse of an underwater transmitter.

'We are trying again to make contact,' Isokov said. 'But first, I have a present for you, Captain.' His eyes were laughing again as he barked an order in Russian down a voice pipe. Across the starboard bow, Jack Quincey sighted an orange marker-buoy bobbing in the swell, its aerial swinging in the motion of the seaway. It was an extraordinary sensation to see *Mars*'s marker-buoy: she must be lying close, crippled in the depths, with George and his men choking out their lives . . .

'Hullo, sir . . .'

Quincey spun round. There stood Culmer, *Mars*'s Number One. He was dressed in a Russian seaman's overall and a grin was crossing the tired, freckled face.

'How many so far, Terence?' Quincey said, not daring to hope . . . 500 feet was deep.

'All survivors from the fore-ends are safe, sir,' Culmer said. 'Apart from a few cuts and bruises, we're all out, sir: sixty-two ratings and three officers.'

Quincey could not believe his ears. '*All* out?' he repeated. 'All escaped and picked up?'

'Yes,' Culmer said quietly. 'Incredibly, only seven men with the bends, sir. Says a lot for *Dolphin* training.'

'The captain?'

So it was that *Mars*'s first lieutenant became the first direct link with the rescue team. On the bridge of the Russian frigate, he described the plight in which he had left his captain, Commander Carn, and the other trapped men.

'They'll not try to escape until the last minute. They've five suits and they won't leave MEM Gallo, sir. The captain, I know, is pinning his faith on the rescue operation. It's a race against time: they've no life-support . . .'

Quincey felt the agony in the executive officer's voice, almost as if he was blaming himself for still being alive . . . the Russian captain had turned towards them.

'Listen, Kapitan,' he said softly. 'We make signals.'

Quincey crouched over the dial which, step by step, was methodically clicking around the bearing ring. It settled, motionless, on a bearing of 126°. A message was being tapped out, in elementary, slow morse . . .

'CAN YOU HEAR . . . ?'

Quincey held his breath. Isokov made a switch: the hydrophone was on circuit: *Mars*, with no power, had no transmitter . . .

Then he heard it, a faint, distant tapping . . . no mistaking that for morse, a rhythmic tapping against their pressure hull.

*Bang – bing – bang – bang . . . bing . . . bing – bing – bing – :* YES . . .

They were in contact at last – they had made the first, real progress, now that the salvage ship and the casualty could communicate.

'May I signal my Admiral?' Quincey asked, unable to conceal the excitement he felt. Once *Kronstad* was in position, he'd set up the rescue ops room on board her, and then her communications organisation could immediately contact FOS/M.

Isokov was handing him a signal pal. 'Write your message,' he said kindly. 'I will send it for you, Captain.'

Quincey sensed the sympathy behind the Russian's words.

Captain S/M4 withdrew the gold pencil from the inside pocket of his reefer jacket. The black capital letters jumped from the white paper:

'COMMUNICATIONS ESTABLISHED WITH MARS,' he wrote.
'65 SURVIVORS SAFE IN FRIGATE.'

He handed the signal to the waiting operator.

'Thank you, sir,' he said, turning to the Russian captain: 'What can I do to help?'

Communications had been established. Now they could get on with the job.

# CHAPTER 13

## *The Eternal Dilemma*

Jacqueline Carn was tidying away the lunch paraphernalia; she had sent the four boys out into the garden to allow her some peace and to give Stephen the chance to sleep. She longed to be alone to ponder the crisis now absorbing her every waking minute: the strain lay, not merely in the terrible choice that might face her and Alastair, but in the agony of waiting for news: the lives of her three men, George, Alastair and her brother Peter, were slowly ebbing away . . .

How was it possible to believe in a God so cruel? She jabbed savagely at the burnt frying-pan – to hell with its surface. If she scoured it away – non-burn, huh! The phone was shrilling in the hall . . . she walked calmly to the instrument, but her heart was racing as she picked up the receiver . . .

'Mrs Carn?'

It was FOS/M's voice, calm, reassuring, but with a false kindness behind the brave words. Vice Admiral Sir Frederick Clewes ought to know better than to fib to her: George had once been Clewes's fourth hand in *Aconite*.

'Yes, Sir Frederick . . . ?'

She allowed the pause between them to linger, praying to her ruthless God that her men could still be spared. The clock was ticking remorselessly in the hall, tick-tocking away their lives . . .

'Jackie Carn here . . .'

93

'I told Jack Quincey that I'd phone if there was any development,' FOS/M said, as clearly as if he were in the drawing-room. 'We're in touch with *Mars*, Jackie. The Russians are being magnificent. Jack Quincey has established communications with . . .' She heard him falter as he searched carefully for his words. He couldn't say, 'the doomed men, those trapped below, suffocating for lack of air . . .'

'With George and the others?' she volunteered, trying to ease his embarrassment.

'Yes. They're passing messages from the submarine to the surface vessels. George and the others are in good heart. We're waiting for the rescue sub now: the Americans should be on the spot very shortly . . .'

The words were confident, reassuring . . .

'How soon?' she asked brutally. She would not let him escape the issue.

'They're due at Zemlya at 1300. They're trying all they know, but the freight aircraft are batting against head winds. They can't do any more, Jackie – and then they've got to lift the mini sub out to *Mars*'s position.'

'Of course, Sir Frederick,' she said listlessly. 'I know you're doing all you can. Thank you for letting me know.'

She sensed the relief in his voice at her unemotional reaction. She carefully replaced the receiver. The line clicked and went dead. Luckily there was an extension in their bedroom if the phone rang again, so she could lie down and try to rest. She'd not slept since Jack's visit this morning, and fatigue was now overwhelming her, as she wrestled with her thoughts. Slowly she mounted the staircase and, trying not to notice George's things all about her, she hauled herself along the corridor and into their bedroom, the room which had witnessed so much happiness and torment over these past months.

She reached her hands behind her to unzip the green Terylene dress that she liked always to wear now: Alastair had first kissed her when she'd been wearing it and she relished shutting her eyes and dreaming . . . she slipped out of the dress and, too tired, allowed it to remain rumpled on the carpet. She'd slip between the sheets, though it was such a perfect summer's day. She unclipped her bra, slung it to the floor on top of the dress and sidled out of her floral pants. She'd sleep nude, dreaming . . . at least, no one could take her reveries from her.

George had never talked about her body, a facet of love-making she had always missed – but, of course, he was a no-nonsense, practical submariner: a down-to-earth, let's get on with it, type of man. She was a sensual woman, but that, surely, was a gift of which to be proud and not ashamed? In those early days, how she had longed for the utter oblivion of real passion – but that was never to be, not with George, she had realised very early on.

She would not be in this dilemma now, if there had never been that appalling accident, the root cause of her misery. She could never, never forget the agony in George's eyes when finally he had pulled himself together sufficiently to enter her private room off the corner of the maternity ward. During the long, dark hours, George had poured out his heart to her. She could remember his words, indelibly etched into her memory as he lay with his head on her breast and his hair brushing her cheek.

'I suspected something was wrong, Jackie,' he had whispered softly in the night, 'when Jack Quincey volunteered to come down with me to the hospital. But I never knew, never realised that the shock could be so terrible.

'Then the nurse – that bloody, hard-faced bitch – she was only trying to take the emotional content out of it, I suppose, but she could have eased the shock a little bit, couldn't she?' He had been unable to continue, as he searched for words that should not hurt her. 'I was prepared for the disappointment of another son, but not for . . . not for *that* . . .

'The nurse had her back to me as I watched her lift something out of the cot. She turned round suddenly and held up the pink child – our Stephen – for me to see.' He had continued swiftly, allowing the words to spill from his subconscious.

'The little mite was hideous: a deformed child, with an empty face staring up at me. Slit eyes and two holes where the nose should have been . . . '

He was lacerating himself and had to stop. He had lain there for how long she did not know. He had sobbed, and the racking of his tormented body had made her cry out.

'It was wrong of me, I know,' he'd said. 'It was the shock. If only I could have been prepared, been warned somehow. I remember saying, "Is this mine"?'

'The nurse nodded, that was all. I stumbled from the room, blind, unable to think. I left the hospital and, half insane, wandered through the town . . . '

The months which followed were the most difficult of their lives. Pathetic little Stephen . . . all the arguments for and against mercy-killing reared their cruel head – but George had been adamant: they would bear their cross, however heavy . . . and, together, they had tried so hard to accept the destiny meted out to them. What she had not expected was her psychological reaction against George's love-making.

The doctors had insisted on sterilisation. The whole process had been so cruelly clinical – physical love between man and woman had been debased into research for the professors.

The doctors had tried to be kind, each in his own way – some trying to ease George's mental stress by jocular inferences; others by cold, medical technology. And in the end they had killed it, their love . . . George had insisted on his vasectomy, but he had refused permission for her sterilisation. 'In case something happens to me,' he had told her. But in the end he gave in to her wishes, and the minor operation had been no trouble.

When they had attempted to enjoy their sex-life again, they had tried too hard . . . He had joked about it, but she had been repelled by his efforts. Her sensuality had dried up – and his personality, after she had had the operation, had begun to change insiduously. 'I'm only half a man,' he'd complained bitterly. He, George Carn, half a man – what a terrible tragedy this had all been, like a tidal wave overwhelming everything in its path. She beat the pillow with her clenched fist, unable to weep. Everything had happened so swiftly. She hated those bloody submarines . . .

She *must* have lost consciousness for half an hour, because the sound of the clock in the hall, striking half past three, jerked her to wakefulness. She ran her fingers through her short hair: her sleep had mussed it up, but she felt better for the thirty minutes' nap. She could hear the shout of the children playing in the garden; with horror, she realised that she had slept away another half hour of life remaining to those men still trapped in *Mars*. Half past three in the afternoon; fourteen hours since the disaster; but how long to go before . . . ? She shut her eyes as she tried to blot out the images flitting through her imagination. 'About a day and a half . . . ' Jack had said, 'thirty-six hours at the most.' And she had been disloyal enough to allow half of one of those hours to slip away.

Poor, dear George: his seed, the ultimate gift which a man could offer his woman, had first fathered a malformed child, and was destroyed for ever. It was not his fault that she was now physically repelled by him, for her mind could not reject the fear. The tragedy, for her part, was psychological, not physical. Instead of a gentle rewooing of her mind and body, George, for all his good intentions, had tried to overwhelm her to prove his virility. Instead of a rapier he had used a cudgel – and the more he tried to prove his manhood, the further he had driven her away from him, until the final, dreadful night . . .

It must have been, she supposed, the misery of all this that had laid bare her heart. Unconsciously, she was yearning for understanding and for the completeness of a perfect union, both physical and psychological, with an ideal lover the man of every woman's dreams. She had been vulnerable; it was then that Alastair had entered her life. Nothing could ever be the same again, not after that Sunday afternoon on Dunbrae Moor.

## Salvage Ship

It was the Englishman who sighted her first: the suspicion of haze below the horizon and then the white cross-trees of the salvage vessel forging into the swell that surged in from the south-west, from Iceland and the Mexican Gulf. Long after the radar report of her approach, Jack Quincey had been straining his eyes for the arrival of *Kronstad*. Ahead of her, her escorting frigate disappeared rhythmically, sheets of spray flying across her fo'c'sle as she dipped into the long swell.

Captain Quincey had been treated with genuine friendliness from the moment that he stepped on board *Krakvilsk*. Kapitan Isokov had pressed hospitality upon him, but, before the mini sub, arrived, Jack Quincey wanted to meet the *Mars* survivors: less than a normal day remained for George Carn and those with him: and all that Terence Culmer could tell him, every detail, would be more shots in the locker for the rescue attempt. So far, nothing tangible had been attempted. The rescue forces were gathering, but, the distances being so great, all that Jack Quincey could do, at this juncture, was to set up the structure for the rescue team when it foregathered.

Quincey had spoke to *Mars*'s survivors who were being cared for in *Krakvilsk*'s for'd mess-deck. They seemed in good heart but uncommunicative, their thoughts being with their mess-mates still trapped below. After meeting them, he had joined Culmer in the ship's ops room, where the Russians regaled them with black rye-bread sandwiches, caviar and a glass of vodka.

*Mars*'s first lieutenant gave him the stark facts: George and six others were trapped in the control room. There had been a total power failure; there was therefore no $CO_2$ absorbent, and the only clean air they could glean would be from the escape air bottles – if the lines were undamaged. From the last slow message received . . . NO AIR . . . it seemed that they were unable to use the reservoir air.

'We're down to basics, then, Number One,' Quincey stated. 'At the worst, I'd give them a total of thirty-six hours from the moment of collision.'

Culmer nodded, his freckled face grey with exhaustion and anxiety. 'They won't leave without Gallo,' he said. 'They've only five immersion suits between them, and one of those has a bad tear in it after the fire in the fore-ends.'

Quincey nodded. Culmer was a good Jimmy: an ex conventional CO and bound eventually for a nuclear command. How he had managed to extricate the whole of his party was a miracle in itself, even though some of them would be suffering from the bends . . .

'Any clues at all about the after part?' Quincey asked, his voice low. 'Where did the collision take place?'

'Abaft 63 bulkhead. The Chief and his boys were all aft at collision stations. There's been nothing at all from them, sir . . . nothing.'

The two men sat in silence in the half darkness, crouched over the chart-table space which they had been allotted. The fluorescent glow from the PPIs reflected the highlights of their faces, as each wrestled with his own thoughts.

'The chief was ready to snort, sir, the moment we got up. The manifolds were open when the collision occurred. The accident must have been catastrophic for them . . . not a chance, sir . . .'

For a full minute Culmer stood motionless, unable to speak. Then he turned slowly towards his senior officer:

'It's a terrible thing to say, sir, but if both halves had survived, our rescue efforts would have had to be diluted. In the time we have, we could never attempt salvage of both – and we couldn't abandon one half for the chance of rescuing the other. We have no choice now. We can concentrate on the captain and those with him.'

Culmer glanced out of the scuttles to where the orange buoy bobbed in the sea, *Mars*'s fore part being only 500 feet beneath it.

'I'm sure they'll attempt a hooded escape, sir, if we can't reach them with the rescue sub.'

'What about the injured man and the other two without suits?'

This was the first time that either men had posed the question. Culmer shook his head.

'Don't know, sir,' he said softly. 'But the captain will be the last to leave.'

Quincey had been in on the development of escape techniques, ever since Jackie Whitton had first conceived his simple brain-child, inverting a bucket in which a man could breathe while he made his escape. His band of pioneers had developed the lessons learned in the Second World War, and he had applied them to the Davis Escape Apparatus, so well tried by pre-war submariners.

*Truculent*'s disaster in the Thames estuary in the fifties, when many of her company had escaped only to drown in the cold tideway, had taught the lesson that the successful escapee must also be able to survive the inevitable exposure. So the immersion suit, like an airman's grotesque outfit, had been designed, a superb piece of equipment with its water-tight zip. Able to breathe clean, dry air from the built-in system until the last moment, the escaping man was not exposed to the fatal consequence of oxygen and carbon dioxide under pressure – as Carn and his men were so soon to suffer. Even if Carn was using the absolute gauge (the instrument provided in each compartment to measure the atmospheric pressure) the internal pressure was bound to increase because of HP air leaks and, perhaps, also of incoming water.

Though there was little Carn could do about reducing the pressure, the instrument *could* tell him how long he dare wait before those without immersion suits must make their suicidal escape attempt. Once the pressure reached two atmospheres, it would be safer for him to order the escape – but everything now depended upon how badly affected they already were by the carbon dioxide poisoning . . .

At *Dolphin*, the drill had been relentlessly plugged into every trained submariner. For five minutes, on the half hour and the hour, the searching surface ships would stop their engines to listen – and that was when trapped men would bash merry hell on the pressure hull – if they had the strength remaining. But now *Mars* knew that help was at hand. Carn was biding his time, balancing the knowledge that life was slowly ebbing away, against the hazard of escape from the conning-tower. It was certainly true that no two submarine accidents were alike.

'*Kronstad*'s clearing away her anchors,' Culmer was saying, almost to himself. 'She's a big ship, sir – all the latest gear.'

So the Russians were doing all they could . . . a miracle, Quincey thought . . . *Kronstad* must have *Mars* in contact on her underwater TV, to be able to anchor so close to the marker-buoy. She was a splendidly functional ship, with her huge well-deck aft, in addition to the two helicopter pads on the built-up flight-deck. Her two athwartship funnels were ugly, but, at this moment, she was the most practical, most beautiful ship he had ever seen. She sported cranes of all sizes, and two giants that extended from huge hydraulic rams. She had obviously been purpose-designed for the recovery of her own nuclear submarines. The hammer and sickle fluttered abaft the bridge; the Russians could well be proud of the superb navy they had built up so rapidly.

Jack Quincey preferred not to ruminate at this moment upon the plight of the Royal Navy, the sure shield which politician-riddled Britain chose to ignore. Instead, he preferred to remember the days when Jackie Whitton's successors had carried on the development of submarine escape.

Believing that submariners, and not scientific experts, should be the driving force (the lesson had been learned when the scientists produced, in about 1950, an escape device that took up the whole of the fore-ends so that there could be no re-load torpedoes), escape development had followed the right road.

The first buoyant ascent was made in 1951. There followed the hooded escape, and, at the same time, the prime requirements to fit a submarine with a prototype escape tower, and to build a training tower. Britain had followed her own devices and had built the 100-foot escape training tower at Blockhouse. With a staff of only thirty-five, the *Dolphin* escape training team trained sixteen thousand submariners a year, from all nations. When the proving trials on the first tower had been successfully completed at sea, the production team at DRS, Bath, had within nine months fitted the first submarine with an escape tower; and this, after the tower had had to be re-designed and re-valved: it had been no mean achievement.

After all this work, the first tragic accident had occurred in the escape tower. The public clamoured for training to cease, and so the submarine service was deprived of one facet of its vital peace-time training. It was fortunate that public opinion had again changed, for *Mars*'s men had been some of the first to recommence escape training.

In the interval, two-men escape towers were being designed; and, consequent upon the enterprise of private firms working on the Atlantic cables and the oil pipe-lines, the Americans and British co-operated in the production of rescue mini submarines: the Yanks were to produce the mini sub; the British, the submarine end of the rescue system.

*Mars*, one of the first nuclear submarines to be so fitted, was unlucky: her attachment had not been completed – the reception platform was in place and so was the air-line connector, but that was all. It would be a miracle if the mini sub (*Lily-One*, they called her) could achieve any results. But the Americans had despatched their best commander, they'd said, so any chance was worth taking.

Quincey heard the rattle of *Kronstad*'s anchor cable. As he turned to make his farewell to *Krakvilsk*'s captain, he recognised the sounds of a boat's falls squeaking in the blocks as the motor cutter was lowered to the water-line.

'Good news, Captain Queencee,' the grinning Russian said, crushing Jack's hand in his bear-like grip. 'The Americans landed at our base at 1420. They are bringing out the rescue submarine in one of our big helicopters. The American commander is in another helicopter and should be landing soon on *Kronstad*.'

As the Russian preceded Jack Quincey to the iron deck abreast the funnel, the Royal Naval captain was silent: the chart-table clock showed 1640. *Only twenty-one hours* remaining to them – fifteen hours had already been frittered away.

## CHAPTER 14

# *No Second Chance*

Kapitan Alexandrei Smirnov was relieved that the American rescue sub had not yet arrived. It was now 1720, but the Combined Rescue HQ had only just convened, in spite of all he had done to urge it on. The helicopters were now pouring in, like hovering dragon flies, upon the landing deck. First, the three American advisers and the commander of the rescue sub; then the Russian experts from base. Even if the sub had achieved its ETA, *Kronstad* would not have been ready to receive her.

That English captain (Quincey, wasn't it?) and that exhausted

– looking officer who had escaped, were the first to set foot on board. Alexandrei Smirnov could sense immediately that those two were practical men, seamen and dependable. Quincey had immediately gone to the heart of the matter and asked for communications to be established between his headquarters in *Kronstad*'s radio room and the British submarine base at Faslane.

Being a salvage specialist, Kapitan Smirnov knew little about radio communications, but he was very proud of *Kronstad*'s superb communication centre, which was equipped to transmit and receive on almost every known frequency. Capable not only of talking and listening on 'voice' to all Russian submarines, the operators, highly trained men, could monitor any foreign ship's transmissions throughout the world. The mini tapes were sent back to Leningrad for memory-banking and, later, for deciphering in those incredible computers he had once seen when undergoing his communications course.

Quincey was talking in 'voice' to his admiral in Scotland. Smirnov was amazed by the familiarity of the conversation: *he* would no more dream of using first names to the bureau in Moscow or Leningrad than of piloting a spaceship around the moon.

Kapitan Smirnov was pleased with himself: like his good friend Isokov in *Krakvilsk*, he was one of the new generation, part of the modern Russian navy. He knew himself to be highly ambitious: but, whereas Isokov had specialised in sonar work and submarine detection, he, Alexandrei Smirnov, of Esthonian extraction had gone a different way. His fisherman father had moved to the old capital of Taallin, and engendered his last son late in life. His third wife, Marguerita, had died in bringing Alexandrei into the world; so the young man had, from his earliest days, been strongly influenced by his aging sailor father. Originating from one of the mistrusted Baltic States which Russia had gobbled up after the Second World War, Alexandrei Smirnov, however competent, was politically suspect. It was therefore to the salvage branch that he had been directed – a specialist activity in which, fortunately, he excelled by reason of the seamanlike qualities it demanded.

Smirnov had graduated from the Russian submarine branch into salvage, after the incident when that new nuclear submarine, *Gorgi Stalin*, had foundered on trials. He had distinguished himself by diving down single handed and attaching the air line. They had saved fifty-eight out of the crew of one hundred and sixty, no mean feat in spite of the tragedy. Mother Russia demanded those sacrifices of her new navy, and there was still no shortage of volunteers for the submarine branch.

Kapitan Smirnov picked up the fo'c'sle phone.

'Keep to the two-hundred-metre line,' he commanded. He was taking no risks here: fortunately, the bottom was rocky, but the weather was notoriously treacherous. He was anchored on the edge of this underwater canyon, and if his anchor dragged, once the lifting gear was out, he would have to slip the lot: that would be the end of his career – and the rescue attempt.

He was still amazed by the incredible volte-face of the Russian naval commissars in co-operating so whole-heartedly with their erstwhile enemies. There could be only two reasons for this new attitude: first, that Russia was so confident that international Communism was winning the economic battle throughout the world (look at the inflation in all the decadent democracies) that there was no more need for the ultra-caution she had previously practised; and, second, that the recovery of one of the enemy's submarine reactors was a prize too rich to be ignored.

'Your objective, Kapitan Smirnov,' his admiral had instructed him, 'is, firstly, to recover the nuclear reactor; and secondly, to try and save those trapped British submarine-men.'

The corners of Smirnov's wide mouth twisted wryly. If he had anything to do with it, he'd reverse the priorities: those men were eking out their lives down there, less than two hundred metres below them. If he, Kapitan Alexandrei Smirnov, made no mistakes (and with all his underwater detecting gear, including the underwater television cameras, he should be dead accurate), he should be able to pass the underwater lifting wires at the first attempt. The mate had already flaked out the huge wires whilst on passage from the base. He could see the bights, neatly stopped off, fore and aft, where they ran the length of the upper deck.

He intended to work simultaneously with the American midget rescue submarine. He, personally, put little faith in that untried gadget, but when men's lives were in the balance, what did it matter so long as one method did not interfere with the other? The American could dive if he wanted to, whilst the lifting wires were being passed: he might even be able to help, with that hydraulically-operated arm with which *Lily-One*, the rescue sub, was fitted. Smirnov looked forward to seeing the thing: he'd give it a close look – its secrets would be added knowledge for the bureau's storehouse of information. A phone buzzed at the after end of the bridge.

'Kapitan here . . .'

'Base Staff Liaison Officer here, Comrade Kapitan,' the voice crackled over the ether. 'The first helicopter with the American rescue sub is on its way. Another, with the remainder of the Rescue HQ staff, three Americans, three Russians and two British, should be with you by 1720.'

'Very good.' Smirnov spoke briskly. He was determined to keep the lines open, in case of emergencies. 'When can I expect the rescue sub and its commander?'

'1800, sir. Its Commander, Lieutenant-Commander Dugan, is in the first helicopter, with the staff.'

'Thanks . . . ' Kapitan Smirnov replaced the combined receiver/transmitter. He hoped he had not been too brusque, but wasn't that the familiar flutter of a helicopter's rotary blades he could hear approaching from the port quarter . . . ?

Lieutenant-Commander Dugan, USN, was present at the first foregathering of the rescue team which took place at 1800 in *Kronstad*'s radio room. The meeting was a brief affair, but indispensable, as was pointed out by Captain Jack Quincey, that plummy-voiced Limey who seemed to be in charge of affairs. Commander Laszlo Dugan was impatient to quit the meeting and happy to leave the others talking: he was determined to oversee the hoisting of *Lily-One*, his precious prototype rescue sub, in which he placed so much faith. He had spent eighteen months of his life – ever since he'd left his command, *Squid*, one of the last conventionals, at Norfolk, Virginia – working on this rescue prototype: since the terrible tragedy of their first nuclear loss at 1300 feet, when an SSN had imploded, the Navy Department had spared no effort to develop a practical rescue system, capable of freeing submariners trapped at great depths.

Laszlo Dugan had always been a man of action – he saw the reason for this meeting, but time was running out. He had to take advantage of this good weather. He pushed back his chair and stood up.

'If you'll excuse me, Captain, I must see to *Lily-One*: I've got my schedules to check before I take the first dip – and that takes time, sir . . . ' He looked the British captain straight in the eye. 'Have I your permission to carry on, sir?'

He smiled that broad smile of his: his bronzed American face was of the traditional pioneer breed: tough, lean, angular, with sharp blue eyes, missing nothing.

'Of course, Commander,' Quincey replied. 'Please carry on. We're absolutely clear about your intentions, aren't we? Your first dive is to be exploratory to see how *Mars* is lying, you will also consider attaching an air line. Is that correct?'

'Right, sir, but I'll have to play it off the cuff. I may not be able to see a thing: depends on the currents and whether there's sand or not.'

'We'll be in continuous touch on the underwater phone. Good luck, Commander ⸱ ⸱ ⸱ ' Dugan interpreted the gesture as a courteous dismissal. The thirty-year-old American hastened from the room; when he stepped out on deck, he felt the cold air off this northern sea cutting his face. Ah, there she was, his *Lily-One*, swaying from the derricks; *Kronstad*'s mate had lowered her gently alongside and was keeping her plumbed six feet above the crests of the long swell. He would board her now, in case of accidents ⸱ ⸱ ⸱

They used another crane to lower him through the mini sub's hatch. He had left his uniform windcheater behind, and, knowing the cold he would encounter at depth, he'd broken all navy regulations and donned his favourite (and lucky) dark-blue polo-necked sweater which Aylmar had knitted for him. He waved to the crane operators to begin lowering; when he felt the sea embracing his *Lily*, he tripped the release gear. He felt the shock and the boat was free, at last in her own element. He'd carry out the checks swiftly but thoroughly: this five-thousand-mile journey could have produced stresses about which he knew nothing.

*Lily-One* was painted orange and shaped like a spatial saucer. She was of advanced design but, built on the same principles as Jacques Cousteau had developed, she looked clumsy when out of her element. Once submerged, she behaved perfectly and was extremely manoeuvrable. Her mechanical arm normally stretched forward like the antenna of some giant insect, but, at the moment, it was folded back and tucked into the streamlined hull. When working, this extending arm, with its lobster claws, could carry out intricate work, even to tightening a nut. He waved to the onlookers on *Kronstad*'s bridge and slammed down the hatch over his head. It was good to hear the water slapping against her hull again and to be master of his own destiny.

First the log: '1919: lowered into water, shut upper lid,' he scrawled. His written record of his day-to-day work was a vital matter. If anything went wrong, he could always depend on the written word, long after his intelligence had become befuddled by the adverse effects of lack of oxygen and excess carbon dioxide. Planes okay; fluid ballast okay; pumps and hydraulics okay; working arm okay – and now for the essential requirement: communications. He took her slowly below the surface, down to thirty feet, to hover there, perfectly under control.

'*Lily-One* calling *Kronstad*,' he called. 'D'ye hear me?'

The response was immediate, loud and clear. '*Kronstad* here; Captain Quincey speaking.'

'You're loud and clear, sir. Strength five. Permission to carry on with my exploratory dive, sir?'

'*Lily-One* carry on,' the English voice answered. 'But from now on, Lieutenant-Commander Dugan, please call me Jack. Understood?'

'Yes, sir – ' Dugan replied, grinning to himself in the solitude of his minute control complex. So the Limey's weren't so stuck up after all . . . 'and my name's Laszlo, sir. But they call me Doc – after one of Disney's dwarfs,' he added. He heard the chuckle at the other end, the first sign of levity he'd encountered during the last twelve hours.

He was lying full length on his stomach in the operating position, his face within a foot of the sighting port, an immensely tough circular glass window, the eye of the little sub. With his left hand, he began to ease her down, 30 – 40 – 50 feet; with his right, he entered up the log:

'Began exploratory dive to 500 feet,' he wrote. As he put down the pencil, a gentle tick-ticking seemed to echo off *Lily-One*'s hull – Tick – tick . . . tick – tick – tick . . . by God, it was *Mars*, couldn't be anyone else, and she was sending out morse by some means or other. He worked the tuning knobs on his hydrophone equipment – and suddenly his mini universe echoed with strong transmissions.

'*Lily-One* here,' he reported briskly. '*Mars* is transmitting.' He flicked a switch and a broad beam of light diffused the darkness enveloping *Lily-One*.

'One hundred feet,' he reported. 'Visibility twenty yards, I guess.' He glanced at the inclinometer: all well, under control . . . He eased up the main motor switch and the hum of the pumps increased to a gentle whine. 'Going on down,' he called. 'Beam me on, please, Jack.'

The bearings were pouring in fast now . . . *Kronstad* and the boys up there were certainly doing their stuff. 250 feet, 300, 400, 450, 480 . . . bearing steady. The adrenalin was streaming in his veins: this was the moment he enjoyed, the instant before location . . .

490 . . . and then he spotted the bottom, twenty feet beneath him, in the pool of light dispensed by the keel lantern. Black rock,

with a fine silt on top . . . and the sand flailing gently in the current like a pennant in the wind. As he nosed the little craft ahead, he saw the underwater cliff falling precipitously into the blackness below. He was on the edge of a vast underwater ravine . . . then, peering into the debris swirling ahead of him, he suddenly glimpsed the huge black mass. It was very close, swaying in the current, its central point balanced on a knife-edged pinnacle of rock.

He pulled back the throttle to the 'hover' position. There, in the searchlight's beams, he saw her, the forward section of SSN 17, the white letters clearly visible on her fin. As he reported into the microphone, he heard the scrunching of metal as *Mars* surged back and forth in the ocean current. She was lying at about a twenty-degree bow-down angle, was pivoted on a fulcrum slightly forward of the fin. He could see the flattened section of the pad on which he was supposed to attach his mini sub. One false move, and *Mars* could overbalance and plunge into the abyss.

He wrote in his log:

'1945: *Mars* sighted 510 feet, balanced on rock pinnacle.'

She must have been here for eighteen hours now – *Half way*, with eighteen hours left to her. The realisation spurred him onwards. He'd circle her and then surface to make his report.

### Radio Operator Dean

Why the hell hadn't he thought of it before? The sudden realisation that he could connect up the transmission side of the emergency sonar to the stand-by batteries in the radio room hit Radio Operator Pinky Dean smack between the eyes. He was recovering from a five-minute session of belabouring the bulkhead with the navigator's wheel-spanner; exhausted by the effort, he lay on the ward-room settee, puffing. He hadn't been so short of wind for a long time: ridiculous, after only five minutes of belting the hull.

They'd laugh at him perhaps? He, the youngest by far, nineteen last birthday, to be offering technical suggestions like this – but the captain had always seemed a decent guy. He'd ask him, anyway, for permission to try.

And so, for two hours, Pinky Dean slaved away in the heat of the radio room, a torrid humidity which worsened with each hour that dragged by. He plodded on, in the knowledge that nothing mattered much any more; and knowing that, if he *could* obtain quick communication, he wouldn't again have to belt away with that bloody spanner . . .

His emergency lantern was losing power: it was difficult to see now – only two more electrical connections to make and, with luck, the transmitter should work. There'd be a limited life because the emergency sonar was greedy on amps . . . but at least they would be able to communicate about the vital decisions with the rescue people up top. Working alone, Pinky Dean had time to reflect on his life so far – not a long one, but fairly full, since the day he'd joined.

With his baby-face and pink complexion, he'd had a rough time during those training days: there was no crueller animal than the young male. Looking back on it, he supposed that, if it had not been for that run ashore in Pompey, when they'd taken him to the brothel, he wouldn't now be in the pickle he was with Poppy Sullivan.

He'd never forget that night: the defiant arrogance of the others as they disappeared down the grotty corridor; the highlight of excitement in Loftie's eyes afterwards; and, while he waited for them in that frowsty ante-room, with its beaded curtains, the self-loathing that had welled up inside him. So when they came back with the laughing girls, they had all looked at him in disbelief.

'C'mon, dearie,' a dark-haired trollop had invited him, 'scared are you, darlin'? I'll show yer the way . . .'

But he'd remained sitting there, toying with his cap, unable to take his eyes off those seductive breasts, so tantalisingly close, beneath their cheap, see-through negligée . . . he had blushed to the roots of his being, but had refused to go with the girl. Jeering and laughing, the lads had followed him outside, to the freshness of a summer's evening on Southsea beach. They'd called him Pinky ever since.

His reaction to those training days had been traumatic. Out on the booze so long as he could afford it, he was not to be outdone any more. And when Poppy had finally given her all, he was the happiest junior rating in Hampshire. The reckoning had come nine months later.

He had not chosen submarines: 'Never volunteer,' the old hands said. He'd been 'pressed' into the branch, but he wasn't the only one, for it was becoming increasingly difficult to man the submarine service which now swallowed up most of the navy's senior rates.

That he had known little about his first submarine did not matter much: he double-banked with older hands and learned the job from them. But now the percentage of inexperienced junior ratings manning these nuclears was much too high: he heard the same moan from all sides and especially amongst the POs and senior ratings. Understudying a Sea Daddy was not conducive to finding out for oneself . . . there ought to be, as in the past, a good grounding in general service ships first. But how else was the branch to be manned?

As senior rates left, they were being replaced by junior ratings . . . and, back aft, where the watch-keeping system was such a problem, very few senior rates were re-engaging. These indispensable men were sometimes serving five years in the same submarine because no one could be found to replace them.

'Back aft' was the problem: there could be no leave until the work was done. The kettle never slept: if a stoker was on leave or on a run ashore, he *had* to be sober when he rejoined.

Manning and personnel were the greatest difficulties with which the submarine service had to contend: there was little point in spending sixty million pounds on a submarine if it could not be manned by sufficiently well-trained personnel. The *treadmill* feeling did not help morale, particularly that of the wives who for three months on end had to bring up the children by themselves. Pinky tightened the last nut and wondered what it had been like in his father's days, with three-year foreign commissions?

He was glad he had joined the boat. He was proud of his job; but if he was honest with himself he had more chance, in these Hunter-Killers, of escaping Poppy. 'It's yours,' she had said the last time, pointing at her expanding waistline. 'You'll have to pay for it . . . ' He hadn't dared tell Mum and Dad, but he'd have to now, after that solicitor's letter from Gosport. How the hell was he to cope?

He slapped on another terry clip and shut-up the tool-bag. He'd request permission to try the transmitter now . . . holding the fading lantern in front of him, he felt his way back to the control room. The captain was sitting at the table, wide awake, his eyes following Dean's every move.

'May I try it, sir?'

'Of course, Dean – give it a go. Make *Mars, Mars, Mars. Do you read?* Got it?' The captain hauled himself from the table and in the dim light groped his way to the sonar room. Dean was already back at the key and had begun to tap out the message.

The response was immediate:

'Rescue attempt starting at 2100. Rescue sub will attempt docking to pass air line through pad connection. Acknowledge...'

Dean was smiling as he turned to his captain. 'Make R for Romeo,' Carn said. 'Well done, Dean. That will cheer up the boys.'

Pinky followed the Old Man back to the control room. Surprisingly, he had turned on the last but one of the three emergency lanterns. The faces in the circle of cold light were like a Rembrandt painting: Commander Sinden's pensive, sensitive profile; the coxswain, wise and resigned to his fate; the navigator, calm but deep in thought, probably worrying about his young family; Soper, worried, his continuous sneer less evident; and poor Gallo, stretched where they had laid him eighteen hours ago. His face was grey and his breathing too fast.

'It's time we had a natter,' the captain began, 'because you all now know how we stand. Thanks to Dean here, we're in contact with the rescue team up top. The Russians must be there, and it's my bet that FOS/M has mounted a major effort: to my knowledge only the Yanks have developed a rescue sub so far.'

'They're sending a sub down, sir?' Hebbenden asked. 'What can she do?'

'I imagine she'll try to get an air line through the pressure hull. She'll have to attach herself to our temporary mounting pad. They're sending her down shortly.'

'If there's a salvage ship up there, they may try to lift us,' Sinden said. 'A *Thetis* type of rescue...'

'It's the air we need most,' Soper added.

'You're right, Jake.' This was the first time the captain had resorted to Christian names; Dean wondered whether he'd been listed in that category.

'When Pinky here,' and Carn smiled as he addressed the young RO, 'you'll forgive me, won't you, Dean? We might as well dispense with formalities...'

Pinky felt himself blushing ridiculously as the captain continued: '... When Pinky has had a sleep, he'll be keeping a continuous communications watch on the sonar set. Until then, will you take over, please, Jake? Let me know if any message is being passed, and then we'll shake you, Pinky...' The captain smiled at him, an open, friendly smile, with no trace of condescension.

'You can all feel the air becoming stuffier: the carbon dioxide is building up, while we are using up the oxygen. Peter has fetched

110

those spare medical cylinders from the oxygen-generating compartment: he will be cracking the oxygen valves when I say so – but we can go on a bit longer yet. So keep still and don't talk . . . I don't imagine anyone's hungry.'

They smiled then: they'd not eaten for eighteen hours and yet no one had thought of food.

'You will all have been wondering how we are to get out . . . Well, it's time I gave you the facts.'

Carn paused, glanced round the table and then told Soper and Dean of the accident in the fore-ends. ' . . . so there are only five suits (and one of them is duff) between the seven of us.'

Pinky knew that everyone's thoughts were now on Gallo. The young RO could sense the terrible truth that must now be stealing into each man's mind.

'One of the disadvantages of being a submarine CO is that sometimes he is forced to choose between two impossible situations.' There were crescents of exhaustion beneath Carn's red-rimmed eyes.

'None of us knows how soon we shall be running out of oxygen; or how badly we shall be affected by oxygen under pressure, or by carbon dioxide poisoning.' He passed his hand across his forehead. 'Don't know about you blokes, but I've got a bit of a head already.'

Pinky sucked his teeth: an insistent ache was thumping at the back of his temples; he had become aware of the pain when he was bending over the apparatus in the sonar room.

'I'll have to decide *when* to make our hooded escape through the conning-tower. I can't leave it too late or we shan't be able to manage it . . . two at a time ought to be feasible . . . ' he added.

'But there must be another one of us in the tower, to shut the upper lid after the two have gone.' Commander Sinden was stating a fact, and Pinky realised that this would be a vital requirement if the others were to have chance.

'Ought to be possible, sir,' Hebbenden chipped in, 'so long as we drain down again quickly.'

'Glad you agree, Cox'n,' the captain said. 'I had reckoned so, but you're an ex tank instructor, aren't you?'

Pinky felt relieved: so it was possible, after all, to escape this nightmare? Provided they kept their heads and didn't foul up the tower . . .

'Yes, sir,' Hebbenden acknowledged. 'The third man will have to signal as soon as the upper lid's shut . . . three bangs on the side of the tower.'

'Okay but speed will be vital for number three,' the captain said. 'Don't forget, he will have been breathing foul air under pressure.'

'We mustn't leave this escape for too long, sir . . .'

The captain was meeting the coxswain's eyes. Both men knew the danger of attempting an escape from this depth. Pinky wished he knew how Terence Culmer and his party had fared: they were either all dead, less than twenty feet away, or some had escaped. *Mars* would know soon enough when the people up top began to pass the facts. Morale would soar, once it was known that the others had made it . . . but what a decision the captain had to make: if he decided to sit tight, a successful lift from the salvage ship, or an air line from the mini sub, and they could be breathing God's fresh air again in a few hours.

'You'll all agree that we should plan for the worst?' Carn was glancing at them again and even Pinky found himself nodding in assent. He didn't want to die yet, even with Poppy's menacing image awaiting him if he reached shore alive.

'I've carefully considered the order of escape, and I'd rather not have any back-chat,' Carn said, his voice hard. 'There are reasons for my decisions and it would not be fair on me to have to explain . . . so . . .'

The captain glanced across at Soper; Pinky saw the officer's mouth twitching at the corners.

'Jake, I want you to go first, with Dean here . . . ' and Carn half turned to the radio operator. 'Happy about that, Pinky?'

Dean felt himself swallowing, finding it difficult to speak. He nodded. He was going to have the best chance of them all then? Soper would guide him out, but it would be up to him from then onwards. He forced himself to pose the brutal question that was at the back of each of their minds:

'What about Gallo?' he asked. 'He's my mate, sir . . . ' He turned away and looked again at the horizontal body. There'd be no chance for El Greco now, not now, even if he recovered consciousness.

'Pinky, no questions,' Hebbenden said gruffly. 'We agreed on that . . .'

'Because of the cox'n's experience,' the captain continued rapidly, 'he will be third man in the tower for the first escape. He'll shut the upper lid and remain in the tower while we drain down. As soon as you can, Peter . . . ' and Pinky saw the imperceptible nod from the navigator's head, ' . . . you'll join the cox'n in the tower for the second attempt. You four will have the good immersion suits and you'll all make a hooded ascent . . .'

Carn glanced then at his friend. 'You, Alastair, will follow Peter into the tower and act as third man to shut the upper lid after Peter's gone . . , I'll drain down as soon as I hear your signal.'

Pinky could feel his heart thumping against his rib-cage as no one said a word. Sinden would have the dud suit, then. The captain was staying behind with the unconscious Gallo: neither would have a suit . . .

'Those are my orders, gentlemen . . . ' Carn was deliberately brutal. 'Gallo and I will join Commander Sinden for the third ascent: we'll be making a rush escape, he and I.' He tried to smile: 'Probably reach the surface before you, Alastair . . . '

In the silence, each man was wrestling with his own conscience; was it fair, in the final count, to allow the captain his privilege of deciding who was, perhaps, to live; who to die?

'Get some sleep.' Carn was the captain again: remote, impersonal.

But to Pinky sleep was a will o' the wisp. He could not switch off his mind: what would it be like, when he swooped towards the surface? If he remembered all that he'd been told, his lungs would not burst – just breathe out normally, they said, if you were making a hooded escape . . . His headache was becoming acute: a constant, dull ache stretching like an iron band across his forehead. He wondered whether he'd stay in submarines, after this lot . . . As a seaman he could sign on for another twelve years, but what was he letting himself in for? A seaman PO had no fulfilling job, because most tasks of importance were carried out by petty officer technicians from other branches.

Yet, Pinky thought drowsily to himself, if he did manage to escape, would he really quit? There were many snags in being a nuclear submariner, but wasn't there a hell of a lot to be said for it? The pay was good and you collected 'hard-liars' when the boat was at sea. The food was okay, being shared by both wardroom and mess-decks alike. Above all (and Pinky was suddenly beginning to realise it now, in the heat of this emergency) was the sense of comradeship. From the youngest and most junior rating, to the captain himself, each depended upon the other for the safe running of the boat and for ultimate survival . . . even he, Pinky, through negligence, could lose the boat, if he really tried.

This fact bred a different discipline – ruthless, but understood by all. There was none of the bull of general service: if a man failed in his duty, the captain's justice was sharp and severe.

Carn would suffer a fool only once – after that, heaven help the offender . . . Pinky turned restlessly in his bunk – of one thing he was sure, if he ever got out of this – he'd have earned his self-respect and learned the meaning of comradeship. Most men never knew this privilege all their lives . . .

A groan, barely audible, escaped from the indistinguishable form lying on the deck in the darkness . . . an unnerving rattle gurgled from Gallo's throat. Pinky slid from his bunk, as someone switched on the emergency lantern. Shocked by the starkness of approaching death, Pinky knelt beside his dying friend and instinctively grasped his hand. He moved away as the captain gently pushed him aside. Carn laid his head across Gallo's chest: he remained there, listening for a long moment. When the breathing ceased, he gently crossed the dead man's arms upon his chest.

Pinky gazed upon the finality of death: El Greco had not suffered, after all.

'God rest his soul,' Carn said.

There was little to add. Gallo was gone. There was one man less to worry about, one more suit available . . .

'Pinky,' the captain said. 'Make to those up top, "One man dead. Six will attempt escape if salvage fails".'

Radio Operator Dean took up the lantern and hauled himself into the sonar room. This was to be his final tribute to the one friend he'd made in the service.

Gallo had had an easy way out: as Pinky tapped at the key, he wondered whether he'd be so lucky . . .

CHAPTER 15

## Dugan's Dive

Laszlo Dugan's exploratory dive had been invaluable for the salvage team up top in determining *Mars*'s position. But there was insufficient exact information on how to pass the lifting wires: some three thousand tons was a huge mass to lift from the ocean bed.

'Take the locating messenger down with you this time,' Captain Quincey had said, 'just in case. It's vital, Doc, to see if *Mars* is safe enough for you to dock on the rescue pad. We could pass the air line by diver if need be: he could go down on the locating messenger, but we'd lose a lot of time.'

Doc Dugan was again on his way down to *Mars*'s trapped position, but this, his second, dive was to include a search of the area to see if he could find the after part of the submarine. There could still be survivors inside: they *could* be waiting patiently for signs of surface ships before making their escape attempt. He'd take *Lily-One* down to *Mars*'s for'd section and carry out a square search from that datum position.

'Four hundred feet,' he reported into his underwater telephone. 'I'll keep up a running commentary and you can plot my position up top. Okay, Jack?'

'*Rescue* to *Lily*,' Quincey's underwater voice bubbled in answer. 'Understood. We're keeping a constant listening watch.'

Visibility was better now, though it had been darker on the surface when Dugan managed at 2100 to break away from the HQ meeting. He had snatched a hot-dog and a coffee from the Russians' canteen, so he felt better, less edgy now that he could get on with the job. It was still touch and go: twenty-one hours had passed, which left only fifteen to go before those men must certainly perish. He turned up the speed control and listened to the whine of the two motors increasing in pitch.

'She's now lying at a thirty degree bow-down angle,' he reported. 'She has a fifteen degree list to starboard.' He could see the mysterious, dark shape ahead now, as she yawed backwards and forwards in the ground-swell. It was tragic to know that one man had died but, even more so that the remaining six were within thirty feet of *Lily*: he felt utterly frustrated, but there was nothing that could be done – not until *Kronstad* was ready. He'd make a quick sweep, first at 500 yards, then at 1,000 from this datum.

'Carrying out square search from datum zero,' he called. 'On my way.'

'Roger.'

And so, as rapidly as he could take her, *Lily* circled the fore-part of the wreck before setting off again into the blackness. He piloted her twenty feet above the sea-bed, which, here, consisted of jagged pinnacles of rock scoured by the sands shifting in the current. A chasm yawned below him, his oscilloscope reading a depth of nine hundred feet: *Mars* must be balanced on the knife-edge of an oceanic mountain whose sides shelved steeply into the fissure five hundred feet below.

Dugan followed the edge of the canyon, the contours of which were running north-south. If the after-part had fallen into that ravine, there could be no chance of rescue – no man could escape from those depths, He motored outwards for five hundred yards, then turned to 090°: he'd proceed clockwise and continue his search five hundred yards from datum zero.

It was bloody cold down here: if only the scientists could really solve this condensation problem, life would be much easier. Four knots was about as fast as he dared take her: the inner square would take him an hour to complete; the outer, at 1,000 yards, two hours – wasn't this exercise a waste of precious time, now that they had positive evidence on the for'd section? He settled down sullenly to carry out the search-sweep as conscientiously as he could.

'2130,' he reported. 'Altering to 180° . . . ' Round she swung, the beam of his searchlight probing before him – it was difficult not to become mesmerised by this unnatural world: but his time was restricted to four hours down here. *Ping – ping – ping . . .* his transmitter continued to pulse its searching finger . . . '2145, altering to 270° . . . '

He continued patiently to report all his depths and positions, but he had to hide his aggravation: Quincey was in this just as much as he was – and the lifting wires took time to lower. They couldn't proceed until *Kronstad*'s cameras had picked up the wreck, which they had succeeded in doing only ten minutes ago. She would have to be right first time . . .

'2200, altering to 360° . . . '

Dugan shivered: he must not forget his other sweater when he surfaced again . . . Another fifteen minutes dragged by.

'2215,' he reported. 'Continuing on course 360°, until search opens up to 1,000 yards from datum zero.'

'Very good,' Jack's English voice replied. 'Keep it up, Doc. We're now lowering the first bight of the forward lifting wire. Take care when you return to datum zero.'

'Right,' Dugan retorted. 'Jeeze, it's mighty cold down here.' He heard Jack chuckling and . . . mercy sakes, what was that . . . ? A distinct echo was bouncing back into his sonar loudspeaker, and, seconds later, a huge black wall came rushing towards him. He slammed the control to right hard rudder, back full power. He felt the juddering from the reversed jets. She came up allstanding in her own length . . . 'I've located the after section, Jack,' he shouted exultantly. *'Wait one . . .* yes, 010°, 720 yards from datum zero.'

Cautiously, keeping the long black wall in his light beam, he traversed the length of the after part. She was gashed open like a sardine-tin forward, pipes and cables gushing from the stricken compartment: no one could have survived in the engine-room. Perhaps the after compartments were intact? The quickest way to find out was to hammer on the hull. His fingers touched the external lever. He watched the lobster claw slowly extending itself. He hovered *Lily* four feet clear of the hull, and fifteen feet from the seabed on which it lay, parallel to the canyon; how far distant she was from the abyss he could not guess . . .

'I'm knocking her hull,' he reported. 'Listen out, Jack . . .'

Clang! Clang-clang! He repeated the signal three times. He pulled *Lily* away, to listen . . . the whine of his motors and the purring of the jet stream were the only sounds. No more. No response. He moved in again. The antenna moved jerkily in the pool of light. Once more the desperate summons – again, only the silence of the deep.

'Try again, Doc . . .' The agony was plain in Quincey's voice. The whole team up top must be listening now. Once more he tried. There was no answer.

'I'm sorry, Jack. Returning to datum zero.'

Communications remained silent as *Lily-One* beamed herself back towards *Mars*'s fore section. Dugan was soon in touch.

'2310,' he reported dully. 'Homing in on *Mars* now: distance three hundred yards.'

'Okay, Doc,' Quincey was saying. 'Get in close and see if there is a possibility of landing on the rescue pad. Secure if you can, and we'll send down the messenger.'

'Aye, aye, sir . . .' Doc Dugan was smiling grimly again. At last, he could use his skill; he'd trained himself so long, for a moment such as this . . . it was going to be tricky . . . look at her there, swaying in the current.

*Mars*'s dark fin was swinging back and forth, an arc of some thirty feet every half minute. As she yawned, she'd strike him as he moved in – but if he could reach under her fulcrum, where the fin joined the pressure hull, there'd be least movement there.

'I'm making my approach,' he said. 'I'll talk myself in . . .' Quincey would know what he meant – like the mine-disposal boys, who reported each move as they worked.

He eased back gently on the throttles. He carefully checked his doppler: rate of advance, three feet per second – now, gently, ease her in . . . there, right under his starboard bow, the circle of the rescue pad – he could even see the red paint on the self-locking air-line connection.

'Six feet . . .'

The black mass swayed above him, the water noises swirling about him and blotting out voice communication. *Lily* edged forwards, foot by foot, until she was poised directly above the pad. She was horizontal, hovering, beautifully . . . if he could nudge up her bows now, and cut the hover at the same instant, she'd settle just right when he cut in the electro-magnets . . .

'Another four feet, Jack . . .'

As *Lily* crept ahead, Doc Dugan was icy calm – this was the moment on which those lives depended. As his fingers groped for the electro-switch, the huge shadow leaped suddenly towards him . . .

There was nothing he could do – the edge of the submarine's fin tipped the edge of *Lily*'s saucer hull, flipping her upwards . . . He sensed the acceleration as she turned almost end-for-end, bow over stern – and then he was flattened against the bulkhead of the motor section. He felt her sliding stern first into the abyss.

'*Emergency* . . .' He had no time to report now. He was fighting for his own life, with *Lily* spiralling downwards, out of control . . . 530, 600, 650 . . . His fingers clawed at the trim and depth controls. He heard the scream as the motors revved to full power. A swift yaw to port and she began to steady, swooping like a swallow – *he had her now* – *that was better*. He yanked the rudder control to the right and saw the ship's head spinning round the compass . . . nothing, no response.

'Emergency surface,' he called. 'Rudder's gone.'

'Okay,' Jack Quincey's reassuring voice answered. 'You're well clear of the wires. Take your time, Doc.'

As Dugan collected himself and his *Lily-One* together, he was astonished to see that the clock was showing 0004, four minutes after midnight. This must be the Fourth of July – goddamit, Independence Day. Not much object in celebrating: not a bloody trick had gone right yet . . . 300 feet and still coming up, thank God.

'*Lily-One*, this is *Rescue*; d'you hear me?'

'Loud and clear.'

'Surface with caution,' Quincey was warning. 'The sea's getting up: the met forecasts a depression on the way.'

That was all they needed: as if a race against time wasn't

118

enough, they now had to fight the weather as well. There wasn't a cat's chance in hell ╗╗╗

## Pilot Officer Soper

2300 exactly: the hands on the ward-room clock were coinciding, if Jake Soper squinted hard enough. He had taken over his trick, for the second time now, from the coxswain. He did not relish trying to remain alert in this eerie half light, but at least they had shifted Gallo's corpse into the control room and concealed it beneath the chart table. It was the sonorous breathing and the sudden, nightmare cries from his sleeping companions that grated on Soper's nerves.

He was, he knew, a loner, probably the solitary soul amongst them. He knew also that his Dartmouth training had perhaps made him intolerant of others, but he *had* tried to conceal his jealousy of Sinclair. The chap had been a trawlerman, and come in through the back door, but what really riled Jake Soper was the familiarity he was certain Sinclair enjoyed with his captain because of his sister's marriage. 'Balls!' had been Sinclair's reaction to Soper's accusation, a retort that had not fostered diplomatic relations.

Jake Soper had volunteered for submarines. His father, a one-time, moderately successful submarine CO, had helped him to complete the specialisation selection form, by erasing every choice, except submarines, which he had doubly and heavily underlined. What else could Jake do, but to volunteer? And this half-hearted enthusiasm had been difficult to maintain at times, even for appearance's sake. This probably explained why most of the other entries had forged ahead of him during sub-lieutenants' courses and submarine training.

He envied the other two lieutenants, Thompson and Macredy, who were in Number One's escape party: they had finished their long training, whereas he had only recently completed *Dolphin*'s specialisation course; in the general service's Principal Warfare Officers' Course he had finished amongst the bottom third in the examinations. The pendulum had swung back: the 'salt horse' had come again into his own, as evidenced by the necessity of a PWO in the fighting ship.

By the time Jake reached the zone for submarine command, there would be no conventionals left. Culmer had commanded his own boat and then endured a shore job before joining the three-months nuclear course; to *Dolphin* next, for another short nuclear-submarine acclimatisation course; and then finally he had been appointed Number One of *Mars*; the next step would be his own nuclear command.

When my turn comes, Soper thought, there'll be no conventionals, because the latest batch of politicians have so decreed. A potential nuclear CO will never have commanded a submarine before he takes over as captain of his first nuclear boat. But what chance had he, Soper, with his unfortunate record, of being recommended for a nuclear COQC? (Commanding Officers' Qualifying Course.)

He'd been in *Mars* only half a dog-watch when that Mark III fish had run amok, with its wire-guidance control system all to hell. That sinister torpedo so reminiscent, they said, of the Germans' Second World War electric fish, was a stop-gap until the new weapons were developed. The Mark IIIs, with their aluminium bodies and their lime-green warheads, were smooth and deadly – and not only for the opposition. Jake's had run wild before the safe range had run off: it had locked on to its parent submarine: if it hadn't been fitted with a collision head, Jake would not be where he was at this moment (500 feet down, trapped and finding it less possible to breathe as each hour dragged by) – which would have been no bad thing . . . and he braced himself against the continuous swaying movement which the boat had taken on.

The uncertainty was unnerving, not knowing what was going on outboard: *Mars* felt as if she was see-sawing in the current, and the motion was nauseous. He wondered what the escape would be like when his time came, locked into the blackness of the swaying fin as the water flooded above his head . . .

The fin, the nuclear-man's jargon for the conning-tower, was an awkward compartment from which to escape. Some thirty feet in height, it was crammed with snorting, radar and W/T masts, in addition to the athwartship periscopes and the ladders. Once he was through the upper lid, he still had to clear the bridge impediments: tricky, if she still carried this bow-up angle. He was lucky to have been the XO's deputy for escape training – which was presumably why the captain had selected him to carry out the first escape. He was thankful now that he'd been one of the first to restart escape training in *Dolphin*'s tank. The instructors' gentle approach in training, even with the most scared of candidates, had probably been responsible for the success of

Number One's party: bloody incredible effort – and if they could make it, why shouldn't we?

The boat was creaking again – an unpleasant rending of metal each time she listed: he wished he did not possess a vivid imagination. If she slipped any more, they'd never get out . . . hell's teeth, that clock was dragging now: seventy-three minutes before Sinden takes over again from me . . . might as well obey orders. What *was* the worst accident he'd been in, apart from this sod?

Undoubtedly, it was the affair which had bequeathed him the troops' nickname for him: Pilot Officer Sooper. Amusing, wasn't it, if you happened to be anyone other than himself?

He was SCOW at the time, half way through the afternoon watch. They had just been passed as operational – about two months after the reactor accident, when everyone had begun to settle down again. He'd never forget the incident.

The Chief EA had been working on the after-planes display unit. He was a damn nuisance standing there; it was difficult to see the bubble, let alone the other indicators, the depth gauge reading 380 feet. The boat was on passage and steaming fast – about twenty-two knots. One of the connections on the unit was loose. A piece flew out suddenly and jammed the after-plane which, inevitably, was at hard-a-dive.

'For God's sake, free it,' he had yelled at the chief who, already, was on his knees and trying to prise out the part with his fingers. Jake had sensed the captain's presence behind him; Carn had probably heard his sudden order, the anxiety in the command. The stick was jammed forward and the more the operator pulled the vital control, the harder the object stuck. In seconds the boat had taken up a 30° bow-down angle and was shooting downwards fast: 700 feet was on the gauge in seconds.

'I'll take her, Officer of the Watch . . . '

Soper stepped aside to allow the captain to take charge.

*'Full astern: both planes in air emergency control . . . '*

The order had rapped out, and now no one could keep his feet. Gear crashed wildly and from aft came the smash of breaking mess crocks.

'Hard-a-rise on both planes . . . '

Carn had not realised how fast they were travelling – suddenly, as the planes went into air control, *Mars* swooped upwards like those terns foraging for fish in the ocean's swell. She stood on her ends, with a 47° bow-up angle – a rating in the sound room nearly lost his head when a unit broke adrift, and the LMA was nearly crushed by a lead sample cylinder. Pilot Officer SOOPER . . . the name would stick now, so long as Jake remained in submarines . . .

2356 . . . life was more peaceful down here . . . stuffy, yes, but not impossible yet; he complained only of a slight headache, whereas poor old Sinclair seemed to have a splitter . . .

He, Jake Soper, was no fool, he was certain of that . . . this was a time to reflect on his record, as all men should from time to time, but no one enjoyed self-analysis – the image might be too distasteful.

*Cherchez la femme*, they said. His chip-on-the-shoulder personality; his arrogance and brusqueness; and his devil-may-care attitude was certainly caused by his over-reacting to Simone's behaviour. She'd crucified him. He'd never wanted to bed a woman since that first and last night they'd battled with each other.

Simone Anstruthers was a colonel's daughter. Not the traditional soldier-father, but a quiet, gentle man who'd served in the quarter-mastering branch. She'd been born in Singapore: the heat must have had something to do with her ardour, because she had, literally, tried to devour him the moment that she'd pulled him into her arms. For her, it was the act that mattered, nothing else – and in the speed with which she'd taken him, he'd bungled the whole affair. Ghastly it had been – and as she tried to rouse him with every barrack-room obscenity which she was capable, he had recoiled, shocked by the degradation. And, as he had lain there, trying to salvage his pride, she had leaned over him. Throwing back her head, the nipples of her breasts brushing his mouth, her throat gleaming in the glow of the bedside light, she had begun to laugh hysterically, with a cruelty beyond imagining – he could hear her still, that wild laughter, from over the years.

'You miserable bloody fraud,' she'd cried. 'You can't even do it, for all your talk.'

He had not touched a woman since: in his private moments, he wondered whether Simone had warped him permanently. Women repelled him now. He certainly had no physical need of them, but did that necessarily make him a queer? After one of his training class had made the insinuation, he'd taken damn good care to be one of the boys when out on a party – but the girls instinctively recoiled, which made him wilder than before. So he had a reputation to maintain – and he knew it to be false. He didn't give a bugger if this balls-up was the end of him – they'd class him as a hero, wouldn't they? *Old Jake Soper chose to stay with his captain . . . Who'd have thought he had it in him?* Perhaps a snigger or two and then oblivion. *Died on active service, in that submarine disaster – how many years ago was it? What was the name of the submarine . . . ?'* Four minutes past midnight, 4 July – the date rang some sort of bell . . .

There was a sudden shock throughout the compartment, then a scraping, rending noise, of metal against metal, immediately above his head. The boat rocked crazily, then slowly resumed her yawing. He switched on the last but one lantern. He held it up towards the deck head. Other staring eyes followed his, along the length of pipes. A cockroach or two, antennae searching, nothing else – no inrush of water.

'Better turn it off,' the captain said. 'Could have been a lifting wire.'

They lay still for a full five minutes. Then, from the radio office, the tick-ticking of the sonar receiver whispered. Pinky Dean slipped from his bunk and in the darkness took up his listening post.

## CHAPTER 16

## *Captain Speaking*

Since the crash, when the rescue sub had damaged herself on *Mars*'s pad, Commander Carn had been unable to sleep. Two hours had elapsed since the report had been received from the surface – but Quincey was despatching the mini sub down again as soon as he could. It was already 0115 on 4 July, the Americans' Independence Day – maybe a good omen, George Carn ruminated, but they'd better get cracking – exactly twenty-four hours now since the collision – and the air *was* getting thick in this appalling heat, which was causing them all to run with sweat. Pools of water lay on the settee cushions, and the smell of their bodies was now fouling the atmosphere – let alone the problem of the heads, which stank from the diarrhoea from which they were now all suffering. Even that function made

123

them sweat and also, panting from exertion, use up the precious oxygen.

If he had not learned from the surface that Jack Quincey was in charge of the rescue attempt, he'd have been more worried than he was . . . but a full day had passed now – twenty-four hours – and the air was undoubtedly much fouler. Each man was suffering the first effects of carbon dioxide poisoning – the thudding ache that slowly encircled the forehead until the pain dulled all decision.

Worse was the problem of oxygen. It was common knowledge, thanks to *Dolphin*'s research since the Second World War, that oxygen poisoning mounted in arithmetical progression proportionate to atmospheric pressure – and *Mars*'s absolute gauge was showing 1.8 atmospheres now. He couldn't vent outboard – and there was no compressor to run in this compartment. This oxygen under pressure was the real danger, because the toxic effect warped men's minds – and, above all else, he needed to think clearly now.

Sinclair would relieve him at 0300; he'd order him then to crack the first of the two oxygen cylinders. Better too early than too late, because they'd have to make their escape within the next eleven hours – he was sure of that, judging by the appearance of his companions. Sinden and Hebbenden, the two older men, seemed to be least affected; but young Dean, bravely facing up to his continuous communication watch, was feeling nauseated; Sinclair had been sick; and Soper had complained suddenly of excruciating pain in his genitals.

George Carn found his eyes mesmerised by the pale oval of the clock dial, less than two feet away from the settee. Remorselessly and silently the hands revolved, while seeming motionless: each second was one less – and nearer to the moment when he had to make his terrible decision. The others had been bloody good: since Gallo had died, not one of them had hinted that they were waiting to learn to whom a reprieve had been granted.

What was worrying him was the possibility that the cox'n or Sinden might fail to shut the upper lid: that would mean a rush escape for the remainder by flooding up the compartment – they'd die before they opened the tower lid, in the toxic condition they were in. The only chance was for number three in each of these attempts to shut the upper lid. Carn turned up the penultimate lantern for a moment to see how the batting order looked and jotted down his thoughts on the sheet of signal pad:

124

|              |                                                                          |
|--------------|--------------------------------------------------------------------------|
| 1st Innings  | Soper — 1 good suit<br>Dean — 1 good suit<br>Hebbenden — 1 good suit – remains to shut upper lid |
| 2nd Innings  | Hebbenden<br>Sinclair — 1 good suit<br>Sinden — 1 shaky suit – remains to shut upper lid |
| Follow-on    | Sinden<br>Me (Carn) — free ascent, no suit |

And then the upper lid could take care of itself.

He smiled ruefully to himself in the darkness. If he survived, he'd be making history for a man of his age: escaping from 500 feet and not a specialist. When he handed over his trick, he'd wake them all; he was sure they were feigning sleep, though the coxswain had been convulsed by nightmares. Carn had shaken him roughly and the older man had jerked upright with a strange cry, his eyes glazed in terror as he stared into the unknown. Wiping the sweat from his dripping brow, Hebbenden had shamefacedly apologised. George Carn was certain that Hebbenden had found no more sleep.

Repellent fantasies and sudden cries during the silent watches of the night were not uncommon in submarines, but for the coxswain to emit such a spine-chilling shriek, was indicative that the strain was beginning to tell. No one had said a word.

Carn felt a disconcerting anxiety more certain, as each minute slipped by, that the boat was balanced on a knife-edge of rock. She groaned as she twisted to the pressures of the current sweeping along on the ocean bed. The sound had at first been unnerving, but it was amazing how swiftly the human mind learned to adjust to danger. He was sure that something had shifted – could she be opening up, under the immense stresses to which she was being subjected down here?

He heard Pinky shuffling along the passage from the radio room. 'Sir,' the lad was whispering in the darkness. 'Captain, sir . . .?'

He could see the lad's spare outline now, faintly visible in the fluorescence of the numerous dials and gauges. 'I'm here, Pinky. What is it?'

A spectre in the half light, the youngster was doing his utmost to keep the unsteadiness from his voice:

'They're sending *Lily-One* down now, sir. She'll try to pass the messengers for the lifting wires. Then they'll send down the bight of each wire, starting with the after one.' Dean could not contain the excitement in his report:

'They're passing five wires. They're all ready to lower, sir, but they've asked us to report our physical condition.'

Carn was silent. If he told Quincey the truth, the knowledge would influence his judgement – he might push the Russians too hard. If he, Carn, made light of their breathing difficulties, they might not proceed with the urgency that was now so vital: 0215 now . . . twenty-five hours gone, ten or eleven left – at the very most – but by mid-day they'd be insensible. No, he'd give Jack the facts. He switched on the lantern again and reached across the table for the signal pad he had just used. Carefully considering each word, he wrote:

*Feeling effects of foul air. Starting first of two medical oxygen cylinders. Imperative escapes attempted within next eleven hours. All in good heart.*

'Make that, Dean, please.'

'Aye, aye, sir.'

Carn could sense the pride in the young man's reply: there he was, a lad of nineteen, a vital link in what could surely become a historic submarine rescue attempt.

'That's good, sir.' The calm voice in the shadow of the corner was the coxswain's. 'They've advanced since *Thetis* days, haven't they?'

'The mini rescue sub makes all the difference,' Soper was saying, also wide awake. 'She'll be able to ease the bights, won't she?'

'Depends on the strength of the current . . . ' It was Sinclair's turn now . . . so they were all awake, but Soper was waiting to have his say:

'I've been thinking, sir,' he said. 'An officer shouldn't be the first out,' he said firmly. 'I'd rather it was the coxswain: he's an instructor, sir.'

Carn looked Jake Soper long in the eye. For some seconds he said nothing. Then, without moving a finger, he said:

'Those were my orders, Lieutenant Soper. You will go first. I want an officer to report the facts to the rescue team.' He drummed his finger-tips on the table top. 'Is that understood?'

'Yes, sir.' Soper's eyes fell and he said no more.

The silence had followed was broken finally by Carn's voice, harsh and brooking no questions now:

'I'll run my submarine by discipline – not by heroics,' he said.

126

'You'll *all* obey my order – that's what discipline is for: when there are impossible decisions to take, I, the captain of this submarine, will take them.' His face broke into the infectious grin they had all once known. 'This is for real, gentlemen: so no bloody heroics. Anyone disagree with me?'

Carn looked hard at each of them, but the silence remained.

'Let's get on with the job,' he said. 'You, Lieutenant Soper . . . you and Dean check your suits for the first ascent. While we're all in fairly good condition, we'd better check our gear.'

'Shall I open up now, sir?' Hebbenden asked. 'The lower lid?'

'Yes, please.'

Both men knew that if they left this until later, they might be too feeble . . .

'Tell Pinky to leave his set, will you, Peter? Get him to check his gear and make certain that Jake goes through the whole drill with him.'

'Right, sir.'

'And Peter?'

' . . . sir?'

'When we've all turned in again, start cracking the oxygen every half hour, please.'

'Aye, aye, sir.'

He watched them, each laboriously setting about his business, the four, Soper, Dean, Hebbenden and Sinclair, holding up their grotesque orange immersion suits, each checking the other's. Alastair, on one side, had his back turned to them. He was holding up the dodgy suit and tweaking at some part of it with his right hand.

'Buck up, all of you,' Carn said, raising his voice. 'This light's going out.'

He watched the feverish haste: the coxswain was the first to finish; then he helped Sinclair, before hauling himself back to his seat, where he lay back, panting for breath. Dean followed, then Soper; and finally Sinden. The greying commander was smiling, an impish light in his eyes:

'Nothing wrong with mine that a little mending won't put right,' he said. 'Anyone a needle and thread?'

'Some here,' Sinclair said. He reached up behind the wine locker and produced the ward-room's communal 'housewife'. 'But no make-and-mend today, sir . . . '

Between narrowed lids, Carn watched his friend trying to conceal the irreparable rent in the suit. Alastair, he knew, would stay with him until the end: you didn't travel along parallel lines so

127

long in the service without building up those loyalties which landsmen could never understand. Sinden turned towards him, as he carelessly tossed the suit into the corner where he was sitting. Their eyes met and Carn had his answer: Alastair would stay until the end.

Sinden would certainly make a free ascent – but Carn knew that Alastair would insist on giving up the damaged suit to his captain – even that ropey article was better than nowt, for it would give the wearer buoyancy and protection on the surface. Then, without warning, the light faded and they were plunged again into the half light thrown out by the fluorescent gauges.

'That leaves us one more lamp,' Carn said. 'We'll keep it for the escapes, I think . . .' and in the gloom, he turned his head in Sinclair's direction.

'You'll have to feel your way around, Peter, to crack the oxygen cylinder.'

'Should be okay, sir,' his navigating officer replied. 'I've got my wheel-spanner.'

Carn smiled to himself in the darkness. He was thankful no one could see him for, with the exhaustion, he was beginning to feel emotional: why was he privileged to lead such a bloody good bunch of men? If he had his time over again, he'd still choose submarines. The chance of a disaster happening to one was remote: it was difficult to take in that they were experiencing reality – and that, at the end of this dreary endurance test, death probably awaited them all.

He was beginning, consciously now, to think of his breathing: he was inhaling deeper and finding little satisfaction. He could hear Sinclair clattering behind the ward-room screen, where he had stowed the first of the two oxygen cylinders.

'Go easy on it, Peter,' Carn said. 'We've still got some ten hours to go. Pity we haven't a gauge . . .'

'Trial and error,' a voice replied from the darkness. 'Better than a foaming pint . . .' That must be Hebbenden.

Carn heard the hiss of the escaping gas, as the wheel-spanner clanked against the valve. Five seconds, that's all Peter was giving them – but the hiss seemed to drag out a long time.

'Keeps your weight down, sir.' The voice was Hebbenden's again, soft and reassuring in the far corner. ' . . . Could do with a pint though, couldn't you, Pinky?'

'Not 'arf . . .'

Carn detected the fear in the RO's voice. Pinky seemed reluctant to crawl back to his seat at the sonar set.

'I've rigged up a loudspeaker, sir,' he said, 'so we can listen from here. Is that all right, sir?'

'You sure we can hear if they call us, Pinky?'

'Certain, sir. Can you hear the speaker, sir?'

Carn cocked an ear and yes, there it was, crackling softly in the passageway. 'Okay, Pinky,' Carn said. 'You win.'

He could hear the audible sigh of relief: the human animal liked to be with the pack if it was in danger. They were all trying to sleep now – even Alastair whom, Carn knew, had been awake since the collision.

Alastair had been unusually quiet this trip: normally he was a ball of fire, a natural *raconteur* whose wit added sparkle to even the dreariest ward-room. But on this patrol he had preferred to remain much in the background. He was probably ultra-sensitive about his station in the boat – he was a couple of months Carn's senior, and obviously he did not wish to cause the captain any embarrassment in what could have been, with any other character, a difficult situation. 'Alastair would get on all right in a snake pit,' Jack Quincey had told Carn. 'And you needn't take him with you unless you want to.'

So Carn had been delighted to share the long watches with Alastair, and was more than ever glad to have him now, even though the worst decisions *had* to be taken by the captain alone. Any fresh ideas could be chewed over with Alastair: it would be good not to be entirely alone when the final test came . . . and George Carn suddenly had a yearning to share confidences with his friend.

Could Alastair, who had known unhappiness in his own life, comprehend the agony through which he, the respected George Carn, was passing with his own wife, Jackie? Perhaps, when they were left alone for the ultimate escape, he could unload it all upon Alastair? He probably had an inkling of the affair already; was it possible to live in such a close community as Faslane and still preserve one's private life? Or were they wagging their tongues, all aware of the collapse of his marriage?

He glanced at the luminous hands of his watch, holding up his wrist before his eyes: almost 0415 – time was moving a bit now. But there was nothing from up top, only an ominous silence . . . what was going wrong? Twenty-seven hours now, nine to go, if thirty-six hours was really their limit. With the headache building up and the hunger for oxygen, he'd be glad when the whole business was over, one way or the other. He wouldn't keep Soper

9

and Dean much longer, but meanwhile he'd try to mobilise his own personal thoughts . . .

Dear, pathetic little Jackie . . . he shut his eyes and, with the balm of Sinclair's oxygen easing breathing difficulties, George Carn stretched his hands behind his head, at ease for a moment from physical discomfort . . .

What had happened to the girl he had married those eleven years ago? He could see the ardent young face before him, the white veil blowing from her dark hair in the blustery April breeze. They had walked so slowly through the primrose-flecked country churchyard where relatives and friends waited to shower them with confetti. Perhaps he hadn't understood how much she had needed him, that lovely bride he had cherished and worshipped so much.

Why was society so strict about the physical side of marriage? 'It's not all that important, a couple's sex-life, once the children have arrived,' his father had said. 'The children satisfy the woman's search for fulfilment, rather than the sensual relationship she craves at first . . . ' Thus the voice of experience, and, after the tragedy of Stephen, he had believed this to be true. He had never needed the abandonment of love-making as much as she desired it . . . he remembered the feeling of surprise, almost of disgust, when she had once torn away, for a brief moment, the veil of well-bred respectability. It had never happened again, that animal night, and he'd often wondered whether she'd been disappointed by his apparent lack of response. It had been ever more of a shock when he had made all the running after Stephen's birth, that she had gently held him at arms' length. The blow had finally fallen, like the guillotine's knife, six months ago now. He could never forget that night, the first of his homecoming after his third *Zed* patrol.

She'd prepared a good meal: pheasant it had been, but she had held back from the bottle of wine he'd opened. Deep down, he'd hoped she would lose some of these new-found inhibitions if she would drink a little, but she had been adamant. He'd gone on to finish the bottle himself, which was why, he supposed, he'd lost his temper when finally he had taken her to their room.

*God forgive me* . . . the memory was still too painful, so that even now the wound opened beneath his heart, when he contemplated his brutal behaviour. She had had every right to behave as she did, but he had been utterly bewildered by the strength of her resistance.

She had stood there, in that nightie her mother had given her,

130

a bell-tent type of thing – 'the canvas tent', he'd once called it jokingly, 'concealing all'.

But she hadn't smiled, the pink floral design efficiently concealing the loveliness that lay beneath. 'I like it,' she'd said. 'Mum gave it to me and it's warm.'

He'd seen red then. Couldn't he warm her enough? He'd ripped off his own dressing-gown and stood there before her, hoping for the effect that once he would have given her.

'Let's go to bed.'

She'd slid between the sheets before he could encircle her with his arms. He'd swept to the top of the bed and roughly pulled at the sheets to vault in beside her. He heard the rip as the linen tore, and heard her complain sharply.

'For heaven's sake, George . . . I've enough to do, without this extra mending. What's wrong with you tonight?'

He had suddenly turned on his side and swept his hands inside the tent, expecting the soft warmth of her body to melt beneath his fingers – instead she had lain rigid, silent, legs together when he had searched for the secret places. Then she had cried silently, when suddenly he could stand it no more and had forced her to his side, half rolling her towards him.

'Oh, my darling,' he'd whispered. 'I want you so, after all this time – what's the matter, my Jackie?' He had ruffled up her hair as he used to do. And when he'd reached the round perfections of her breasts, she had suddenly, with a bitter cry, recoiled from his embrace.

'Take your hands off,' she'd sobbed. 'You're hurting me.'

The stab of pain that racked his heart had snapped the control that had always held him back. He'd show her, his passionate Jackie, that the accident had made no difference – couldn't she feel him now, searching for her, demanding, no gentleness now, fierce, brute male seeking his mate . . . ?

She had resisted all the way, and when suddenly the pent-up tide had overwhelmed him to spill its force upon a barren waste, he'd known the anguish of a broken soul. They'd lain there in the darkness for hour after hour, wrestling with the monstrous psychological block that the birth of pathetic little Stephen had engendered. When the grey dawn had stolen across the red-brown shoulder of Dunbrae Moor, she had told him that he repelled her now, with his violent, ceaseless demands . . .

He had not touched her since.

George Carn lay there in the darkness, the pain in his heart as acute as the throbbing band across his forehead. That night had

131

changed for all time the relationship between Jackie and himself: the breakfast the next morning had been monosyllabic; he behind his paper, trying nonchalantly to stir his coffee, she, the middle-class mum correcting the children's table-manners; whilst all the time Stephen's grotesque little face had mumbled unintelligibly. The podgy cheeks had, as always, become smothered before his mother could cope with his demands.

The boat juddered suddenly, her hull trembling from the stem to 63 bulkhead. He could feel the tension in the darkness, as each man grappled with his own thoughts. The breathing was heavier now, as each of them drew in his lungful of what oxygen there was left, each breath a conscious effort.

Carn would have seriously to consider mounting the first escape soon, before it was too late for Hebbenden and Sinden, who would be shutting the hatch . . . but he could not fathom why there was nothing from up top – nothing for two and a half hours: 0345 now, twenty-seven hours breathing the same air, the six survivors steadily fouling what was left with their own carbon dioxide exhalations. Why the devil had he been so weak in allowing Number One to leave those protosorb trays in the dockyard, merely because they took up space? That decision, four months earlier, could be costing them their lives – but that was the period when he had almost stopped fighting . . .

Jackie had changed so suddenly: she had even altered the tone of her letters, the pages now being full of children's and mother-in-law's chit-chat . . . He had once, in a spasm of contrition, poured out his soul into seven pages of air-mail paper and despatched it with the mail collected by the chopper off Lerwick – but to his endearments she had not once alluded, when seven weeks later he had returned to Faslane to pick up the mail that had been following *Mars*.

It was the mercurial metamorphosis which had thrown him most. Jackie had been absolutely honest about the cause. When they had consulted the trick-cyclist in Glasgow, an embarrassing interview for them both, the learned man with the rimless spectacles had told them that six months would probably see a change back again – but four months had elapsed now and, if anything, his Jackie was more remote than ever. Protecting herself behind a polite shell of indifference, she might have been a complete stranger. As attentive as ever to his domestic wants and to the efficient running of Dunbrae House, she was endeavouring to substitute the love of a companion for that of a lover.

He was trying to understand. There were so many sudden and inexplicable changes in her life-pattern that he was utterly confused when he returned home: homecoming was once a pleasure to which he had looked forward with enormous longing – but now . . . if he cared to search his soul deeply enough, he knew that he'd be happier if he did not have to face the hideous frigidity of a stranger-wife.

When he was on leave, she made a habit of leaving the children with him when she went into Glasgow once a fortnight to have her hair done . . . a hell of a long way and damned expensive merely to visit a hairdresser . . . and always she seemed on edge, strung like a taut wire, taking the telephone calls and saving him the trouble of opening the mail . . . there were moments when he seriously wondered whether she was involved in some sort of affair. He wouldn't mind, if the catalyst would only restore her to him, with the warmth and love that once bound them together so firmly . . . how, he wondered, was she taking the news now, with a sub-smash in full tilt and he at the heart of it?

Perhaps this was God's judgement on them both for not accepting the cross of their Stephen? If he came out of this, perhaps they could start again, she and he? Perhaps the shock of this disaster might sweep away the mental blockage? And when he got home, he'd be so gentle with her, his own Jackie, lying, her head on his chest, at peace against his heart . . . but, if nothing were to change?

If she remained repelled by him, her abhorrence of his physical contact surmounting even her intended love, what was he to do? These long absences were bad enough, but if abstinence was to be enforced for the rest of his life, how could he cope? He was miserably aware of the quicksands beneath his feet – he, who had been a solid citizen all his life, an ascendant star in the submarine world, suddenly had no foundation beneath him – he was as shallow and as insecure as the rest of mankind . . . but now, quite suddenly, a strange calm swept over him, a peacefulness that engulfed his mind as he submitted totally to whatever was to come. Those words kept on recurring in his mind: ' . . . The peace of God . . . ' how did it go? . . . 'which passeth all understanding, keep your hearts and minds in the love of God . . . ' The beautiful prayer had come before the blessing at evensong, the one service he had enjoyed in his youth.

He was aware then of a distant, scratching noise, like a mouse scrabbling in an attic . . . He sat up slowly, trying to identify the sound – yes, there it was again, a distinct scraping as if some

133

object was crawling across the casing . . . the boat lurched viciously and he was thrown across Sinclair's recumbent body.

'Pinky,' he ordered quietly. 'Man your set and get in touch up top, please.'

It was time now to act. He was at peace and he could think objectively: 0605 by his watch, the air becoming more poisonous with ever half hour that passed . . .

*. . . South-East Iceland,
Faeroes, Fair Isle, Viking . . .*

It was fortunate, Doc Dugan thought, that the communication frequency between *Lily-One* and *Kronstad* was not common to that being used by the stricken submarine. The anxiety caused by the steady fall in barometric pressure was infectious: a desperation was now added to the urgency already provided by the time-scale. *Kronstad must* start lifting before the depression arrived: the 0400 met report was disquieting in the extreme, and the barometer was confirming their worst fears.

Working beneath the arc-lights in the well amidships, those Russian welders had been magnificent. As Doc piloted his *Lily-One* into the depths (it was now 0545), he could see them in his mind's eyes, arc-lights reflecting blue-violet flashes on their visors, as their probes welded the new fin after *Lily's* accident; and still working on the mini submarine as they swung her over the side on the crane, they had refused to give up until the last moment. The waiting for the weld-seams to cool before he submerged had been the worst ordeal.

350 feet: his probing searchlight was steadier now, at this depth freer from the ground-swell lunging in from the south-west, a sure sign that bad weather was on its way.

'Dive now,' Quincey had ordered him. 'Secure the bights of the wires in place, if you can. We've got to start lifting, Doc, before the gale arrives.' The Limey was cool, in spite of the stress: amongst those six men were two of his best friends.

'What about the air line, Jack?'

'Take it with you and button it on if you can – but that's secondary. We've *got* to start lifting: *Kronstad* has the capacity for a quick lift.'

'Even if I have to secure on the pad, sir, with *Mars* so unstable?'

'You'll have to risk it. It's our only chance.'

So here he was, 380 feet and almost on top of *Mars*; the echo was showing clearly on the PPI – 160 feet distant – 140, 120 – he eased back the throttle to allow *Lily* to coast in on her own impetus . . . there *Mars* was, the loom of her black hull massive in the aura of his searchlight.

His eyes ached as he searched again for the landing pad forward of the fin. *Mars* had shifted since his last recce: she was more upright and had lost that bow-up angle. She was swaying like those fronds of oceanic seaweed festooning the submarine shadows of this unknown world – and below her, off on her port beam, he could see the gorge that slipped away from her . . .

There was the first bight – it was neatly placed, thanks to *Kronstad*'s underwater cameras. It was looped, like a child's skipping rope, a few yards from the bulbous bow – a touch to starboard, a few more fathoms veered, and he was sure he could ease the wire along the hull until it came up against the fin . . .

'Okay, *Kronstad*,' he reported. 'I can see the first bight. Veer ten fathoms . . . I'm going in now.'

He watched the life-saving tentacle slowly descending until it was poised a few yards ahead of the porpoise-headed bows – and beautifully judged it was, as it hung, looped beneath *Mars*'s keel. A pluck now from *Lily*'s extendible arm and the ocean current would do the rest . . .

'Hold it,' he ordered, the note of excitement impossible to contain. 'I'm closing in now. Stand by to veer smartly.'

He felt the palm of his right hand enfolding the stumpy stick – a gentle nudge ahead, and *Lily* moved forward; as she closed, he worked with his left hand the control stick of the extending arm. There it was, the claw fully open now to push against that huge wire . . . he felt the resistance as the boat came up all-standing – he slowly increased the revs . . . heard the crescendo of the thrusters' motor . . . watched the loop slowly swinging across the bow . . .

'*Now*,' he yelled. '*Veer smartly* . . .'

He jerked the stick into astern. As the little craft backed out, the wire dropped suddenly: with immense satisfaction, he watched the bight settle below the keel, the current swinging the loop neatly around the hull – those boys up top were bloody good.

'We're there with number one,' he yelled exultantly. 'Stand by to heave taut when I've got the bight anchored abreast the find.'

'Right . . .' the bubbly voice of Quincey came down from the strange world up top. 'Standing by on number one. We're sending down number two . . .'

They weren't wasting a second up top . . . he shoved the stick

135

forward; nudging and pushing, tweaking and twisting with the extension arm, *Lily-One* slowly eased the first bight aft, along the pressure hull. Then, as Dugan was about to report the first wire in position, he spotted that the bight had snagged against a twisted plate on the far side.

'Hold it,' he shouted. 'It's fouled on the other side. I'm crossing over to clear it.'

He ignored the risk of becoming entangled in the wire. He steered his craft directly over the casing: there it was, the wire caught by a jagged plate that hung like a broken limb from the severed after section. He snatched the wire in the lobster claw – saw the pincers close as he worked the controls. He went astern and slowly built up the revs. The wire held solid.

'It's fouled,' he cried. 'Can't shift it.' His heart was pounding against his rib-cage.

'Try again,' Quincey called. 'We've got you in the camera.'

The motor whined, reached a high-pitched scream, painful to the ears. *Lily-One* was trembling from the strain.

'Keep it up,' the voice above urged.

'It's moving . . . ' Doc yelled.

Suddenly the little craft catapulted forward – the wire was free. *Lily-One* was caught in her own tentacle. She began to fall, out of control, as Dugan slammed the emergency release button of the extension arm. He gave her full surface boost when suddenly she freed herself – then, spiralling upwards, he quickly regained control. As he glanced below him, he saw the monstrous black shape sliding down the mountain side, a plume of debris spouting in her wake – then she stopped, poised on the edge, balancing on a jagged tooth of rock, held by the first lifting wire.

Another shock like that, Doc Dugan thought, and she was done for . . .

'Send down number two,' he shouted.

The time was 0605; the long ground-swell was stirring up the sea-bed. Visibility along the ocean floor was deteriorating rapidly and now it was difficult to see.

# CHAPTER 17

## *First Attempt*

Jake Soper had known for the past half hour that his trial could not be far off. Since 0700 the captain had from time to time turned on the emergency lantern, the last there was, for a few precious seconds, when Sinclair was struggling around the compartment to open the valve of the first oxygen cylinder.

At first, when fresh oxygen had flooded the ward-room, the relief had been immense – but now, at each half hour when Sinclair cracked the valve for five seconds, the effect had diminished. For a brief few minutes one could breathe naturally; after ten minutes, each breath was laboured – a long, deep intake of air to the depths of the lungs, but still Jake did not feel satisfied – and, God, my head . . . when would this splitting ache, this steel band searing his temples, ease up? The pain was so acute that it dulled all thinking – how long before their reasoning was impaired?

Pinky Dean had been magnificent. He had stayed by his sonar transmitter until the last minute, when the captain had ordered him to rest. This had been the first clue that Jake had rumbled: their moment for escaping was imminent. Then, speaking slowly and deliberately, the coxswain repeated, step by step, the drill they were to follow when once they were in the tower. He, Jake Soper, had the sequence word – perfect, but so much depended on Pinky – and in these prolonged intervals of darkness it was impossible to judge the reactions of one's companions.

Dean seemed composed and ready for meeting the unknown. As for himself, the Almighty had it in His power to snuff out Jake Soper's life – 'In the twinkling of an eye', the scriptures said, didn't they? He'd had time to prepare himself for death – he'd tried to remember the confession recited each Sunday in the college chapel: 'We do earnestly repent and are heartily sorry for these our misdoings . . . the burden is intolerable . . . have mercy upon us . . . ' but Jake could only achieve a few sentences. He could see the model of the square-rigged ship, hanging high above the congregation's heads and running downwind towards the altar.

He wished now that he'd had the guts to take his belief more seriously. Did God really forgive? Did he really sacrifice His son on that cruel cross, to save miserable sods like Jake? He'd been bloody selfish, but he'd never deliberately hurt anyone – and he was sorry, bitterly ashamed for his failure with Simone – but was the bungling *his* fault? Had it been a sin, a mortal one, to renounce the physical charms of women since then? God knew he wasn't a queer, but supposing he had been, would He forgive him? Had He hung on that tree, ready always to forgive if only His children could have the humility to plead for pardon?

Jake shut his eyes and prayed, the first real supplication he had ever made. He lay still for he knew not how long. And then he felt an unmistakable strength welling back into him, a serene courage he'd never known before. The cynics would sneer that this was a last insurance, act, hypocritical, but he couldn't care less now: he was at peace and ready to die – and if the eternal mystery of death was shortly to encompass him, he certainly was no longer dreading the final steps across the mystical divide . . .

'Jake and Pinky,' the captain's voice spoke from the darkness. 'Better get ready now.'

Jake Soper rolled from the settee and stood up, as the lamp snicked on.

'Aye, aye, sir. Ready, Pinky?'

He was amazed by the steadiness of his voice. 'You'll follow us up, Coxswain?'

'Yes, sir. I'll check your suits first.'

The clock showed 0715 when they began to dress, but the minute hand had moved past the half hour before they were ready. Before zipping up, they stood by the fin ladder, waiting for the captain's 'Go'. From the radio room echoed the voice of Alastair Sinden, who had relieved Dean at the sonar set.

'*Kronstad*'s standing by for the first escape,' he said. 'They're ready when you are, but watch out for the lifting wires: they are about to heave in and are not waiting for the escape.'

'Thanks.'

The captain turned to the waiting men. 'Okay, Jake? Tell 'em up top, please, that we'll hang on for a little longer, in case the lift's successful.' He was holding on to the ladder himself, to counteract the persistent rolling that the boat had taken on. 'And tell Captain Quincey that Commander Sinden and I will be escaping last, after the coxswain and the navigating officer. Quite clear?'

Soper nodded. Pinky shook hands with the remaining men, then zipped up. 'Don't be too eager, Coxswain,' the captain said, grinning for once. 'Remember you've got to shut the upper lid.'

'I'll give three taps on the fin ladder, sir,' Hebbenden said, 'as soon as it's okay to drain down.'

'Right. Off you go . . . Check that both gags on the stole are in the down position.'

The three men left open the hoods of their immersion suits. Soper went first; then Dean, clumping up the ladder; and finally the Martian figure of Hebbenden disappearing through the lower hatch.

Soper waited half way up the tower, on the small platform where the second ladder began its ascent to the upper hatch. He heard the clang! of the lower hatch shutting beneath them.

'Lower lid shut, sir.' Hebbenden's confident voice was as matter-of-fact as that of an instructor in the *Dolphin* tank.

'Very good, Cox'n. I'm going on up,' Soper panted, 'Follow me, Pinky.'

'Right, sir. Good luck, sir.'

'Standing by the floor valve,' the coxswain reported from the pitch blackness. Good – so Hebbenden had found the main flood. He'd climb to the upper lid as soon as the deluge began.

'Stand by, Cox'n.'

Soper felt the chill of the rungs as he slowly hauled himself up the endless, slippery ladder. Step by step he felt his way: no second chance if he fell now in this darkness. He must not waste time, for the air was foul here and under pressure.

'You okay, Pinky?'

'Fine, sir.'

'We'll stop here to get our breath.' They waited a full two minutes, each breath an effort as they tried to force the oxygen to the depths of their lungs –

'Ready?'

'Yes, sir.'

At last Jake felt the hatch above him – there were no more rungs to clutch.

'Hold on to my feet.'

He felt the RO's firm grasp around his ankles.

'Once we're through the hatch, use one hand only for holding on, the other to protect yourself – there may be a lot of gash about . . . Good luck, Pinky.'

'Thank you, sir – same to you.'

'*Open the flood* . . . shut the vent,' he shouted.

His words sounded strange, not his own, as they echoed through the massive tower. He heard the coxswain repeating the order; then the ring of the wheel-spanner as he opened the valve; the scrabbling of his feet as he began to mount the tower – and, finally, the roar of incoming water as it deluged into the tower. They were on their own now: utter darkness; no communication because of the deafening roar and the hissing of the air . . . And the mounting pain in their ears as the pressure began to build up.

Thank God for *Dolphin*'s drill . . . none of them would zip up until the last moment – the only air to breathe was being compressed above their heads – and the poisonous mixture was becoming worse under pressure, more and more lethal. They'd have to be bloody quick, Pinky and he, if the cox'n was to have any chance of survival – and what of the others who were to follow?

Pinky's hand was gripping his ankle; and then he was aware of a third presence, invisible, squeezing up alongside but just below. Hebbenden must be doing his balancing trick, edging as close as he could to the upper lid, ready to shut it as soon as Pinky and he were clear.

The pain in his ear-drums made him cry out – but what did burst ear-drums matter so long as they reached the surface? The breathing was more difficult, with the mounting pressure – three hundred and fifty pounds per square inch, wouldn't it be, at this depth? His brain was mushy . . . difficult to think – Hell, shouldn't the pressure be equalising now, because the noise had decreased; there was a general hissing but the roar of flooding water had vanished – ah, here it came – his feet were wet and he could feel Pinky and the cox'n squeezing up beside him . . .

'*Try the hatch* . . .'

He thought he heard Hebbenden shouting. He yanked at the long clip of the upper lid – he nearly fell from the ladder, as the clip came away easily.

'*First clip off!*'

The habit of training asserted itself, dispelling the instinct to panic. ' . . . Zip up hoods . . . on nose clips . . .'

He was entirely cocooned, zipped from toe to head: only a few breaths and he would lose consciousness. He reached for Pinky's head with his other hand, felt the enclosed hood as Pinky fumbled with the zip.

He pulled at the second clip. He felt it give, flick clear. He pushed against the upper lid. Not a bloody movement . . . nothing

. . . solid . . . oh God . . . Shove, *heave*, every ounce I've got . . . he straightened his trembling legs, anchored tightly by Pinky's arm . . . then suddenly the oval hatch swung open above him. He hung on to the handle as the lid opened. The water swirled about him. Beneath his feet he could feel Hebbenden fighting for the handle of the hatch . . .

*Thirty seconds ascent for 500 feet, they'd said* . . . let the bubble take you, breathe OUT, breathe OUT . . . OUT . . . OUT. They'd said it was easy, but they didn't tell you of the pain – oh God, I shall pass out – this ear of mine; why is the right worse than the left? Try to swallow, clear the tubes . . .

And why was Pinky hanging on so tightly, damn his eyes. It was all he could do, not to kick himself free – *they were going up in tandem, bloody funny, bicycle made for* . . . God, oh God, *was death like this, all pain* . . . *and breathe* OUT – OUT – OUT . . . *and is this wetness blood, blood, my blood – and if I don't exhale I'll burst, like a balloon around the Christmas tree, shining, scintillating sparklets and smell of candle grease; those mini electric bulbs – the tinsel and the red-crepe parcels stacked around the tub.*

How many seconds gone? OUT . . . OUT . . . *hold my breath, now, there's more to exhale – only collapsing lungs and a red mist, a bloody great flux before my eyes; His blood, that Man they nailed upon a tree* . . . and Pinky, for Christ's sake, let go of my legs . . . I'll kick your teeth in, if I get out of this – *but who cares anyway – least of all my Mom and Paw – and that bitch, that Simone, my love, I'd have loved you so if you'd been kinder* . . . I can't hold on any longer – *the water can swirl into my lungs, fill up those collapsed balloons and I'll drown, down,* DOWN, *again, back to the black monster lying there so deep* . . .

There was a roaring, angry gushing about him. He felt the intense cold as he shot through the surface and into the exquisite clean air – the first icy stab of arctic air that bit into his lungs. He collapsed back into the water, floundering in the buoyancy of his suit. He was aware then of the angry seas, white and curling as they broke about his head. He gasped, glimpsed the grey masts of plunging vessels; then all swam dizzily in a sickening spiral of unreality as he drifted into oblivion.

'*. . . the Depth and Dream of my Desire*'

Rudyard Kipling had expressed it best, the hidden secret that consumed her being, each hour of every day and night.

> The depth and dream of my desire,
> The bitter paths wherein I stray –
> Thou knowest who hast made the Fire
> Now knowest who hast made the Clay . . .'

She'd looked up her Kiplings, that blue and gold collection which her mother had given her. She had found it again in *My New-cut Ashlar: The depth and dream of my desire, the bitter paths* . . .

Jackie Carn rolled over on to her side, her knees drawn up as she sleepily opened her eyes to the new day stealing across the purple moors of Dunbrae. She normally lay drowsily for a delicious few minutes, slowly awakening to the loveliness of another day, her subconscious savouring the passion of his touch, even now, though it was nearly a month ago – but she could feel the sweet pain in her breasts that lay, lonely and impatient, for his return . . .

This was Friday, 4 July. She'd slept through the early hours, drugged by the sleeping draught the doctor had given her, dulled at last to the agony of waiting – but now it was already eight-fifteen. A quarter past eight – thirty-one hours, wasn't it? She'd been ticking them off in the diary she kept by the bed – and FOS/M had said they could have little hope after thirty-six hours – five hours – only five hours left to them, her precious three . . . could fate ever have been so cruel to anyone else?

The inescapable self-condemnation prodded persistently at her soul – a just punishment, was it, for what they'd done, she and her beloved Alastair? Why wasn't He satisfied with damning them, her and him only? Couldn't He spare the others? This love of theirs could not be sinful, this incredibly precious, once-in-a-million thing that so few people could ever know. This love came from God, she was sure: no human agency could fabricate a gift so precious and so pure – whatever the world, in its impurity, might call their relationship. *Alastair*, oh *Alastair* . . . she whispered his name, and closed her eyes the better to see him before those waters snatched him for ever, the fishes to destroy his body so strong, virile and beautiful . . .

She would not regret the sadness now, the recriminations, the deceptions of her double life – those agonies could wait, for there would be plenty of time. But their total gift to each other, no mortal could comprehend: the love they'd shared between them had surged like a tidal wave, overwhelming reality as it swept them headlong towards disaster . . .

Of course, it had to be Sunday – one of those incomparable

naval Sundays, the sun shining, the ensigns clean, the boats at the lower booms and the church pendant drooping from the depot-ship's yard-arm. The gulls, wheeling and squawking above the gash-chutes; and the terns hovering above the loch's dark surface, before they plummetted to their invisible prey: these would always be the memories of a Service Sunday for her. But, now, the Sundays could never again be the same.

This was a contrived, deliberate meeting of theirs. They had shared the decisions, knowing that they had crossed the Rubicon on that Friday, nine weeks ago now. She met Alastair in Glasgow and he had driven her to Aberfoyle. They left the car and walked down the track skirting the sparkling loch on the far side of the village.

'I want to be yours, totally,' she had whispered to him as they sat together by the loch. She could smell now the scent of the crushed bracken and the sweetness of the heather where the bees buzzed away their working life. He was tickling her ear with a sprig of heather, but when he heard the words she had spoken so softly, he turned away so that she could not witness his torment.

This had been their second chance, when they could still have retreated. She could feel his hands now, as his arms had enfolded her.

'I want to be yours . . .'

He had succumbed, taken her at her word. When they had kissed a flame had licked, kindling her passion. She had flung herself at him, devouring him with the sensuality which had for so long been locked inside her. They had spoken not a word, where they clung together by the loch. Oblivious to the world, both knew the hunger that the other craved to satisfy.

'We'd better go,' he had said, glancing at his watch. He had gently freed himself, silently leading her by the hand, back towards the car.

He had driven fast, anxious not to make her late for Jeremy coming home from school. He had let her do the talking but, once through Glasgow, he had suggested the picnic. Then and there, they began to lay their plans. The days dragged interminably. She had persuaded her mother to take the children for the night in her Glasgow flat. Alone in Dunbrae House, Jackie had slept lightly and woken with the dawn. She'd thrown the lunch into the picnic basket and was out and away before eight o'clock. She took the sandy track that led through the larch wood and on to Dunbrae Moor.

Their trysting place was to be the birch grove in the Sma' Glen

– the clump of trees nestled by the burn that tumbled through the purple heather from the upper regions of the moor. The grove was four miles from the house and utterly isolated, even from the climbers who regularly attacked Dunbrae Cairn, the granite peak which drew the Glasgow mountaineers. Her feet flew, her heart raced as the love she bore him tugged at her, leading her onwards to the moment when, for the first time, they would be entirely alone for any length of time.

She didn't count the cost now: she wanted only to be enfolded in his arms, to give herself totally. She was snatching at the opportunity of being his utterly – if he wished to take her, he could do with her as he willed. She longed to lose herself in his embraces, out there, under the white galleons of cloud sailing so majestically across that blue, blue sky.

What could the world know of beauty such as theirs? When Alastair was apart from her, each was a separate part of the whole – but when together, the two halves bonded into one soul, a completeness beyond human understanding. Their love had brightened all that was beautiful: for the first time in life she was fully alive, intensely aware of the colours in a sunset, the joy in old people's faces. Everything, everyone had an added lustre, difficult to explain; and when Alastair and she were together, laughing with the world, those around them caught their infectious joy. For the first time in her life, she had found it easy to love those who previously had seemed so difficult and so impossible . . .

She knew she had reached the heights of happiness. It was easy to thrust the mundane world behind her, but she was keenly aware of her responsibilities to George and the children: they needed her too.

But today she would ignore the clamour of her conscience: she had deliriously accepted the love that Alastair had offered her, but one day the reckoning would come. She would have to choose, but, dear God, not yet, please, not yet . . . She couldn't let Alastair go – she needed him so; what would there be for her to live for? A mediocre marriage for the rest of her days, after having tasted paradise . . . ?

She reached the burn and cut off through the heather, her footsteps sure as she forged across the rise that hid their secret rendezvous from the glen. She followed a straight line; no detours today, no one would be up there on a Sunday. As she crossed the sky line of the rounded hummock, she looked down at their retreat four hundred yards below – the birches were swaying gently, their filigree leaves dancing in the morning's breeze. A cry

144

of joy escaped her lips as she found herself running through the heather, uncaring whether it scratched her legs. Then she was there, out of breath as she leaned against the silvery trunks. She threw herself down in the shade and felt the soft turf beneath her. They'd picnic here, share their veal and ham pies, savour the strawberries, the last of the season. She had prepared this picnic with care: he was an appreciative man, sensitive to the wishes of others. To see him happy was to her the greatest joy.

The wind was in her face and she tossed her head for the breeze to blow through her hair. She knew he adored her, relished her wildness and disarray; but why did she love him? She didn't know, couldn't begin to give reasons – she loved him and yearned to show him how much . . . Perhaps it was his sparkle, his gaiety, or was it the contempt he showed for the inconsequential trappings that made her a prisoner, unable to laugh as once she did?

She jumped to her feet when she heard his whistle carried by the wind. There he was, arm waving as he came bounding through the heather, in his open-necked blue shirt and old grey trousers.

She smoothed down her green cotton skirt as she ran towards him, her blouse crisp with the care with which she'd ironed it, loosed at the top button to reveal the separation of her breasts. They kissed, hugging each other in delight. He held her at arms' length, the better to drink in her loveliness, and she knew that after today, she could never be more beautiful in his eyes.

'I thought you'd never come,' she said.

'I was afraid you'd not be here,' he replied, his eyes laughing that gentle smile creasing his tanned, sensitive face. It was those eyes, so intensely blue, that made her heart stop: how could any man affect her so . . . ?

They had fallen upon their lunch, voraciously gobbling it down while the sun climbed higher into the heavens. The tomatoes, peppered and sliced, the cucumber sandwiches, the two tins of cool beer – their tastes were heightened that day, food for the gods, where they laughed and hugged and kissed together, beneath the whispering leaves and the hot, hot sun . . .

And all the while, the excitement had mounted inside her: why couldn't he hurry his eating? She'd begun to collect the bits and pieces to hasten him, but in sheer contentment he had slowly munched at the last sandwich. In desperation she'd watched him, and then he'd laughed, blatantly teasing her, as he flung the half-eaten piece of bread into the heather . . . she continued to loosen her blouse and looked away as she felt his glance upon her. A

145

delicious warmth suffused her limbs, as she pulled him to his feet.

'Come on, my darling dear,' she'd said. 'Let's wash in the burn.'

Hand in hand they'd hurried to the burn that plopped, laughing and gurgling, through the peaty banks of heather. Shamrock green was the downy moss that moulded the banks; where the water undercut the peat, pools of shade darkened the brown water which was the brook trout's universe. The current trickled between the pebbles; and over the granite rocklets, cascades spluttered down, waterfalls of diamonds splashing into the gold-flecked eddies below . . . cool and clear it was, this crystal miracle, where the trout-fry lived – and Alastair had laughed as they buried their faces in the coolness.

And when he'd dabbed her dry, he took her hand. Gently leading, he strode towards the granite rocks in the bracken that covered the slopes of this fairy glen. With his other hand, he parted the green fronds, the heads of the fern five to six feet high, a bracken roof above their heads.

'Here it is,' he said softly. 'Our secret home.'

He had turned towards her, his eyes calm and serious, not laughing now.

'Our little house,' she'd said. And hidden from the world was their secret place, a circle of green turf framed by a coronet of purple heather, for the ling was now well passed. He spread wide his arms, a gesture that was both a courtesy and an invitation: she fell to her knees and stretched herself beneath him as she felt his hands. Above them, high, high in the blue heavens, a lark was soaring, ever upwards, its song a paean of praise.

'I want to be yours,' she'd whispered fiercely. 'Oh, Al, I want to be yours . . .'

No shame; no excuses for the lick of lust that fanned them both; no looking back and no regrets . . . that was what they whispered to each other afterwards. This precious miracle was something in which they both exulted with a deep thankfulness . . .

She had known what he had wanted, even then . . . not a swift conquest by him. She had felt him beside her, his passion as overwhelming and as fierce as her own. Each caress she gave to him was more than matched by his own until, suddenly, she had felt the surge of his manhood exploding inside her. Fiercely she had held him against her, savouring the miracle until she could feel the pulse no more . . . and there, in the bracken, his hands upon her uncovered breasts, his head tucked into her shoulder, she had lain motionless, in total submission to his will. Entwined together and silent, they had searched the depths of each other's eyes, his with the clear blueness of the northern Scot, culled from the lochs and the freshness of the northern seas.

The practical problems of afterwards had held no embarrassment: they had laughed together, like children, over the naturalness of life; when they had finished, he had gently pulled her to her feet to hold her at arms' length. Smiling, he had gazed into her excited eyes.

'What have you done to me, my Jackie?' he had asked. 'It's a long time since that happened to me.' She had turned and picked up the basket. 'We'd better get back,' she said, taking his arm. 'The children will soon be back.'

Something was ringing far away, a familiar sound she could not recognise . . . Jackie Carn sat upright in her bed; she shook her head as she glanced at the clock again, half past eight – heavens, she'd nodded off again and that was the phone down in the hall. She jumped out of bed and, throwing on her rose-coloured dressing-gown, ran barefoot down the stairs. What terrible news now? Or had they managed . . . ?

'Jackie Carn . . .'

'FOS/M here, Jackie,' the familiar voice said. 'Can you stand some more news, old thing? It's good, from one point of view . . . '

'Go ahead; I can take it . . . ' She felt herself trembling. Had they saved them . . . had they got them out?

'Jake Soper and one rating have been picked up. They're being decompressed now, but they'll be all right, apart from the inevitable damage to their ears. They escaped through the fin.'

It was difficult not to betray her disappointment. What about Al? And George and Peter?

'That's good,' she said softly, waiting . . .

'And the others are going to have a go, two at a time, Jackie.'

'When . . . ?'

'We've had all the news from Soper. The coxswain and your brother are next. George has been adamant.'

'When will . . . ?'

'Try to stop worrying, my dear,' the kindly voice said. His confidence was wearing thin, but she knew how hard he was trying to help. 'George and Alastair Sinden are okay – they'll escape last.'

'What about the lifting operation, Sir Frederick?' she asked timorously. They said they'd be lifting *Mars*, didn't they?

'Impossible at the moment, Jackie. There's a gale blowing there

147

now,' the voice said at the other end. 'We don't know yet whether the Russians can stay on the billet.'

'Oh . . .' She tried to arrest the cry that had welled to her lips.

'I'll ring you, Jackie, as soon as I know anything.'

She slowly replaced the receiver.

This ghastly *Mars* nightmare would pass . . . she would become another forgotten widow, left to her dreams. But to lose all one's heart suddenly, in a single cruel sweep of the knife . . . ? Wasn't this too much, even for her to bear as retribution?

But why, God, why such a punishment for the miraculous beauty Alastair and I have shared and for which we have searched all our lives? This love can be no sin . . . and she stared at the drawn face in the hall mirror.

Was that the woman she'd known as Mrs George Carn some nine weeks ago? Was that tired face reflecting the secret that now consumed her life?

The pigeons were cooing down in the wood. The wind was rustling the birch leaves in the drive outside. She must cook the children's breakfast, or Jeremy would be late for school.

CHAPTER 18

*The Coxswain*

The tower, it seemed to Submarine Coxswain Ronald Hebbenden, was taking a mighty long time to drain down. Twice since he'd shut the upper lid (a close shave that), he'd almost fallen from his ladder. His head went on swimming even after he'd unzipped the hood; he had to lean with his back against the side of the tower, in case he passed out. He felt desperately sick, nauseated by the near-loss of consciousness; all he wanted was to climb down out of this terrible, dark void, back to the control room compartment in which he could at least breathe, however painfully.

The captain and Commander Sinden had heard his three raps on the side: the draining down had begun, and at last, with the vent open, he could begin to breathe again . . . his chest was aching, a poniard-like pain, excruciating in intensity . . . his head was splitting open and he was about to vomit. The water level was falling fast now, draining to the bilges in the bottom of the boat – and then he heard the clattering on the lower hatch beneath his feet: they were doing their utmost, those three – and suddenly the water swirled from under him and he was sliding, feet first, through the hole, where a dim, pale light glowed: three men were peering down at him, revolving, each with a pale, anxious face . . . and slowly, shaking his head, recognition dawned – the captain, the navigator and the passenger . . . God, I'm going to be sick.

He crouched over the bucket they held for him. He retched up his insides, his sweat running like a river in the heat and the stench. His knees gave way as he tried to move towards the ward-room. He slumped across Gallo's cold softness under the sheet. Lieutenant Sinclair's arms were under his armpits, and then he was being half dragged, half carried to the settee in the ward-room.

'I must put this out . . . ' Those were the captain's words: calm, reassuring . . . ' . . . well done, Swain. We'll soon have you round.'

He felt the water between his lips. He shook his splitting head again, passed a sticky palm across his forehead to wipe away the stale sweat, salt to his taste as it dribbled from his nose.

' . . . a-ah . . . ' The nausea diminished when oxygen hissed beneath his nostrils. ' . . . Bloody good of you, sir.'

Slowly he pieced together his account of those minutes in the tower. Sinden was bending over him, asking questions, repeating the drill, item by item: it was his turn next to be number three . . . he and the Old Man would be last – there was just a chance for a rush escape, if they really knew their stuff.

'I don't think we'll wait, Cox'n. Air's much worse.' The captain's breathing was heavy and he was gasping from his recent efforts. 'When you feel up to it, we'll get you and the navigating officer out . . . okay?'

Hebbenden grunted: all he wanted was to be left alone. He longed to sleep, to be rid of this terrible head and the agony of fighting for breath. He wondered whether he would have the strength to have another go . . . ? He sat up, propped on one elbow.

'Captain, sir?'

'Yeah. What is it, cox'n?'

Hebbenden swallowed, gasping for oxygen.

'I know the drill now, sir. Commander Sinden ought to go next, with Lieutenant Sinclair.'

In the darkness, he felt the pressure of the captain's hand on his shoulder.

'Shut up and lie down, Cox'n. Get some rest, and then you can go.'

Hebbenden stretched out his long body: he could do no more. Carn was rustling in the passageway. 'The sonar's calling,' he was saying. 'I'll see what they've got to say. I'll warn them of their impending good fortune to welcome the coxswain and the navigator.' Hebbenden chuckled. Well, there was nothing for it. Rest he must, if he was to be of use to anyone, let alone himself.

Each breath was a prolonged physical effort now: however long one inhaled, however deeply, one's lungs were never filled. For a long time he had been trying to harness his thoughts.

He knew he was a simple man, as his beloved Madge had so often told him. For a short spell, during that phase after the war when everyone was getting out, he'd left the service to try the sweet life outside. They'd soon found out, she and he, when running that fish-and-chip shop, that in civvy street dinner wasn't piped at noon. He'd been too kind, trusted everybody, given away too much fish to the old dears who hadn't a penny to bless their hearts with . . . 'You'll never make a businessman, dear,' Madge had said so often, her eyes wet behind those pink plastic-rimmed spectacles she'd got on 'the health'. He'd been lucky: the service had taken him back. It had been a near thing, with the nippers growing up so fast: a pair of shoes, when he could afford a new pair for 'em, had lasted only six months.

But in that short spell, the navy had suffered a metamorphosis: the change had been too rapid, that was the trouble. The navy was traditional and did not, surely, have to act the 'popularity Jack' part for the yobbo ashore?

It had been very different when he had joined. The submarine branch had not yet received its first nuclear: it was a proud trade, and to have volunteered was the secret pride of all of them. He remembered being appalled when he reported back to the drafting office in the barracks. The RPO was dealing with a new entry:

'Right,' he cajoled. 'Who wants to volunteer for subs?'

A long silence.

'Who wants to volunteer for the Royal Marines?'

A few hands shyly went up, mostly from the rear rank.

More silence . . .

'Who'll volunteer for general service?'

More hands.

'Off you go, you lot, to general service. This class to Royal

Marines.' The chief had paused, grinned, then said:

'The rest to submarines.'

That's how they manned the boats now: the press gang again, like the war . . . but once in submarines, few voluntarily came out.

Ah! that was better . . . he felt sick no longer. He'd try to sleep for a few minutes, to refresh his tired brain: he could always cat-nap, any place, any time. 'You're like Churchill,' Madge had teased him once. She was a grand girl, his Madge, plump, roly-poly, a warm, passionate woman; though most people would have called her plain, to him she was lovely.

'I don't mind, dear, what happens to us,' she'd whispered once to him in the early hours when he was home on a twenty-four-hour leave, 'so long as you've got lead in your pencil . . . ' He had lain there and laughed with her, deliciously, until they made love again, while the grey dawn broke over dreary, ugly Sheerness . . . his Madge, how would she take it, if he didn't make the next escape?

A Hunter-Killer was more demanding on everyone than a boomer . . . and particularly for the first lieutenant and himself. The turnover of hands was so rapid that the paperwork was immense – and no one else could do it. He hoped that he'd per-formed adequately as coxswain because, secretly, he hoped one day to qualify for fleet chief: not only was the new rate better paid, but its status meant a lot to a man with pride . . . and Madge would love it, wouldn't she?

It was 63 bulkhead that made life so bloody awkward. That ruddy division was no mere physical barrier between the after part and the fore-ends: it was a psychological block. One day, the powers that be would surmount the difficulty, but they'd have to look slippy. Too many good men were going outside, fed up with the instability of routine in the SSNs – the wives were at the bottom of the restlessness – and who could blame them?

As for leave, and football teams, and watchkeepers – oh, gawd – and he clasped his head again. He'd be thankful to escape, whether dead or alive.

The senior ratings in the SSNs were working to the limits of their endurance. The life was almost worse than an operational boat in wartime: sleep was all they craved, when the key men were coping with anything out of routine – and that was more often than not. No one else could do the job – this was the root of the matter: these boats were highly technical, and, on top of that, their operational life was too complicated. It was tempting for the Staff to keep her running around the clock: sixty million, sterling, was an expensive mass of junk to lie around idle.

In the end, it was the human factor that mattered: what was the use of producing these incredible monsters if there was no one to run them? And, one day, there'd be an accident . . .

Ron Hebbenden laughed softly to himself: what the bloody hell was *this*? That day when they nearly lost *Marlin* had been a tea-party compared to this; but, in its own way, that accident had been more alarming: it had happened so suddenly.

*Marlin* was exercising with the NATO fleet: some ship up top was operating a variable-depth sonar, so they went deep to elude the trap. She was passing the 500 foot mark when a half-inch-diameter pocket blew in the engine-room. He'd been talking to the chief at the time. He'd never forget the terrifying speed of events . . .

At a pressure of about 300 pounds per square inch, the deluge gushed into the compartment at an incredible rate. They went to collision stations and closed the hatches, with him, the coxswain, trapped back aft . . . Both ends were shut off and they began to pass round the orange suits.

When *Marlin* hit the surface, she shot straight out and rolled on to her side: back aft they didn't know they were surfacing, so they fired their red grenades – then everyone was struggling on the deck as she rolled on her beam-ends. They thought they were diving again, so the clips had been taken off the after escape hatch – and on her way down, there was only the weight of water keeping the lid shut. The ward-room steward, a doubtful quantity normally, was a big, effeminate type with, fortunately, five children. He hauled himself up and slapped on the clips . . .

Hebbenden found himself sweating again – even *Mars* was rolling now – and he smiled to himself . . . but those air bursts could be upsetting.

He'd always been amazed at the speed with which a youngster adapted himself to the life: like Dean. Only nineteen and yet he could operate the W/T as well as 'voice'; and shortly, when the radio operators and radio plotters amalgamated, he'd be a trained plotter too. And old Crumm, the thirty-six-year-old radio supervisor, a friend of Hebbenden's since they were boys together, was also a maintainer. A good job, for anyone going outside . . . the difficulty was now that these monsters were too technical for everyone to be able to carry out everyone else's job, unlike the old days . . .

'Rested, Cox'n?'

He heard the query from the depth of his bunk. His stomach

kicked in revulsion: how easy now, to jack it in. He was not up to it; too unwell – and, anyway this *was* the truth. He felt none too good: he shook his head to clear the dizziness that still afflicted him.

'All set, sir . . . ' He hadn't the guts to refuse. He glanced at his watch: 0952 – there wasn't much more time left to them down here, anyway – three hours at the most, he reckoned.

The pale light came on again. As it did so, the round emergency lantern shot across the table. He steadied himself from the boat's sudden lurch by grabbing Sinclair's shoulder. The navigator was checking his suit, and his friendly smile gave Hebbenden back his confidence. And there, waiting in the passageway, was Commander Sinden, in his torn suit, which was an excuse rather than a practicality. The three men moved towards the control room.

As they reached the screen dividing the plotting from the control section, a shuddering, whipping motion contorted groan ran through the length of the stricken boat. She seemed to sway to her beam-ends, more of a lay-over than a roll, as if some giant hand was pulling her down. They heard the scrape of wires along the pressure hull; the screech of shearing metal; the wrench of steel plating as it sundered.

The bows shot up as she catapulted across on to her port beam-ends; then she was away, her bow-up angle soaring to 70° as the sundering howled its agonising cacophony: Hebbenden watched the luminous pointer on the depth-gauge beginning to swing – 550 – 580 – 595 – and his stomach once more came up to meet him. The sensation was like swooping downward in a New York elevator – down, dow-w-w-n, and then, as they slithered into a helpless mass in the corner, the light went out.

## A Seaman's Decision

Kapitan Alexandrei Smirnov wondered how much more his *Kronstad* could take. Since 0930, when the front hit them, the seas had been mounting steadily. Now, twenty minutes later, she was pitching steeply in the troughs of the advancing seas. He glanced across at the plunging frigates: he'd *have* to send them home – but there, less than fifty metres on his starboard beam, danced crazily the orange marker-buoy which had been their datum point for the past seventeen hours.

Smirnov swore obscenely. How could fate deal such an appalling hand? Those last two men had escaped: they had even survived, thanks to the speed of his motor-cutter – but now, when the wires were coming home nicely, this gale, so typical of this savage Barents Sea, had swept in from Iceland to dash their hopes.

Against his own judgement, he'd permitted Captain Quincey to send down the rescue sub once again. That American, the sub's pilot was a brave man – but how were they going to recover him now? *Lily-One* would have to surface and Dugan would have to bale out. They'd have to sacrifice the rescue sub.

*Kronstad* was plunging into the seas. From the corner of his enclosed bridge, he watched the spray leaping in plumes across the fo'c'sle head. The well-deck was awash and the men were finding difficulty in keeping their feet, in spite of those special anti-slip thigh boots. It was dangerous down there. If one of those huge lifting wires parted – he shuddered at the thought of the carnage it would wreak, both to his men and his ship. It couldn't be long now before the gear would part, with the crazy snatching of his anchor cables. He would have let go both anchors, but it was pointless now to risk his emergency kedge: soon nothing would hold in these seas. He turned as he felt someone standing behind him. It was Quincey, and it was lucky that English was the world's common language.

'How long can you hold on, Captain?' the Englishman asked.

The voice was carried away on the howling wind, but Smirnov caught the sense: the query was only too clear in the man's agonised eyes.

'I must slip my cables,' Kapitan Smirnov shouted, 'or we'll lose the gear.' He picked up the fo'c'sle-head phone. 'Buoy the starboard cable,' he shouted. 'We'll come back as soon as the weather moderates.' He turned again to Quincey. ' . . . sorry, Captain,' he said, shaking his head.

'Can't you wait another half hour, Captain? I'll order them to escape . . .'

Kapitan Alexandrei Smirnov knew that Quincey had understood. The weather had beaten them. The trapped men must die.

'I'll heave to and keep the frigate here,' he yelled. 'We may see them when they reach the surface.' He shook his head again. The ordeal was too much for him: he was not a ruthless career man, never had been.

'Weigh port anchor,' he shouted. 'Full speed.'

The men jumped to it on the slippery steel decks. The cable came pounding inboard, the brake-drums squealing as the winches revolved. A seaman spun a wheel-valve and the cable rattled down the navel-pipe. Smirnov thrust his hands deep into the pockets of his greatcoat. He could not face the Englishman: but he knew that the man had understood. Quincey was a sea-man too; he would know that you couldn't risk many men's lives for the chance of saving four . . . and a miracle had already been achieved, hadn't it?

A sudden juddering trembled through the ship. He slid across to the starboard side to watch the hands preparing to slip the wires from the snatch-blocks on the derricks and the cranes. Then he felt the angle coming on . . . *Kronstad* was being heeled over by some monstrous weight.

'The submarine's shifted,' he spoke out loud. 'She'll take us with her.' He jumped outside to the starboard wing, where the force of the wind smacked him full in the face.

'*Emergency slip*!' he yelled through his megaphone. 'Let go all wires. Slip the starboard anchor . . . '

He watched the pigmy men, marionettes, slithering on those heaving decks, leaping to their stations. From behind him, a voice was calling from the sonar room:

'Kapitan, sir. Sonar's dead. There's no reply from *Mars*.'

## Diminishing Returns

'You don't have to go, of course . . . '

Peter heard the captain's voice, desperately tired now, resigned. They were lucky to have escaped serious injury when *Mars* had come up all-standing from her 200 foot plunge. Apart from bruising, miraculously, there were no bones broken.

Six hundred and eighty feet, that was a hell of a long way down – lower by eighty feet than the depth from which any other ascent had been made, Peter thought. The coxswain was waiting for him, and, in the shadows thrown by the dimming lantern, he could see Alastair Sinden crouching there. He was suffering from his breathing more than the rest of them: he was gasping now, a bad colour as he fought for oxygen.

'I'm ready, sir,' Peter said, barely recognising his own voice. 'I'll follow you, Swain.' He turned to shake George Carn's hand.

'Tell Jackie . . . ' Carn for a moment was losing control. He spoke softly, the words choking in his throat. 'Tell her I love her . . . Be sure to tell her that, Peter,' he said, barely audible. Peter nodded, unable to trust himself, as he felt the bearlike grip of Carn's hand.

As Peter felt his way towards the control-room ladder, he was surprised to find the coxswain hanging behind. Peter waited, standing by the ladder, eyes averted as Hebbenden shook hands, first with the orange-suited Sinden and then with his captain. For these two men, each the senior representative of his own world, this was the moment of parting: each was a professional: each knew that the chances for all four of them were now non-existent. Of the choice of deaths, remaining behind would be the least messy – and the captain hadn't made clear yet whether he was going to make the attempt – he had no immersion suit, and Sinden's was US anyway.

'Shall we be expecting you, sir?'

Peter could not refrain from posing the question: it was impertinent of him, he knew, but Jackie would want to know how her husband had perished – and those up top would want to know when to give up hope. Peter, if he reached the surface alive, would be expected to furnish the answers. 'They'll need to know up top, sir . . .'

Peter caught the glance passing between the two men who would be left until last. Sinden nodded imperceptibly; Carn hesitated, deep in thought for a long half minute. Then he turned towards Peter. 'Yes,' he said. 'We'll have a go, before it's too late.' He turned to Sinden: 'I'll wait for the same signal, Alastair, before draining down.'

'Three raps,' Sinden said. He smiled as he held up the wheel-spanner. 'I've got my tool,' he said. As he raised the steel implement, Peter glimpsed the long rent stretching the length of his suit, from armpit to hip: the cobbler's stitch barely held the material together.

'What are you waiting for, Swain?' There was an edge of impatience in Carn's query.

'I thought I'd be better at the bottom of the tower, sir,' he said quietly, ' . . . seeing as how I've done it before. Once I've opened the flood and the vent, I've got loads of time to climb to the upper lid. That would give Commander Sinden plenty of time to get set, sir – for shutting the lid again after we've gone.'

'You'll follow the navigating officer?'

'Yes, sir – that'll cut out as many human errors as we can . . .'

Carn nodded. 'Okay, makes sense to me – any objections, you two?'

Peter felt relieved when Sinden shook his head.

'No objections at all, sir . . .' he heard himself saying.

'Off you go.' Carn's words were hoarse and brusque. 'Good luck.'

The effort of releasing the two clips of the lower hatch caused Peter to grab the rungs of the control-room ladder. Sweat was pouring from him and his mind reeled as he gasped for air – great, long draughts that left him exhausted. There was nothing left to breathe now, nothing reaching the depths of his lungs.

'Get up them stairs, for Christ's sake, get moving . . . ' that's what they longed to bawl at him; but this was no TV show, this was for real . . .

He turned his back on them and hauled himself upwards, hand over hand, into the dark hollow gaping above him. When he had struggled through the lower lid, he groped for the wet rungs of the lower ladder – a pale light flickered below him, then went out. He began the long haul upwards, hearing the clang of the lower hatch being shut by the solitary man left in the control room. All was silent now, save for the groans of gasping men heaving themselves upwards, some fifty rungs, to the invisible upper hatch.

'You okay, Peter?'

Sinden was not far below him. From the bottom he could hear Hebbenden clattering on the lower platform as he searched once again for the main flood . . . he was obviously feeling his way, intent on making no errors now. Then Peter felt it: the top rung and, above it, the horizontal roof of the tower. His fingers felt the oval upper lid, offset on one side, the gateway to survival. His hands groped: ah, there it was, the long handle, the first clip to release. If he fumbled the clips at the last moment, they'd all perish: Sinden would be unable to shut the lid after them . . .

'You there, sir?' he panted.

'Yes – all set . . . I'll keep hold of your ankles,' Sinden said.

There was a sharp cry from the bottom of the tower: the coxswain had rammed against some protrusion . . . the proximity of death seemed to be affecting his unique flow of language . . .

'Is there room for the cox'n to pass you, sir?'

'Yeah – all set.'

From the depths of the tower Peter could still hear the clumsy movements of the big man – Hebbenden was wuzzy, perhaps – but from up here, it was impossible to tell what was going on . . .

'All set, Cox-n?' Peter heard his query echoing through the hollow tower that could become their tomb . . .

There was no reply – the Swain was impatient, waiting for the expected order . . .

'*Open the main flood . . . *' Peter gasped the vital command. *'. . . Open the vent.'*

Their moment had arrived at last, the instant for which they'd

157

been waiting for thirty-three hours and thirty minutes . . . the roar of rushing water at 300 pounds per square inch would force his brain to work, instead of dwelling on maudlin memories of Jeannie and the kids . . . what the hell was keeping the Swain?

'*Open main flood . . .*' he yelled again. As his order reverberated in the stillness, he felt Sinden tugging at his ankles.

'Something's wrong, Peter. I'm going down.'

Peter bit his lip. Hell's teeth, at the critical moment . . . Sinden was slithering fast down the ladder. Peter heard him flop at the bottom, but there was no sound from Hebbenden.

'Peter . . .' The call was sharp, urgent. 'Come down . . . *quick*.'

The hairs prickled at the back of Peter's neck. As he reached the half-way platform where the two ladders joined, there were three sharp, metallic clangs . . . Opening up? What the hell's Sinden playing at? Peter heard the scrabble of the clips being released from below by the captain in the control room. A vague circle glowed, and there, in the shadows above the lower lid, he saw Sinden crouching over a large, shapeless mass.

They had eased the unconscious bulk of the coxswain's body through the lower hatch, Carn taking the weight from below, while Peter and Sinden held each arm from above. They gave up the useless struggle of trying to lift him. Frantically they unzipped Hebbenden's orange suit while Carn tore at his shirt. 'Oxygen, Peter, quickly.'

The captain clapped his ear to the unconscious man's chest. Sinden grabbed the right wrist, feeling for the pulse. By the time that Peter returned with the cylinder, Hebbenden was not breathing.

'For God's sake – *oxygen . . .*'

The precious life-giving gas hissed beneath the jowls of the prostrate man until the cylinder was empty. Hebbenden's lips were already blue and his chest had ceased to heave.

'He's dead . . .'

Carn threw himself astride the motionless body. He crossed his hands and pounded the breast bone . . . three times . . .

'Mouth-to-mouth, Pete . . .' Carn gasped, pressing thrice again, in the hope that cardiac massage might prevail.

Peter had never before applied his knowledge of mouth-to-mouth resuscitation. He'd always been repelled by the idea, but now, surprisingly, he felt no qualms, as he knelt by the cox'n's shoulder. Pulling back Hebbenden's chin and pinching his nose, Peter opened the cold, blue mouth. He breathed in a long,

agonising draught, then sealed the blue lips with his own. Once –
twice – his will fighting the revulsion that came to him. '. . . they
usually vomit,' the Doc had said during first-aid training, but
could dead men . . . ? Peter choked, sucked another deep breath,
shut his eyes, blew again . . . he was sweating now, nauseous . . .
*five* – pause – *six* . . .

'He's dead,' Sinden said softly. 'No pulse.'

Carn removed his weight. He slid one knee across the dead
man; remained on his knees, his eyes closed. 'God rest his soul,'
he said.

Sinden, too, was bowed. 'Amen,' they murmured, joining
together in the final act of respect.

He knew not how long they knelt there. Carn rose and
staggered to the ward-room pantry where they kept the napery.
He found a tablecloth and gently spread it across his coxswain's
corpse. 'We'll lay him alongside Gallo,' was all he said.

By the time they had completed their melancholy task, they
could not stand, beaten by nausea and exhaustion. For a full five
minutes, they leaned against the periscopes, their legs stretched
out before them. The ache across Peter's forehead was now a
steel band, each throb of his heart a stab of pain between his
temples. Their breathing at last became more regular – then, each
of them, a grim follow-my-leader, crawled back to the ward-room
settee. In the darkness they laid themselves down to recover and
try to think.

This failure of the thought process, Peter realised, was so
dangerous. Already Soper and Dean had made reports entirely at
odds, in the sincere belief that they were right. Two and two made
five; and an 'open' valve would be reported 'shut'. This effect on
the brain was the result of oxygen poisoning under pressure and
was lethal.

'They'll be cooking their dinner up top,' Sinden said, glancing
at the luminous hands of the clock. 'It's eleven o'clock.'

'They'll be too sick,' Carn said.

Nobody laughed. Carn went on:

'I wasn't far out – thirty-four hours gone.'

'You gave us thirty-six . . . '

It was Sinden, his old mate . . . Peter smiled ruefully in the
darkness . . . was death stealing upon them as easily as this?

'Captain, sir?' Peter couldn't imagine why he hadn't thought
of it before: 'You can use the cox'n's suit.'

In the darkness, the silence was profound. Each man was

listening to his neighbour's laboured breathing, endeavouring not to betray his own agonising pain.

'I wasn't proposing to do that.'

Peter blundered on, amazed at his own effrontery – but there were no barriers now . . .

'What d'you mean, sir?'

'It either stays on the cox'n – or Commander Sinden wears it.' The firm voice directed itself in the darkness towards the passenger's corner. 'Give me yours, Alastair, please.'

The tension fused again into silence. Peter heard Sinden struggling to his feet.

'Sorry, George,' the passenger said quietly. 'I'm fond of this suit. I'll keep it, if you don't mind.' Sinden was directing his voice now towards the navigating officer. 'Sinclair . . . ?'

Peter shook his head . . . was this some ghastly nightmare? ' . . . fetch the coxswain's immersion suit, please. Then give it to the captain.'

Peter held his peace. He rolled from the settee and scrabbled through the darkness to the ward-room entrance.

'Lieutenant Sinclair . . . ' Carn was gasping but his words were crisp.

'Sir?'

'Disregard Commander Sinden's order. Return to your bunk.'

The captain was rising to his feet. As Peter continued towards the control room, he heard the crash of a ward-room chair.

The two men were face to face in the darkness and, for a moment, were alone.

# CHAPTER 19

# *The Sands Run Out*

The ringing of eight bells floated down upon the wind. Captain Quincey, muffled to the eyebrows against the bitter wind, was surprised to hear the familiar sound, where he sheltered in the port wing of *Kronstad*'s bridge. Though the guts seemed to have gone out of the gale, it was still blowing hard: it would be some time before the seas moderated . . .

*Kronstad*, now hove-to and riding out the storm, could be swiftly back on station again, as soon as Kapitan Smirnov could risk it. Life was proceeding as usual 'tween decks: soup, fish, and then meat perhaps – and coffee afterwards? Did communist sailors drink coffee after their meals? And 680 feet below, three men were eking out their last hours of life . . .

George Carn, Alastair Sinden – both had served with him at one time or another, either as third or fourth hand. And Sinclair, the reliable ex-trawlerman – they were just being allowed to die. Quincey felt the blood oozing from the palms of his hands where he clenched his fingers in a paroxysm of frustration.

It had been a near thing . . . that chap Soper and the young RO . . . both had been optimistic when they signalled through the port of the decompression chamber. Those two had survived remarkably well – blood from the ears and symptoms of the bends – that was all – but they'd got out before the gale had shoved *Mars* down another two hundred feet.

Soper had confirmed that Carn was basing his decisions on a limit of thirty-six hours – but Soper had wondered whether the trapped men could last that long. He had been sure that their coxswain and Sinclair would make the next attempt and follow soon – but what the hell had gone wrong? Five hours had dragged by since then: not a sign, not a word, not even a morse message with a spanner against the hull. Those emergency sonar batteries must have spilled in the two-hundred-foot drop: Carn must not waste air and energy on useless communication. He would be relying on *Kronstad*'s remaining on station.

Soper had reported that George would have no suit – and that Alastair's was ripped. They hadn't a chance by free ascent from a depth of 680 feet, not those two, reaching their forties and only normally tank trained. They had probably decided to die decently – but what of Sinclair and the coxswain? *They* had suits and a chance in a thousand . . .

Jack Quincey watched the seas leaping, white and angry, across the horizon. What were they going to tell Jackie Carn? Perhaps it was best to remain silent, with a possible hour of life left? What was the point? The telephone call would not bring her George back. It might be fairer to prepare her for the worst . . . and anyway it was time he reported to FOS/M.

As he opened the door to the radio room, he saw the solid figure of *Kronstad*'s captain staggering towards him across the pitching deck.

'I'm going back,' the Russian said. 'It's moderated enough now to recover my anchor.'

As the Russian seafarer jangled the telegraph, an American doughboy approached him, a Joint Rescue Team message in his hand:

'From *Lily-One*, sir,' he said. 'Intermittent tappings being received from *Mars*. Investigating. TOO 1302.'

Quincey's heart leaped: was there a hope? They were alive, that was all he knew . . . they were running out of minutes in which to make their last bid . . . He, of all people, knew how slim were their chances: four men to escape in one hour – two attempts and one drain down – their thinking would have gone, addled by oxygen under pressure – and by carbon dioxide poisoning . . .

Thank God he'd been persuaded by that maniac, Doc Dugan, to leave *Lily-One* deep while the gale was on. But Dugan, also, would be short of air soon and would have to surface.


### The Fierce Light of Truth

What had transpired between those two, Peter realised, as he gasped away his life on the ward-room settee, would never be known. Suffice it that, when he'd returned with Hebbenden's suit, his lungs burning from the exertion of fighting for air, Carn had held out a hand for the life-giving suit. He had pushed it across to Sinden who, already peeling off his damaged clothing, had silently accepted it.

'We're too flaked to stand much chance at the moment,' the captain gasped. 'It's now 1210 – we'll get our heads down for a spell. The sleep should pull us together. We'll make a better job of the escape . . .'

Peter sighed with relief: he'd been fighting the insistent demands of his sleep mechanism – his lids drooped and it was painful propping them open in the gloom. Blessed, divine sleep. He could rest for ever . . .

'Couldn't agree more . . .' Sinden had already stretched himself out, Peter felt certain from his passenger's corner: the breathing was already sonorous, breaking into nasal snoring . . .

'Get some sleep, Peter,' Carn said. 'I'll keep watch, just in case . . .'

Peter could not remember whether he'd been grateful: the courtesy mattered little now. In this demi-world, his thoughts had for a moment spanned the oceans to where they lapped the shores of Morecambe Bay. A white-walled cottage nestled against the sea-defences . . . their first home. Jeannie was there, with the first of their brood, Peter Junior . . . the tide was running in across the white sands and overhead the terns were mewing. Smoke spiralled from the chimney, and, in the meadow, sheep sheltered in the shade beneath the elms, where raucous cawing from the rookery proclaimed an English summer's day . . .

. . . He heard it, that frenzied cry in the darkness. Peter jerked himself on to one elbow – but why this unfamiliar, utter darkness, this terrible pain in his chest? What was this stabbing pain in his skull? And why was he gasping, choking, unable to breathe? And who was that, blast him, shrieking his head off with his nightmare hallucinations . . . ?

'. . . *Jackie – Oh Jackie, where are you?*' the terror-struck voice was gabbling. The words were unmistakable now: 'Oh Jackie, Jackie . . . ' The insane babbling petered out. There was a moan of despair – and then a whispered, 'Oh, my God . . . ' from Alastair Sinden's corner in the darkness of *Mars*'s ward-room.

Peter Sinclair lay motionless, his body rigid – utterly still. He was an interloper, an unwelcome guest, an onlooker into some Machiavellian tragedy born of a distressed mind, a hell which could not exist. He would feign sleep. He'd heard nothing. He'd remain asleep until Carn shook him . . . *Prepare thyself for death*, but I want to live, dear God, how I long to live – but how can I now prevent the poisoning of my mind by this terrible secret?

He fought for breath, deeper now; ah, deeper . . . trying to grab every atom of oxygen from this putrid atmosphere that was rapidly killing them. He shut his eyes as the dimming light of the last lantern came on to bathe the ward-room in its pallid gleam.

Peter was sure that no words passed: only this cruel silence, as full realisation of the tragedy filled the vacuum of their minds. Then, as the seconds slipped by, Peter watched, through half-opened lids, the two men who now faced each other and to whom existence was now irrelevant.

The scene was like a Rembrandt. The models frozen; the contrast of light and shade emphasising the drama of the awful moment. 'Chiaroscuro' the artists called it, didn't they?

Carn was slumped against the settee. His white shirt was grey with sweat, his arms stretched before him on the table, sleeves rolled up, fists clenched. His hair was ruffled, his unshaven, heavy face dark with dirt and beard. He stared before him, his eyes bright, looking through his friend, as if he were a spectre.

163

'It's you, Alastair . . . ?' he whispered.

Peter watched the protrusion in Sinden's throat, an Adam's apple more prominent than most. It moved as he gulped and nodded, unable to speak. Alastair's head swung slowly from side to side, rhythmically, like those fat, lead-filled toy clowns that could not topple . . .

'We love each other . . .' Sinden whispered the words, his blue eyes glazed with compassion for the hurt he was causing his friend.

Carn remained there, a marble statue. He peered at Alastair, trying to see through the haze that blinded him. The brown eyes softened and a faint smile creased the corners of his mouth.

'Thank God it's you, Alastair . . .'

That was all that was said. He rose slowly to his feet, and stretched across to Peter's bunk. He shook his navigator's shoulder, as the last flicker of the lantern threw the occupants of the ward-room into relief against 63 bulkhead. The light faded and the ward-room was plunged into darkness.

'Shall we go, gentlemen?' the captain said. 'They'll be waiting for us up top.'

## CHAPTER 20

## *To Everyman, A Different Exit*

'The weight of the flood water will keep it shut.'

Carn's words echoed downwards to Peter, who was standing at the bottom of the tower: Carn, in the damaged suit, was heaving himself slowly upwards. He had to stop every few rungs to regain his breath, and Peter wondered muzzily whether the captain would make it. Carn would be first out because he would virtually be making a free ascent. After Peter had opened the main flood and the vent, he was to climb past Sinden, who would be tail-end-Charlie and hold open the upper lid.

Peter pushed against the lower hatch, felt it drop down against its spring. He'd stand on the lid when the water gushed in – then he'd move, bloody fast if he could, up the ladder to the top. 'Lower lid shut, sir,' he called into the darkness.

Peter could not resist the notion that this was some insane play-acting, the 'stiff upper' jargon that was carrying them through to extinction . . . they'd be crushed to death in seconds – and the captain, in that ripped suit . . . he hadn't a cat's chance in hell . . .

'All set, Peter?'

Carn's voice reverberated now, echoing in the chilly vault. They'd have to hurry: Peter's head was swimming already and his brain was muzzy; difficult to string together his words in the right sequence, though he knew what he wanted to say . . .

*'Standing by, sir . . .'*

*'Open main flood. Open the vent . . .'*

Peter leaned against the wheel-spanner; felt the valve spin open. As he repeated the order, his final words were drowned by the explosion of the deluge foaming at his feet. In seconds the water was above his knees, a fine spray enveloping the lower section of the tower. He'd had to move fast if he wasn't to drown in this boiling cauldron. Though the air was non-existent, he summoned all his strength to heave himself up the ladder, hand over hand.

Alastair Sinden waited in the darkness, four feet below his friend. The appalling truth had been exposed, and, in the blackness of the tower, the enormity of his guilt came home to him . . . it couldn't happen, not in real life, they said – but how frequent was this tragedy, when the best friend completed the third corner of the triangle? And what a contrast between his conduct and that of his best friend . . . *'Thank God it's you . . .'* was all that George had said. Betrayed by his best friend, George had the magnanimity to forgive, even during these final precious moments of life . . .

A man's life passed before him in those few seconds before death, so they said . . . the roaring of the flood water was thunderous now, and he felt the ladder shaking from Sinclair's desperate scrambling upwards. Sinden's Eustachian tubes were giving him terrible pain as the pressure began to build up: 300 pounds per square inch would rip his ear-drums open.

He could stand that, even bear the pain of destroying George, but he could not face death with tranquillity if this gulf remained between himself and his Maker. He and Jackie had deliberately flouted His law, believing deeply that their love had come from Him. So it had, but they had been wrong in excusing themselves for the way in which they had used His love. The joy and the beauty could have emanated only from Him, but now, in a few seconds, he, Alastair Sinden, would be crossing the threshold – to forgiveness or eternal damnation?

In the darkness, Sinden prayed, ripping the veil from his soul. With the singing of the pressure in his ears and the cascading water roaring about him, he besought the absolution that only He could grant. ' . . . *forgive me, Jesus. Forgive us, Jackie and me; have mercy on our souls, have mercy . . .* ' and, as he uttered the supplication aloud, he was aware that the rushing of the flood water was slowing up.

Sinclair's hands were groping at his ankles. Alastair leaned backwards, his shoulders pressed against the tower to allow him to pass: Carn had proposed that Sinclair should be the second man out, because the younger man would have the better chance of reaching the surface: and Sinclair had re-qualified the most recently in the tank re-scrub. The water was flooding slowly, now, as the pressures began to equalise . . . in a few seconds, George would be taking off the first clip and he, Commander Alastair Sinden, Royal Navy, would have to zip up his hood. A few seconds of life left . . .

The water had stopped flooding now. George's foot was pressing against his shoulder. Alastair heard the first clip snap off, then felt the struggle as George wrestled with the second – the pressure *must* be equalised now. He zipped up the hood of his suit – a few breaths were all that remained now between himself and the Great Divide.

The sudden pressure made him scream involuntarily and then he felt George kicking above him. He sensed Peter's exit, felt the body sliding upwards past him – but what was holding George? Alastair's hands shot upwards to prevent his head smashing against the roof of the tower. In that split second, he felt George's left leg entangled in the longer of the two clips; the head of the lever was jammed into the rent in his suit.

Sinden tore at the fabric, his hands pouring blood. Oh God, so nearly there – his senses were reeling, his heart bursting inside him, an explosive, billowing pressure building up . . . *breathe out, calm, for God's sake, keep calm – There! The fabric was free now* . . . With a last despairing effort, he heaved himself upwards to grab George's flailing body around the shoulders. *Hang on to him; don't let him go, whatever happens. My own suit will take us both up, up, upwards now on our way* . . . OUT *out, breathe out* . . . and the red mist swirled about him, a rushing, overwhelming aura of flailing, fiery lights, pure and clean and all-consuming.

Carn assumed they would add *Mars*'s crest to those already

adorning the walls of the submariners' chapel in Blockhouse. A subscription might even be raised to mount a plaque in the museum above the chapel; fixed to the wall in polished brass, it would read: 'The shoulder epaulets of the late Commander George Carn, Royal Navy, Commanding Officer of SSN *Mars*, lost in collision off Novaya Zemlya in the Barents Sea.'

As he had opened the upper lid, he'd felt the long clip snagging the rent in his suit . . . He couldn't free it, not now. He hadn't the strength, and who cared, anyway?

So this was death?

No agony, save for his ears. The serenity of acceptance, a swift oblivion as his senses begun to swim, swirling into unconsciousness . . . that must be Peter gliding by, swooping upwards . . . God speed, brother-in-law – give her my love. Don't forget, she's your sister, too – take good care of my Jackie . . .

What was Alastair playing at? Trying to free my trapped leg, before the air bubble gave out? He was such a bloody good guy. Jackie would have been happy with him . . .

I've tried: steady, stupid, trusting George Carn, who couldn't take a little adversity when it came his way. But I tried, reckon I did . . . So, God, take me as I am, but don't let Jackie be lonely – anything, anything but that. If Al makes it, let them find peace together: it'll be easier for them without me . . .

He felt Alastair grasping him around the shoulders: realised they were shooting upwards now, towards those green, grey waters – oh God, this agony is crippling me, but exhale as they said – *breathe out. You're escaping from only 680 feet, huh . . . ? Jackie, my dearest Jackie . . .*


When the upper lid flipped open, Peter Sinclair held on for an instant to the ladder rung: the captain needed a moment to extricate himself through the hatch. Fortunately, in an SSN there were no jumping wires, so the ascent should be free of snags . . .

He'd zipped up his hood in the nick of time – and now there remained those few breaths. He must not use them, but exhale . . . He did not relish bursting, with portions of his lungs ballooning through his mouth and nostrils – but why was the captain so long in getting out?

He felt, then, the wild kicking of Carn's legs: he was stuck outside the lid – and as Peter began to float upwards, he felt Sinden's hands clawing at the snagged suit. What an appalling end to a terrible tragedy – why couldn't Carn free himself? Sinden was sacrificing himself trying to extricate him. They were both lost now . . .

Peter surged upwards, towards the surface . . . Those two had deliberately given him the chance to live, he, the youngest man – and he'd snatched the opportunity without even a thank you. But, God, how I long to live . . .

His lungs were inflating, he was beginning to burst as the pressure decreased during his rapid ascent. Breathe out . . . *out*, OUT. The instructors in the tank could not have explained the drill more fully. He could never have attempted this escape without that training – but he'd never make it – 680 feet and he was losing consciousness from the agony of his lungs and the terrible pain in his ears and his head. His chest was bursting – he could no longer breathe out, for he'd reached the depths, the farthest corner of his lungs. He knew that he'd never see Jeannie and the kids again . . .

A sudden blurring of his senses, roaring in his head, and he knew no more.

# CHAPTER 21

## *Negative Sub-Smash*

Captain Jack Quincey peered through the starboard bridge window. Alongside him stood the broad-shouldered *Kronstad*'s Russian captain. Both men were silent, as were the remainder of *Kronstad*'s bridge personnel. There was no sound, save the whine of the radar aerials revolving on the bridge-deck above. Amidships, between the PPIs, the second hand of the clock glided remorselessly around its dial: 1350.

Thirty-six hours, twenty minutes . . . they could be conscious no longer: George, Alastair, and Peter Sinclair. They had decided to die with dignity, in their submarine tomb, deep beneath this treacherous sea, that now, so perversely cruel, had calmed to a long, oily swell.

'I am sorry, Captain.'

The Russian, in his bluff fashion, was extending the sympathy of the seafarer. He, too, knew the fortitude that was required to sacrifice friends for the good of others.

What was his lookout pointing at, there on the starboard quarter . . . ? He followed the seaman's outstretched arm, saw the man calling excitedly towards the bridge: there it was, an orange speck, riding gently in the swell. There was a ragged cheer from across the water where, along the line of *Krakvilsk*'s guard-rails, *Mars*'s men had been keeping their vigil.

Quincey watched the motor-cutter swaying towards the orange immersion suit; unashamedly he brushed away the tears – but why, for God's sake, why only one orange suit?

The R/T on the bridge-screen began gabbling in Russian, the coxswain of the boat reporting to his captain. Then Culmer came on the air. He'd been in the cutter for the past three hours, directing the search – and now, the wash of the cutter churning white as she nudged alongside the orange speck, the XO's voice was tense:

'*It's Sinclair* . . '

There was an interminable delay while they hauled the helpless form over the gunwale. The cutter listed dangerously, and then the body was inboard, lying flat on the bottom boards.

'He's unconscious,' Culmer's voice reported, 'but he's breathing. Returning him to the ship, sir.'

Quincey turned towards the Russian captain, relief on his face. But the Russian was gesticulating, pointing abeam . . . and *there* was another, a larger, orange blob . . . it dipped in the swell, barely buoyant.

Quincey couldn't speak, while the second motor-cutter streaked towards its goal. He held his breath, measuring the distance as it decreased so agonisingly slowly. The sequence was repeated and the bundle, this time on the far side of the boat, was man-handled over the gunwale.

The loudspeaker snicked on. The voice was Soper's and he sounded very English.

'We've recovered the captain and Commander Sinden, sir. I'm bringing them back.'

Quincey grabbed the microphone which *Kronstad*'s captain was extending to him:

'Report their condition,' he snapped. 'D'you need the decompression chamber?'

The loudspeaker crackled again:

'For Commander Sinden: yes, sir, certainly.'

Damn Soper, why couldn't he . . . ?

'What about the captain?' Quincey rapped the question.

'The captain's dead, sir.'

The R/T snicked off. Quincey walked slowly through the bridge door, to the wing outside. He lifted his eyes to the western sky: there, coasting up from the horizon, white clouds gathered, great galleons of cumulus, sailing majestically through the heavens, their reflections shimmering on the sea. Across the swell a gannet glided, its black-tipped wings kissing the grey-green water.

## CHAPTER 22

# Mrs Jacqueline Carn

She had been sitting by the grandfather clock since its chimes had pealed mid-day. Joan Martin, Commander S/M's wife, had taken the children and was feeding them in her own house.

Jacqueline Carn wanted to be alone when they told her. She'd ensconced herself in the hall, not far from the phone; refusing to look at it – she loathed the thing, this harbinger of tragedy.

She'd realised, deep down, that after the one-o'clock news had ended, there could be no hope ... and still the phone remained inanimate ... and two o'clock ... and now three ... could they not release her from this agony? She stared before her, unseeing, oblivious now of time ...

At four twenty, she slipped into the kitchen. She flung the tea-bag into the pot, switched on the kettle – then she heard it, the shrill summons, ringing, ringing in the hall.

She was out of breath when she reached the phone: she stared at the shiny thing – hating it. She reached forwards, slowly folding her fingers round it – then snatched it up, clasping it between her hands.

At first she could hear only the singing of the wires down the line. There was a 'Thank you, I'll take it,' and the deep voice she had grown to know so well was speaking, as clearly as if he were in the drawing-room.

'Jackie ...?'

'Yes? It's me.'

'FOS/M here, Jackie.'

'Yes, Sir Frederick ...?'

She could hear his breathing, all the way from Faslane.

'Jackie . . . '

She felt numb. She'd know it all along.

'I can take it, Sir Frederick,' she said. 'They're dead, aren't they?'

'They've got out, and we've picked them all up.' FOS/M's words came more easily. 'Peter's okay, Jackie.'

'Yes, Sir Frederick . . . '

'And Alastair is alive.'

'Yes . . . ' she whispered.

'Jackie: George died on the way up: he was wearing the damaged suit . . . instantaneous . . . known nothing.'

She stared through the open door at the birch leaves shivering against the white bark of their mottled trunks.

'He's dead . . . ?' she whispered. The scent of the bracken was sweet on this summer afternoon, carried by the breeze and wafting through the house.

'He gave his life, Jackie.'

She listened to him, gentle, simple words, trying to comfort her . . . useless, bloody silly, platitudinous . . .

'Sir Frederick . . . ?' Her heart raced beneath her breast as she asked softly:

'Is Commander Sinden hurt?'

' 'fraid so, Jackie, but he's lucky to escape with his life.'

She dared not ask, could not probe further. She must *not* lose control.

'He's paralysed from the waist down,' FOS/M was saying. 'The doctors say he may recover, but they can't tell yet.'

She rammed the handkerchief into her mouth, stifling the cry that escaped her. She heard a pheasant chuck-chucking in the spinney; from far away, down the glen, a dog was barking.

'Are you there . . . ? Are you all right, Jackie?'

She slowly replaced the receiver. The clock chimed the half hour, the pendulum tick-tocking rhythmically behind her. Soon it would be time for supper and she had not collected the children yet.

# PQ17 – CONVOY TO HELL

## by Paul Lund and Harry Ludlam

In June, 1942, Convoy PQ17, consisting of thirty-five merchant ships, set out for Russia with an escort of cruisers and destroyers. They had a reasonable chance of success until the order came to 'Scatter!'

What followed represents one of the most terrible and tragic blunders of the Second World War.

Authors Ludlam and Lund give a first hand account of the horror and despair that faced the men left to the mercy of a cruel enemy. From thousands of sources and recollections they have built up an unforgettable picture of what it was like to be in PQ17 – and survive . . .

**NEW ENGLISH LIBRARY**

# THE FLEET THAT HAD TO DIE

## by Richard Hough

In 1904 the Tsar ordered the Russian fleet to seek out and destroy the Japanese navy. The fleet consisted of about fifty out-dated men-of-war, ill-equipped, badly manned, incompetently officered. They had to sail half-way around the world to engage the armed might of the Japanese navy under the formidable Admiral Togo.

This is the magnificent chronicle of a suicidal venture, doomed to disaster from the start – a voyage that went from catastrophe to catastrophe, ending in bloody and final disaster at the Battle of Tsu-Shima.

**NEW ENGLISH LIBRARY**

# TIRPITZ
## by David Woodward

The *Tirpitz* was the biggest warship in the Western
Hemisphere and her influence on the war was immense.
The British did not dare leave her alone for fear that she
would break out into the Atlantic and repeat the terrible
havoc of her sister ship *Bismarck*. This gripping and
authoritative book tells the dramatic story of how the British
achieved the seemingly impossible task of sinking the
*Tirpitz*. First came the torpedo bombers, then the R.A.F.,
then the frogmen. Yet still the *Tirpitz* survived and it was not
until the R.A.F. had carried out three attacks with 10,000
bombs that she finally, but slowly, turned over, taking the
lives of all but seventy of her crew of a thousand.

'A first-rate story of adventure' – **Daily Telegraph**

On sale at booksellers and newsagents everywhere.

**NEW ENGLISH LIBRARY**

# NEL BESTSELLERS

**Crime**

| | | | |
|---|---|---|---|
| T031 306 | THE UNPLEASANTNESS AT THE BELLONA CLUB | | |
| | | *Dorothy L. Sayers* | 85p |
| T031 373 | STRONG POISON | *Dorothy L. Sayers* | 80p |
| T032 884 | FIVE RED HERRINGS | *Dorothy L. Sayers* | 75p |

**Fiction**

| | | | |
|---|---|---|---|
| T034 879 | CRUSADER'S TOMB | *A. J. Cronin* | £1.00 |
| T034 925 | HATTER'S CASTLE | *A. J. Cronin* | £1.50 |
| T027 228 | THE SPANISH GARDNER | *A. J. Cronin* | 45p |
| T013 936 | THE JUDAS TREE | *A. J. Cronin* | 50p |
| T015 386 | THE NORTHERN LIGHT | *A. J. Cronin* | 50p |
| T034 755 | THE CITADEL | *A. J. Cronin* | £1.10 |
| T027 112 | BEYOND THIS PLACE | *A. J. Cronin* | 60p |
| T016 609 | KEYS OF THE KINGDOM | *A. J. Cronin* | 60p |
| T029 158 | THE STARS LOOK DOWN | *A. J. Cronin* | £1.00 |
| T034 852 | THREE LOVES | *A. J. Cronin* | £1.25 |
| T031 594 | THE LONELY LADY | *Harold Robbins* | £1.25 |
| T038 114 | THE DREAM MERCHANTS | *Harold Robbins* | £1.50 |
| T031 705 | THE PIRATE | *Harold Robbins* | £1.00 |
| T033 791 | THE CARPETBAGGERS | *Harold Robbins* | £1.25 |
| T035 239 | WHERE LOVE HAS GONE | *Harold Robbins* | £1.25 |
| T032 647 | THE ADVENTURERS | *Harold Robbins* | £1.25 |
| T038 130 | THE INHERITORS | *Harold Robbins* | £1.25 |
| T035 427 | STILETTO | *Harold Robbins* | £1.00 |
| T038 092 | NEVER LEAVE ME | *Harold Robbins* | £1.00 |
| T032 698 | NEVER LOVE A STRANGER | *Harold Robbins* | 95p |
| T032 531 | A STONE FOR DANNY FISHER | *Harold Robbins* | 90p |
| T037 053 | 79 PARK AVENUE | *Harold Robbins* | £1.25 |
| T038 084 | THE BETSY | *Harold Robbins* | £1.25 |
| T035 689 | RICH MAN, POOR MAN | *Irwin Shaw* | £1.50 |
| T034 720 | EVENING IN BYZANTIUM | *Irwin Shaw* | 85p |
| T031 330 | THE MAN | *Irving Wallace* | £1.50 |
| T034 283 | THE PRIZE | *Irving Wallace* | £1.50 |
| T033 376 | THE PLOT | *Irving Wallace* | £1.25 |
| T030 253 | THE THREE SIRENS | *Irving Wallace* | £1.25 |
| T033 171 | SEVEN MINUTES | *Irving Wallace* | £1.25 |

**Historical**

| | | | |
|---|---|---|---|
| T022 250 | THE LADY FOR A RANSOM | *Alfred Duggan* | 50p |
| T017 958 | FOUNDING FATHERS | *Alfred Duggan* | 50p |
| T035 050 | LEOPARDS AND LILIES | *Alfred Duggan* | 90p |
| T035 131 | LORD GEOFFREY'S FANCY | *Alfred Duggan* | 75p |
| T024 903 | THE KING OF ATHELNEY | *Alfred Duggan* | 60p |
| T032 817 | FOX 1: PRESS GANG | *Adam Hardy* | 50p |
| T032 825 | FOX 2: PRIZE MONEY | *Adam Hardy* | 50p |
| T032 833 | FOX 3: SIEGE | *Adam Hardy* | 50p |
| T032 841 | FOX 4: TREASURE | *Adam Hardy* | 50p |
| T028 092 | FOX 14: CLOSE QUARTERS | *Adam Hardy* | 50p |

**Science Fiction**

| | | | |
|---|---|---|---|
| T027 724 | SCIENCE FICTION ART | *Brian Aldiss* | £2.95 |
| T030 245 | TIME ENOUGH FOR LOVE | *Robert Heinlein* | £1.25 |
| T034 674 | STRANGER IN A STRANGE LAND | *Robert Heinlein* | £1.20 |
| T037 045 | I WILL FEAR NO EVIL | *Robert Heinlein* | £1.20 |
| T030 467 | STARMAN JONES | *Robert Heinlein* | 75p |
| T026 817 | THE HEAVEN MAKERS | *Frank Herbert* | 35p |

| T035 697 | DUNE | *Frank Herbert* | £1.25 |
| T032 663 | DUNE MESSIAH | *Frank Herbert* | 75p |
| T023 974 | THE GREEN BRAIN | *Frank Herbert* | 35p |
| T023 265 | EMPIRE OF THE ATOM | *A. E. Van Vogt* | 40p |
| T027 473 | THE FAR OUT WORLD OF A. E. VAN VOGT | *A. E. Van Vogt* | 50p |

## War

| T027 066 | COLDITZ: THE GERMAN STORY | *Reinhold Eggers* | 50p |
| T020 827 | COLDITZ RECAPTURED | *Reinhold Eggers* | 50p |
| T012 999 | PQ 17 - CONVOY TO HELL | *Lund & Ludlam* | 30p |
| T026 299 | TRAWLERS GO TO WAR | *Lund & Ludlam* | 50p |
| T025 438 | LILIPUT FLEET | *A. Cecil Hampshire* | 50p |

## Western

| T017 892 | EDGE 12: THE BIGGEST BOUNTY | *George Gilman* | 30p |
| T023 931 | EDGE 13: A TOWN CALLED HATE | *George Gilman* | 35p |
| T033 945 | EDGE 14: THE BIG GOLD | *George Gilman* | 60p |
| T022 706 | EDGE 16: THE FINAL SHOT | *George Gilman* | 35p |
| T024 881 | EDGE 17: VENGEANCE VALLEY | *George Gilman* | 40p |
| T026 604 | EDGE 18: TEN TOMBSTONES TO TEXAS | *George Gilman* | 40p |
| T028 135 | EDGE 19: ASHES AND DUST | *George Gilman* | 40p |
| T029 042 | EDGE 20: SULLIVAN'S LAW | *George Gilman* | 45p |
| T029 387 | EDGE 21: RHAPSODY IN RED | *George Gilman* | 50p |
| T030 350 | EDGE 22: SLAUGHTER ROAD | *George Gilman* | 50p |

## General

| T020 592 | SLAVE REBELLION | *Norman Davids* | 35p |
| T033 155 | SEX MANNERS FOR MEN | *Robert Chartham* | 60p |
| T023 206 | THE BOOK OF LOVE | *Dr David Delvin* | 90p |
| T028 828 | THE LONG BANANA SKIN | *Michael Bentine* | 90p |

## Mad

| N862 185 | DAVE BERG LOOKS AT LIVING | | 70p |
| N861 812 | MAD BOOK OF WORD POWER | | 70p |
| N766 895 | MORE MAD ABOUT SPORTS | | 70p |

---

**NEL P.O. BOX 11, FALMOUTH TR10 9EN, CORNWALL:**

For U.K.: Customers should include to cover postage, 19p for the first book plus 9p per copy for each additional book ordered up to a maximum charge of 73p.

For B.F.P.O. and Eire: Customers should include to cover postage, 19p for the first book plus 9p per copy for the next 6 and thereafter 3p per book.

For Overseas: Customers should include to cover postage, 20p for the first book plus 10p per copy for each additional book.

Name ......................................................................................................

Address ...................................................................................................

...............................................................................................................

Title ......................................................................................................
(NOVEMBER)

While every effort is made to keep prices low, it is sometimes necessary to increase prices at short notice. New English Library reserves the right to show on covers and charge new retail prices which may differ from those advertised in the text or elsewhere.